The Girl from the Tanner's Yard

By Diane Allen

For the Sake of Her Family
For a Mother's Sins
For a Father's Pride
Like Father, Like Son
The Mistress of Windfell Manor
The Windfell Family Secrets
Daughter of the Dales
The Miner's Wife
The Girl from the Tanner's Yard

DIANE ALLEN

The Girl from the Tanner's Yard

MACMILLAN

First published 2020 by Macmillan
an imprint of Pan Macmillan
The Smithson, 6 Briset Street, London EC1M 5NR
Associated companies throughout the world
www.panmacmillan.com

ISBN 978-1-5098-9524-3

1 3 5 7 9 8 6 4 2

A CIP catalogue record for this book is available from the British Library.

Typeset by Palimpsest Book Production Ltd, Falkirk, Stirlingshire
Printed and bound by CPI Group (UK) Ltd, Croydon, CR0 4YY

MIX
Paper from
responsible sources
FSC® C116313

Visit **www.panmacmillan.com** to read more about all our books
and to buy them. You will also find features, author interviews and
news of any author events, and you can sign up for e-newsletters
so that you're always first to hear about our new releases.

Dedicated to the memory of Ellis Irene Allen.
You left this world too soon but you have
left behind you six sons that you
would have been proud of.

1

Flappit Springs, Denholme, West Yorkshire, 1847

'Don't cry, Lucy, take no notice of them.' Ten-year-old Archie Robinson scowled at the three girls who had just called the girl he had known since birth horrible names, teasing her with hurtful taunts and jeering. Archie tried hard to console Lucy by putting his arm around her shoulders to hug and comfort her.

'Leave me be, Archie. You aren't helping. You are even worse than me – look at you!' Nine-year-old Lucy Bancroft pulled a face at her companion and glared at him. 'I'm fed up of being called names like "Stinky" and hearing, "Hold your nose, Smelly is here" every time I try and join in with some of them.' She looked back at the three girls who always ganged up together, leaving her out, when she attended Sunday school in Denholme. Despite her tears, Lucy turned and retaliated by sticking her tongue out at the giggling trio, then marched off sobbing, with the penniless but faithful Archie by her side.

'They are not worth your tears. You are loads prettier

1

than any of those three. They are only jealous. And besides, you don't smell. It's only because you live at the flay-pits that they yell that at you. Betty Robson can't say anything to anyone – her father's butcher's shop, when he's slaughtering in his yard, smells just as bad as the tannery.' Archie put his hands in his pockets and looked across at Lucy, who had now stopped crying and had decided to sulk.

'I hate the three of them. They all look alike anyway, with their fancy bows in their hair and their sickly smiles. I'd rather be on my own than pretend to be something I'm not. Anyway, one day I'll show them. I'll be far more important than all of them put together,' Lucy mumbled as they crossed the wooden bridge over the stream to the place where she lived. She stopped in the middle of the bridge and looked around her, then glanced at her friend. 'I'm sorry, Archie, I didn't mean to upset you. You can't help being badly dressed; after all, you've no father to look after you.' Lucy regretted her hard words to the lad who was always by her side. She shouldn't have let the three empty-headed, spiteful girls get to her.

'It's alright. We all say things we shouldn't. Besides, you're right: I do look like a scarecrow. I haven't even any boots to put on my feet at the moment.' Archie looked down at his bare feet and remembered the better times when his father was alive, before an accident at the nearby quarry where he worked had taken his life. 'My mother's trying to save enough money to buy me a pair. She's just glad it's summer now and that I'll manage for the next few months.'

Archie smiled and looked at Lucy. He was right when he said the other girls were jealous of her. Despite their families having more money, Lucy Bancroft was the bonniest lass in the Worth valley, and it made no difference to him that she came from the nearby flay-pits, where her father worked as the tanner. They were alike, he and Lucy: both had been handed a bad deal in life, but he had a feeling Lucy would not let that stand in her way – unlike him.

'I'm sorry, you must miss him, and your life must be hard. I shouldn't feel so sorry for myself.' Lucy leaned over the wooden bridge and looked down into the stream; the woods around it were full of bluebells and white wild garlic, the smell of which filled the air. 'I'll ask my father if he can make you some boots, or at least something to cover your feet for the summer. We've plenty of leather about the place – it's about the only thing we do have. Mam says we've no money, and she's worrying because she's got another baby on the way.' Lucy sighed and threw a twig into the stream from an overhanging tree and watched it float downstream.

'No, don't worry about me. I'll be fine until autumn comes, and then I'll be old enough to go and work for somebody, and can bring some money home for my mother. I can just about read and write, so that's a lot more than some can do at my age.' Archie leaned over and looked into the river, then turned and smiled at Lucy. 'I'd better get back home – my mam will be waiting for me. We always go and see my grandmother on a Sunday, and she's an old stickler and we will both get a good tongue-lashing if we are late for our dinner. It's the only decent meal we get all week, so I'm fair looking forward to it. I can almost smell that boiled brisket, and happen she'll have made Yorkshire pudding, if we are lucky.'

Archie slurped as he nearly dribbled into the stream, thinking about his one good meal of the week. Lucy waved as she watched him take off back through the spring undergrowth to his home, high up on the wind-swept moor. He was a good friend to her, and she felt pity for the near-penniless soul that he was.

'Well, has the church saved your soul again for another week?' Bill Bancroft looked at his daughter as she kicked off her boots and sat down next to him in the small kitchen of Providence Row. 'I don't know why your mother makes you go. It'll not help you in any way – God's never done owt for me.'

'Be quiet, Bill Bancroft, and thank Him for what you do have – which is a lot, and you know it.' Dorothy folded her hands and looked at her daughter. 'Have you been crying? Your eyes look red.'

'I fell out with Betty Robson and her friends – they were calling me names,' Lucy whispered.

'So much for religion,' Bill muttered.

'You take no notice of them, Lucy. You give them back as much as they give you. Everybody's the same on this earth; we all have the same habits and needs.' Dorothy turned and went to the drawer where the cutlery was kept and started to lay the kitchen table for dinner.

'Father, I walked back from Sunday school with

Archie Robinson today. He'd no shoes on his feet, as they can't afford any. Could you make him some, do you think? We've plenty of scraps of leather about the place.' Lucy looked up at her father, hoping he'd say yes.

'Nay, lass, I can't make shoes; he needs a cobbler, and brass, and you should know that.' Bill shook his head.

'Then will you take him on in the yard this back-end? He'll be old enough to work for you then – he'll be eleven in September.' Lucy was going to help her friend out, one way or another, of that she was determined.

'We'll see. I can't promise, but we will see.' Bill looked at Dorothy. The Robinson family had fallen on hard times, but they weren't the only ones who were struggling in the bleak surroundings of the Worth valley. Bill and his family were just scraping by, but at least there was always food on the table, and his family were dressed and shod so far.

'Go and get changed out of your Sunday best, Lucy, and then come down for your dinner,' Dorothy said to her caring daughter as she checked the pan of boiling potatoes on the hearth.

Lucy got up from sitting next to her father and gave him a quick hug, before climbing the stairs to her room. She loved her father; even though he drank he was always there for her, whereas her mother was always nagging or chastising her. Once there, she sat on her bed and looked out of her bedroom window at the flay-pits and tannery that blighted all their lives with their smell and filth.

She hated where she lived, and she hated being the lass

from the flay-pits; when she said where she was from, people wrinkled their noses and pulled a face at her. One day she would be free of this place. She would meet a wealthy man and marry him, and then she would breathe in clear air and would have pretty dresses and ribbons in her hair, just like Betty Robson. Yes, of that she was sure: a dashing, good-looking man, with a clean home to call her own and, hopefully, money in the bank – after all, that was not a lot to ask. She didn't know how, but that was her dream, and nobody was going to take it away from her, not even Betty Robson and her shallow friends. However, right now she was the smelly lass from the flay-pits, whom nobody gave the time of day to, and her dreams were simply that: dreams with no substance.

2

Flappit Springs, 1857

Adam Brooksbank looked around him and questioned why he had returned to the godforsaken wilderness that used to be his home. The rain was coming down in stair-rods and the wind was blowing so fiercely that the sign of The Fleece, the hostelry that he and the hauliers had just passed on their way to his family farm, creaked and groaned, trying its best to break free from its hinges.

He'd forgotten how dark and foreboding the moors between Keighley and Halifax were, and how repressive on a day like this. Yet they were wild, with a strange attraction that pulled you into them and enveloped your very soul, if you let them. He stood and looked back down into the Worth valley and watched as candles and lamps were lit in the windows of houses, in readiness for the coming evening. The smoke from the industrial towns of Keighley and Thornton wasn't reaching the moorland today; instead the wind was driving it down the valleys, making visibility into the surrounding mill towns impossible, despite the howling gale. Adam shook his head. Poor buggers, he thought; he'd rather be sodden and frozen up here, where the wind blew free, than slogging his life out in a cotton or steel mill – a life of drudgery and toil. And what for? A back-street house that belonged to the mill owner, and a privy shared by all the street. No wonder there was so much crime and discontent in both towns.

He swore again as a large drip slid down his neck, and the wind blew more fiercely as he put his head down and walked up the long-derelict path to his ancestral home of Black Moss Farm. The hauliers, with his earthly possessions piled high upon their horse and cart, followed him, cursing at such a place on such a wild night. The farm looked even more desolate and wild than he remembered it, as he glanced up and saw the familiar outline of the low-roofed house set under the moorland tor, and the dark silhouette of the sycamore tree that he had played in and around as a child.

Memories of his childhood came back as he stood in the once spotlessly whitewashed porch and put the key into the heavy, locked oak door. He had to twist it a time or two before the door yielded, but on entering the old farmhouse, Adam's heart beat fast, as his mother's and father's faces came rushing back into his memory – as if it was only yesterday that he had said goodbye to them both. He glanced around for an oil lamp to throw light upon the old home, lighting the one that hung from a low beam and watching the flames flicker and make shapes on the old walls as the hauliers came back and forth with his goods. They were eager to get home; the moors were no place to be on a wild night like tonight. It took them all of thirty minutes to unload the few possessions Adam had bothered to bring with him.

'We're off now, mate, before the night gets any worse. Everything is unloaded now – we just need paying.' The haulier and his lad stood in the bare room, their hair wet through and the hessian sack around their shoulders giving them little protection from the fierce elements.

Adam quickly trimmed the wick on his oil lamp as it started to splutter and die, before placing it on the mantel and replying to the haulier. 'My grateful thanks, gentlemen. I'm sorry the weather's not been kind to you. How much do I owe you?' He reached into his pocket and took out his money.

'A guinea, mate. That furniture took some hauling up that bloody hill, and my horses will appreciate the downhill journey – it nearly broke their backs coming up.' The haulier held out his hand in readiness for payment.

'Aye, well, here's the guinea in payment, and a shilling each for your help. I couldn't have done it without you.' Adam patted the back of the haulier as he quickly pocketed the coin, hardly believing his luck.

'This is a godforsaken place. You can't smell it today, but the stench from the flay-pits nearly knocks you down, if the wind is blowing in this direction, not to mention the noise of them blasting from the quarry at Denholme. What's a gentleman like yourself wanting with a place like this?' the haulier asked with a wry smile on his lips, as he watched the lad, dumbfounded that

9

he'd been given a shilling just for doing his job, go out of the door. 'The farm's been empty for some years. I've never known anybody live here as long as I've been around here.'

'I needed to come home – be my own man. I've had enough of being at somebody's beck and call. This was once a good farm, until I turned my back on it more than ten years ago,' Adam answered honestly, although he didn't give away too much.

'So you're from here?' The haulier was inquisitive. Who was the man who was foolish enough to move into the farmhouse that caught all the wilds of the weather and moor that could be thrown at it? Nobody ventured near Black Moss Farm, which stood brooding and forbidding, alone on the path just past the crossroads between Halifax and Haworth, Keighley and Thornton.

'Aye, I am. Now, if you'll excuse me, I've much to do before nightfall, and your horses are waiting.' Adam ushered the man out of the door and into the gale that was battering the fellside. He didn't mind people knowing that he was back on his old patch, but not yet. He needed time to get settled, to get the house back into habitable order and to look at what shape the forty acres of land were in. He knew the local folk would be gossiping as soon as they saw a light in the old homestead, but for the next day or so he just needed peace.

'Goodnight to you then, sir. And good luck, because you'll need it. You'd not find me staying here the night; it's too wild and remote for my liking!'

'Aye, perhaps you are right – I'll need your luck. But

I know the countryside's ways and I could do with some peace, so I'll embrace my old home with open arms. I'll be fine here on my own; in fact I will relish it. Take care, and thank you again for your hard work.'

Adam watched as boy and man covered themselves with more sacking and whipped the horses into motion, once in their seats. The steam was already rising from the horses' backs, and he couldn't help but think they'd need a good rub-down and the hand of a diligent stable boy on their return to Keighley. He closed the door behind him and looked around at the dirty grey walls, which used to be spotless, and the filthy flagged floor that was once polished to within an inch of its life. He remembered that his mother always had chequered curtains at the windows and a pegged rug by the hearth, with a vase of wild moorland flowers on the table, as she and his father sat next to the blazing fire discussing the day's events, while she knitted and he smoked his pipe. But those were in the good old days, when he had not been so headstrong and selfish.

Adam felt a cold shiver run down his back and realized quite how cold the old home was. He found and lit yet another lamp, then searched for something to light a fire, to get some warmth into the old place. He then looked at the fireplace: the remains of a crow's nest filled the hearth, having obviously fallen down from a previous spring, along with one of its now-mummified occupants. Should he take a chance and hope that the chimney was not blocked by the troublesome pests? He pushed the twigs and their occupant into an orderly heap and reached for an old newspaper that had been left by the side of the fireplace, glancing at the headlines and the date of *The Keighley Chronicle* and smiling as he screwed up the paper, placing it under the ready-made kindling sticks. The headlines reminded him of his close friend Ivy Thwaite, as he read: 'Police Confiscate Mechanical Fortune-Telling Device'. Ivy had no time for suchlike; she was a true spiritualist and hated the hoaxers who preyed on the vulnerable and heartbroken that searched for their loved ones after death. Without her, he would have been lost after the death of his beloved wife Mary, and might have been tempted by the hoaxers' convincing deceits, in his search for forgiveness for not saving Mary from her death. Ivy had been a close friend for many years and at one time Adam had thought of courting her, but she had been too headstrong for him. He shook his head, thinking that it would never have lasted; and besides, Mary had appeared in his life and he'd known instantly that she was the one for him.

He rose from his knees and braved the gale outside, walking to what he knew was the coal house, hoping there would be at least a cob or two still remaining in the dark corner of the stone-built shed. Finding a small pile of coal still there, he quickly returned into the house, built the fire up and placed a mutton pie that he'd bought from a street seller in Keighley into the rusty side-oven to warm. He sighed and looked around him, and it was then that he realized how thankful he was that he had been brought back to his roots. Now it was time to rebuild his life and try and forget the past.

With the fire lit and the mutton pie warming in the side-oven, Adam sat back and gazed into the flames of the fire. So much had happened since he had left Black Moss as a younger man: he'd lost both parents and his wife, and had seen quite a bit of the world, but now he was home and he meant to settle down. Tomorrow he'd go to the nearby flay-pits, where they tanned hides, and buy some lime to whitewash the walls, then advertise his need for a local lass to clean and do the housework. She'd have to be a quiet one, a lass who didn't gossip; he'd no time for flibbertygibbets who chattered all the time. He aimed for a quiet life compared to the last few years – God willing!

Adam felt himself dozing, his head getting heavier and his eyes closing, as the heat from the fire warmed his bones. The events of the day jumbled in his mind and, as the cloak of sleep overcame him, memories of his past came flooding back. The fateful day when his life had been torn apart by the act of a thieving beggar and his own actions.

Slowly his mind replayed the day.

It had been a warm summer's day and by his side was his beautiful smiling wife, Mary. She was blossoming, after just giving him the news that they were to become parents and she was carrying their first child. Adam was dressed in his police uniform; even though it was his day off, he'd decided to wear it, as he was proud to be part of the constabulary within Keighley organized by the Borough Council. He enjoyed the position, even though it meant that he witnessed the darker side of life, and still couldn't quite believe the depths of deprivation within the slum areas of his beat. Although the force had not been formed long, he had built himself a good reputation within it – one of fairness, and of carrying out well the letter of the law, even though sometimes he did it in his own way.

The locals, however, viewed him with suspicion and were not as keen on their protectors since they had agreed to carry out and enforce the local Poor Law. There was rioting in some places to defend the beggars and poor of the area, who they said were being hounded by the constabulary and made to live in the newly built workhouses, in order to keep the streets tidy and ease the government's conscience. Adam had paid no heed to the situation, ignoring even his mother and father's sympathies for those less fortunate than themselves, and had gone out dressed, proud as Punch, in his police attire.

Mary and he had enjoyed dinner with his mother and father at Black Moss and were on their way to the Piece Hall at Halifax, excited about the fair that was being held there and about watching Blondin, the renowned tightrope-walker, walk blindfolded the height and width of the Piece Hall. Adam smiled in his sleep as he remembered the hall bustling with visitors from far and wide, and with stallholders, traders and performers competing with one another, shouting their wares within the large, three-tiered high, square building that was still used by the woollen trade. Its name depicted its origins, as a 'piece' was the name for a thirty-yard length of woven woollen fabric produced on a hand-loom in a weaver's home, then brought for sale within the walls of the mighty hall.

The Piece Hall was packed with traders most weeks, but that day was one of gaiety within its old stone walls and everyone was celebrating, as ribbons and banners fluttered in the wind and people cheered and talked along its ancient corridors. Mary had gasped as, far above their heads, a narrow wire was strung from one corner to the other, in readiness for the mighty Blondin to perform his daring feat. Both of them were laughing and giggling as they climbed the four flights of twisting steep stone steps to the very top of the hall, to be as close to the performer as they possibly could be, squeezing their way into the edge of the balcony that overlooked the cobbled market place far below. Once there, Mary regretted not looking around the market as she spotted a chestnut-seller and turned, pleading with Adam to go back down and buy her some chestnuts. In his sleep Adam mouthed the words, 'Stay there, I'll be back', before his dreams took him down the steep stairs to the chestnut-seller and looking up to his beloved Mary, before re-climbing the stairs.

His smile turned to a frown as he remembered hesitating for a moment. Something was wrong; somebody was running amongst the crowd along the floor that Mary was on. There was a murmur being emitted from the crowd, and Adam watched as he saw Mary turn and shout for him as she tugged and argued with a pickpocket who was trying to relieve her of her posy bag.

15

'Let him have it,' Adam shouted, his voice lost in the crowd, but echoing around the kitchen of Black Moss Farm in his dreams. Then Mary disappeared and screams rang out, telling Adam that something terrible had happened.

Every step he took back to where Mary was felt like climbing Everest. The hot chestnuts lay discarded on the ground as he pushed his way through the gathering crowd. Reaching the bottom of the last flight of stairs, he barged his way through the gasping people. There lay Mary, motionless and dead, with blood pouring from her head and the posy bag that she had fought the pickpocket for still attached to her wrist. Bending down, he picked up Mary's body and nursed her head on his knee, rocking back and forth while tears and sobs erupted into an almighty declaration of grief. 'No, no. Why, my Mary? Why didn't you let him take it?'

The crowd was staring at the peeler who hadn't been able to protect his wife from a common pickpocket. Adam would always remember the look on the crowd's faces as they gazed down upon the sight. He woke up with the scream still on his lips. He wiped his eyes and brushed away the tear that had escaped in his unconsciousness. His body was shaking and a feeling of doom had overcome him. It had been bad enough that he'd lost his wife to a worthless pickpocket, but the reaction of some of the crowd to him had hurt as well. When he heard a voice call him a 'peeler' and asking what did he expect, if he was enforcing the unpopular Poor Law, he'd started questioning his role in society. 'No wonder folk have turned to crime,' he'd heard a second man jeer at the back of the crowd.

His pride had been the cause of their downfall that day, with his decision to wear his uniform in the struggling mill town of Halifax, where everybody had to fight for every slice of bread they placed on their kitchen table. Had the pickpocket chosen Mary on purpose, being able to spot Adam in his uniform and having a grudge against the newly formed police force? That he'd never know, but the day had set his life in a different direction and had made him turn his back upon his father and mother, who had told him right from the start not to leave the family farm for the sake of the money offered by the constabulary. Adam had scoffed at their concerns, but looking back now, they had been right; he'd learned that people and friendship were more important than anything money could buy. After burying Mary and her unborn child, he had left far behind him his family at Black Moss Farm and the life he knew, and had tried to bury the jeers and cries that haunted him. His parents had been correct, but he'd been too proud to admit it.

'Damn, damn!' Adam jumped up from his chair as the smell of burning alerted his nostrils to the fact that the oven worked too well. Smoke filled the room as a blackened mutton pie was rescued from the side-oven. He sighed; that just about summed up his day. He'd go to bed hungry. Tomorrow was another day; and hopefully, in the light of day, his old home would look more welcoming.

3

Adam woke to the sun shining through the bare window and squinted as he rubbed his eyes, before sitting on the edge of the bed on which, the night before, he'd hastily placed his feather mattress, pillows and blankets, before realizing that some of the springs were loose, causing it to squeak every time he moved. That was the first job of the day; he couldn't endure another night of torture.

He sighed as his left leg started to give him pain. It had never been the same since his injury, and the damp weather of late had made it worse. He reached for his one dependency in life and looked at the near-empty bottle that usually kept the discomfort away and made life more bearable – another hour and the pain would have subsided and he could go about his business. He swallowed back the drop that was left, then ran his hands through his thick mop of dark hair, before going through the motions of his morning ablutions. Looking into his mirror, he stared back at the man fastening a garnet tie-stud into his high collar, and wondered what his Mary would have thought of him now. He had kept himself in good shape; standing six feet two and weighing no more than twelve stone, he looked fit. His hair had kept its colour, being still as jet-black as the day he was born, as were the sideburns and the moustache that adorned his face. It was his eyes that belied his state of mind. Their hazel colour told a story of sadness and regret, if they were gazed into deeply enough. The eyes truly were the windows of the soul, he thought, as he quickly stopped himself from feeling too sorry for himself.

He walked down the bare stairs and made his way into the kitchen, relighting the troublesome fire before placing the kettle over it to boil, and placing a pan of porridge oats and milk on the side of it for his breakfast. Stirring the pan occasionally, he looked round his new home. It wasn't too bad, given that it had been empty for a number of years. Nothing that a lick of whitewash and a good scrub of the floorboards wouldn't fix. A week of hard work, with a lass to help him, and he'd have got on top of it; and then he'd tackle the land, just as spring appeared back on the moor.

He looked across at his heap of hurriedly unloaded furniture. He'd tackle that later in the day; it could stay put for now. One of the first jobs that he had to do was to whitewash the walls and fix the glass in the window where the wind was blowing through. He'd visit the flay-pits after his breakfast. They would have a ready supply of lime and, as they were his nearest neighbours, he'd make himself known to them. That was the worst thing about coming back home – if the wind was blowing in a westerly direction, the smell from the pits and vats that the animal hides were initially soaked in, to loosen the hair and soften the hides, was offensive to the senses and tended to cling to the fibres of your clothes. It was a smell he disliked, but thankfully it rarely reached the moorland heights of Black Moss. He was well aware of the flay-pits, but it was of little concern, because coming home was hopefully going to save him: a new way of life, and a home whose security he craved, was worth a few days of unpleasant smells each year.

After mending the squeaking springs on his bed, Adam stepped out across the rutted road in the direction of the tannery and the small line of cottages called Providence Row. The sun lit the surrounding moorsides, giving them a completely different feel from the previous day. Even a flitting skylark was rejoicing as he walked into the tannery yard. The smell hit his senses and his stomach churned as he looked around at the pile of hides waiting to be processed, before being placed in the huge pits of lime and local spring water to be softened. He watched as a rat nearly ran across his feet, unbothered by his presence, as there was an abundance of convenient food in the form of the fat and offal still attached to the piled-high hides. The rat's life was soon cut short, as a man clad in a leather apron hit it over the head with a spade that he was carrying.

'Bloody things – the yard's wick with them; big as cats they are. Easy pickings, you see.'

'Aye, it was a bit large. I think that was the best end to it.' Adam looked at the burly man who stood before him, then pulled his handkerchief to his nose.

'The stench is a bit bad today. It's always better to come on a wet day, if you want my advice.' Bill Bancroft, the owner of the yard, grinned at the well-to-do gentleman who stood in front of him. 'Now then, what can we do for you? You don't look the kind of man that's looking for work here.'

'I've just moved back into my old home at Black Moss. I've been away too long, but now I'm back. Adam Brooksbank.' He held out his hand to be shaken, but it was dismissed. 'I thought you might be able to supply me with some lime. I'm going to limewash the walls, freshen the old place up a bit.'

'I'll not shake your hand, else you'll stink of these hides all day. I'm Bill Bancroft – I own this tannery. I, my missus and five children live in the first cottage of Providence Row. I can supply you with some lime. I'll send one of my lads up with a bag or two for you. But it'll be more than lime you'll want for that place, as it's not been lived in for some time. You say it's your old home, but you must have been away a long time, because I can't remember you. Although now that I think about it, my father did mention you; it's just that I've never met you before.' Bill waited and looked at the man who was taking in the workings of his tannery, and whom he now remembered being mentioned by his father, because he recalled the day of Adam's wife's death.

'Aye, it's been a good few years. But the old spot

pulled me back. Time to make roots and settle down, as I'm not getting any younger. How much do I owe you for the lime? I'm grateful that you'll get one of your men to deliver to me.'

'Nobbut a bob or two; pay me whenever – there's no rush. We all help one another out around here, it's the only way to survive on this wild hillside. Wild men and wild weather, that's what makes Flappit Springs. You've got to be tough, so I hope you are prepared.' Bill grinned.

'I've known worse. I've just been discharged after serving in the Crimea. Believe me, I can take care of myself.' Adam seldom talked about his experience in one of the bloodiest wars England had ever fought, but this time he thought it would do no harm for the men at the tannery to know that he could stand his ground.

'The Crimea – now you must have been hard to survive that. Flappit Springs will be heaven compared to a winter spent before the Siege of Sebastopol. Is it true that thousands died because of the cold and conditions you had to endure?'

'Aye, thousands died out there, and not only from the cold, but also because of the inadequacy of the generals in charge, friendly fire, disease and madness. Take your pick. Our soldiers were outnumbered and outman-oeuvred. I was stupid enough to get involved because of a friend. I wasn't even a military man when I joined. He sweet-talked me into it, assuring me that it would be an adventure – just what I wanted in my life at that time; plus I already knew a little of the Russian language, as my grandmother was originally from Tomsk and I had heard the language spoken by my mother and her since I could toddle. I found the Russian language easy to learn, so I ticked all the boxes to help in the fight for intelligence-gathering over there.' Adam had felt betrayed by his friend, Captain Linton Simmons, whom he had gone to support, with his detecting and linguistic powers, at Simmons's request. At the time it had seemed like an escape from death and the grief of losing Mary, so he'd jumped at the chance of becoming a scout for the British military, working for intelligence – until the death of Charles Cattley, head of intelligence, just before the fall of Sebastopol. Adam's bitterness concerning the war, which Britain was now feeling guilty about, poured out. 'At Balaclava and Inkerman we were almost slaughtered, as we didn't know enough about the Russians. But thank heavens, with the help of our Allies, we turned it around to become a victory. However, if I'd known about the loss of men, then I'd never have gone.' Adam waited while the boss of the tannery took in his words.

'It seems like you didn't escape without injury yourself, by the look of the limp you've got.' Bill stared at the man, who had obviously been through hell.

'Sword wound, top of my leg at Sebastopol – ensured my discharge, thank God.' Adam smiled.

'My thanks go out to you for risking your life for our country. We could do with more men like you. I'll make sure you don't get any bother from any of my men here at Flappit Springs. They might be a rough lot, rowdy and outspoken, with a few dimwits amongst them, but they'll give you the respect you deserve.' Bill watched as Adam glanced at the hard-looking men of the tannery going about their business. 'Now, is there anything else I can do for you?' Bill asked.

'Not unless you know of a likely young lass to become my housemaid?' Adam joked.

'Well, if you're asking, my eldest – Lucy – would be your person. She's twenty and she's got the cheek of the devil, and she could do with something to keep her out of mischief. She's at an age when she turns men's heads and doesn't know what she does to them. Get her working for you and it'll get her away from here. She'd be ideal for you. You look after her, mind; I'll not have her being abused by you, else you'll have me to answer to. It'll do her good working for an older man, and not flirting with half the empty-headed ones that work in my yard. She'll get herself into bother yet.'

Adam leaned on his stick. 'Send her up to visit me and we'll see if we are right for one another. She might hate the sight of me.' He grinned.

'Nay, I don't think she'll do that, especially when there's some money involved. She's beginning to like the finer things in life and, with five children, we haven't that much brass to spend, even though the tannery is mine. Talking of which, what would you be willing to pay her?'

'Haven't had time to think about it. Let her come and see me, and we'll take it from there. I promise she'll get paid what she's worth, and I'll look after her. You have my word.' Adam liked the straight-talking tannery owner, and at least he looked after his family.

'I'll send her up with Archie Robinson, when I send

24

him with your lime. It'll be this afternoon, will that be alright?' Bill waited for a reply while he shouted at a worker to 'Put your back into it!'

'Aye, that will be fine. I look forward to meeting her.' Adam watched as one of the tanners lifted hides out of the flay-pit and took them into one of the large sheds that stood within the tannery. He could see, through the partially open doors, that a tanner had spread one of the soaked hides across a smooth, curved beam and, with a sharp knife, was scraping away the hair to make the hide smooth and ready for the next stage in the process. 'It's interesting to see how you all work,' Adam commented.

'Aye, it's not the most pleasant of jobs. But the world would be lost without leather. It makes your shoes, sharpens knives, keeps your horse in harness and even helps rock babies asleep within their cradles, while they are suspended on leather straps. There will always be a need for leather. Now, if you'll excuse me, I'll have to sort this bugger out. Look at him, it'll take him all day to shift that pile of skins.' Bill walked off and shouted again at his worker, who was making hard work of moving a pile of hides into an empty lime-filled pit.

Bill Bancroft was a hard worker, proud of his job and family, and he'd make a good neighbour – somebody Adam felt he could count upon, if need be.

Adam watched through the farm's window as Archie Robinson unloaded into his outhouse the two sacks of lime that Bill had sent him. A stunning, giggling Lucy

Bancroft was sitting on the edge of his cart, chattering away while swinging her legs freely under her long skirts and watching the good-looking young man do his job. She jumped down suddenly as Archie closed the outhouse door and made his way over to knock on the farmhouse door. Adam watched as the young woman teased the lad who was trying to get his job done, and smiled as Archie asked her to stop tempting him and behave, else her father would have his hide tanned. So, Lucy was a flirt – a flirt who would have to be taken in hand, if she was to work for him. Adam straightened his face as he opened the back door to the knock of Archie and his temptress.

'Mr Bancroft sends his regards, sir. I've put the two bags of lime, sir, in your outhouse. Mr Bancroft says to take care with it. It can burn your skin if you splash it on yourself and don't wash it off quickly.' Archie stood in the doorway as Lucy stood behind him, composing herself for the man her father had told her to respect. Archie turned and decided he'd better introduce Lucy. 'This is Miss Bancroft.' He nearly shoved Lucy in front of Adam and stepped back.

'Thank you, lad. I appreciate you delivering the lime so fast.' Adam looked at the pretty blonde girl, who could hardly keep her face straight as the lad she'd been flirting with announced her presence. 'Now, Lucy, you'd better come with me and let him get back to work. We wouldn't want him to get in any bother with your father, now would we?'

'No, sir. My father will be timing him. He knows how

long it takes to come here and back. He's walked here and back plenty of times in the past – here and The Fleece down the road. My mother says he might as well live here.' Lucy smiled and looked back at her muse as Archie made good his escape.

'Now, Lucy, let me tell you what I want done, and you tell me if you are up to it.' Adam held back a smile, before setting out his stall concerning what he expected from the flirtatious young woman. 'I'll expect you to clean and cook, and make sure my house is tidy at all times, and do what there is to do when I ask it of you. In return, you'll find that I'm not an unreasonable soul. I won't ask too much, I will keep you fed, and I will praise you when I think praise is deserved. On the other hand, step out of line and you'll soon find out that I can be scathing with my words and actions. Do you think you could cope with that?'

'I'm a hard worker, sir, I'll not let you down.' Lucy looked straight at her new master. 'My mother says I should feel lucky that I've been given this chance so near home. And besides, we need the money because my mother's carrying another baby. Not that my father knows yet, let alone me knowing it for sure. I've just seen her being sick in a morning and she's been crying of late – a sure sign another baby is on the way. My father will go mad when she tells him, as he doesn't want another baby in the house.'

'Well, perhaps we should keep that to ourselves for the moment, Lucy. At least until your mother tells your father. I'm sure we are going to get along fine. Now, how

27

about I pay you two shillings a week? You can start straight away by making me a sandwich, and then while I start to whitewash these walls with the lime your father's so kindly sent me, you can go and scrub the kitchen floor. All you need is in the back kitchen, and there's some water heating in the copper boiler in the outhouse.' Adam watched as Lucy's eyes widened at the thought of two shillings to call her own. He'd make sure she earned it; she seemed an empty-headed girl, who was rather open with her views, but at least she wasn't a sullen bit of a thing; and she'd be company for him, without any commitment on his behalf.

'Yes, sir, that would be wonderful. Thank you very much, sir.' Lucy found her way to the kitchen and then came back quickly, her face aglow with embarrassment. 'I'd like to make you a sandwich, sir, but there's only a loaf of bread in the kitchen. So I've nothing to put in it.'

'My fault, as I've not unpacked properly yet. Here, there's a crate of basic food, which I should have put away this morning when I made my breakfast. It needs placing into the larder, and then later this week I'll make my way down into Keighley to stock us up.' Adam walked over to his unplaced pile of items and pulled out a wooden crate filled with flour, sugar, butter, cheese and other essential items, which he had bought before his journey from Keighley. 'You'll find some cheese in there, Lucy – that will do just grand.'

Adam carried the crate into the low-set kitchen that was at the back of the house, with the larder leading off from the main room. 'The range in the front room is best for cooking on at present. This kitchen is going to have to be made my priority. There's no water in the whole of the place; it is outside the back door in a trough and runs straight down from the moor, but I aim to pipe it into the house. It should have been done years ago. You'll have to make do and mend until I get things in order, but the main thing to do first is get the old place clean and habitable for now.' Adam smiled and looked at Lucy as she stared up at the kitchen ceiling, which was near collapse. 'I'll soon get the place straight, don't you worry. It'll be a different place in six months' time, if I have my way.'

He left her to open the crate and make him a sandwich as he gazed out of the window and questioned the foolishness of his decision to take on the old homestead. In the distance he could hear the Flappit Quarry men at work, hewing out the York stone that was in demand for all the buildings being erected by busy industrialists in West Yorkshire. The ring of hammers echoed around the hills and moors. At least he wasn't going to be beholden to someone telling him what to do, all day every day, and so he would just have to be content with his lot in his life. He'd nowhere else to go and, apart from Ivy Thwaite in Kendal, nobody cared whether he lived or died; but Adam had not even heard from Ivy in a while. He breathed in deeply; he'd eat his sandwich and then at least mix the whitewash for the one room that was habitable, before asking Lucy for her help in rearranging throughout the house what possessions he had. His old home needed time and patience spent on it – a bit like

29

himself, he thought, as Lucy entered with the best-looking sandwich he'd eaten for a long time.

'That'll do grand, Lucy. Thank you.'

'Pleasure, sir.' Lucy smiled. She was going to enjoy working for Adam Brooksbank. He might be a slightly older man, but he was good-looking, with charm. Her father had been right: he was a man with money and manners, and she could do far worse.

4

Adam stared up at his bedroom ceiling and yawned. His body was aching all over from placing his belongings into their allotted place in the old house; his right arm and his injured leg were giving him the most gyp, after whitewashing the main living room. He roused himself. Lucy would be making her way up from Providence Row and would be knocking on his door, if he didn't move. She'd been good company, for a lass so young, and she'd worked just as hard as himself, so he'd no complaints so far. He dressed in an old pair of trousers and a striped twill shirt. Today was not a day for finery, as he was about to tackle the hole in the back kitchen roof, if he could find some spare slates to fit the job. No sooner had he reached the bottom of the stairs, which creaked and groaned with every board trodden on, than there was a quiet knock on the door and Lucy walked in.

'Morning, sir. I've collected some sticks for kindling from out of the hedgerow. They are good and dry, and they will soon get a fire going in the hearth. It may be early March, but the wind still cuts through to the bone up here.' Lucy gave him a quick glance up and down, noticing that he hadn't bothered to shave yet and was not dressed as finely this morning, before she took off her cloak and set about cleaning out the previous day's embers from the still-warm fire, placing the twigs that she had gathered from the hedgerow into the fire's grate.

'I could have done that. Lighting the fire is no hardship.' Adam smiled at the lass as she raked the ashes away and soon had the fire blazing.

'Now, it's no good having a dog and barking yourself – that's what my mother would say. I'll see to it every morning. Besides, it gets me away and out early, before my siblings are awake. I swear the noise the youngest two make, shrieking and crying, is enough to waken the dead. Lord knows what home will be like when there's another mouth to feed.' Lucy went over to her cloak and produced two newly laid eggs from its pocket. 'I picked these up on my way here. Old Moffat has a field full of hens, just next to the crossroads; he's not going to miss two eggs, so I brought them for your breakfast, seeing that your pantry is not full to bursting.' She grinned as she went out into the yard with a pan and the kettle to fill with water, then placed both on the fire to boil.

'Now, you mind what you are doing – no more stealing of eggs. You could go to prison for that.' Adam looked concerned, but could not chastise her too much as Lucy had been kind enough to think of breakfast for him. 'Like I said, I'll go down into Keighley, probably tomorrow, and stock up the pantry. But today I'll try and fix that kitchen roof and put slate on it at the front. You can see the stars through the ceiling in the spare room, I noticed, when I made my way to bed last night.'

'I don't know what possessed you to come and live here, sir. It's been unlived in for such a long time, and it's so out of the way and right on the moor's top – it gets so wild up here in winter.' Lucy dropped the eggs into the pan to boil and placed a plate and mug on the table, which had found a home in the main room of the house.

'It was my family home, Lucy. I was born here and lived here as a boy with my parents, right up to getting married and leaving them for what I thought would be a better life in Keighley.' Adam looked at his new maid as she sliced him some bread and buttered it for him to eat with his eggs.

'Oh, I thought you were from off. I didn't know you were born here. So where's your wife at, sir? Did she not want to join you?' Lucy asked inquisitively.

'She died a long time ago, and I've been on my own ever since. Now enough of me. Tell me who's who in the area: who should I get to know, and who should I keep at arm's length? I'm out of touch with some of the folk who have moved in while I've been away. However, I'm sure a bright girl like you knows everybody around here.'

'The biggest family around here is the Fosters; they live at Whiteshaw in Denholme and own the cotton mill in Denholme. Then there's the Bucks at Godmansend; they own a lot of the land around here, and Mrs Buck was one of the Dawson family that have woollen mills in Bradford. They have a second home in Wales, so they are only here part of the year. And then there's . . .' Lucy reeled off the names of all the relevant families in the area while Adam listened and watched, as she spooned his boiled eggs out of the boiling water onto his plate. 'I'm sorry you've no eggcup – I never thought,' Lucy apologized as she watched him juggle and peel the hot hard-boiled eggs.

'It's not for you to apologize. The eggs are fine as they are. Now then, you are a mine of information. You should have been working with me over in the Crimea – with your intelligence, we'd have won in the first year.' Adam laughed.

'I earwig what my mother and father say, and I talk to all the men in the yard; they tell me everything. Everybody, that is, except Thomas Farrington. I give him a wide berth as he frightens me, and lately he just stares at me and says nothing. I think he's got a bit missing.' Lucy fell quiet.

'Who's Thomas Farrington and where does he live?' Adam pricked up his ears, concerned that this man was worrying his hard-working maid.

'He's my father's foreman, and he lives at the other end of our row. Father says he's a good worker, but I don't care – I don't like him.' Lucy's face clouded over.

'If he bothers you, you let me know,' Adam said to her.

'No, you are better off not crossing him, he's a nasty piece of work. He's too handy with his fists. He's always

34

fighting with someone or other, especially when he's drunk too much at The Fleece. You said you were in the Crimea – is that where you got your limp?'

'Aye, it was. I didn't move fast enough to get out of the way of a hussar and his sword; the bastard ran me through, and that was the end of my time serving in Her Majesty's army. Good thing and all, too, else I'd have frozen to death, like thousands of others who were left to rot in the Balkans. Men would have fought to have eaten the eggs you've just fed me, we had so little food. Now, while I make a start on mending the roof, you make a list of what we need in the house and I'll see that I buy it in the morning.'

'I will, and I'll make some bread, if that oven is to be trusted, once I've given it a good clean and worked out how to regulate it.' Lucy motioned to the oven range, which on the first night of his arrival had burned Adam's pie.

'I wish you well with that. I only fell asleep for a brief minute or two and my supper was ruined. I'm more at home mending the roof, mind. I leave the women to cook for me.' Adam grinned.

'Are you sure you'll be alright going up and down the ladder – won't it cause you pain?' Lucy looked at Adam as she cleared his breakfast table and watched as he put on a leather jerkin to keep him warm.

'Well, there's nobody else going to do it for me. So the sooner I make a start on it, the better. It's a good job I brought all my tools with me from Leeds Barracks, because I'm going to need them to get this old place in

35

order. But once it's done, Black Moss will be back to the home it used to be. I'll have some hens of my own, and sheep and a milking cow, once I've finished with the house and seen to the walls and fences.' Adam stood in the doorway and looked back at Lucy. He found her easy to talk to – too easy, for he had to get on with his work around the house. However, he noticed the look of concern on her face.

'But your leg, won't you struggle with the job in hand?' Lucy protested.

'I'll be fine, I can't let a thing like that stop me. Men with a lot worse left the fields of the Crimea and they've still to make a living. But thank you for your concern.' Adam smiled to himself as he closed the door behind him and left Lucy to tidy the breakfast table and go about her baking. She was proving to be a good lass, and he was glad he had stumbled across her. Despite her saying what she thought, there was no harm in talking straight; in fact it was a good trait of the Yorkshire man to say what he thought, Adam mused as he struggled with each rung of the ladder, balancing nails, slates and hammer as he gingerly made it onto the kitchen roof. She was right, he thought, when he caught his breath and stopped himself from shaking with effort as he sat upon the ridge tiles of the farmhouse. The climb had taken more out of him than he'd realized, and he looked around him as he rubbed his painful leg. How he'd missed his true home, he thought, breathing in the dank, peaty smell of the moors that lay around him. There was no smell like it, and no view like it on a good day. He was glad to be home; it was where he belonged.

Lucy organized herself in the kitchen. She had soon made the dough for the bread and then placed it next to the fire to rise, before looking around her for the next job that needed doing. She'd make a list of items required, as the bread baked in the temperamental oven. She sighed; she was going to enjoy her work here. It was no way as hard as working for her mother, and she could run the house as she saw fit. The pile of furniture that had been delivered the previous day had now found a home in each room, and she decided to give the oak furniture a polish while waiting for the bread to rise.

Black Moss was beginning to look like more of a home now, she thought, as she tried to regain a shine on the ancient Welsh dresser that had made its home in the main room of the house, rubbing it with beeswax and then buffing it up with a polishing rag. Then she unpacked and placed the blue-and-white willow-pattern plates on the tall plate rack, and that immediately made the cold, newly whitewashed room into a home. She stood back with her hands on her hips and smiled. The old place would look nice if it was given some love and care, and she was going to take some pride in helping Adam Brooksbank get it into shape.

The hammering of nails being put into the slates to secure the roof could be heard from above, and Lucy listened as she heard Adam stop and start again as he balanced himself precariously on the roof. Then she heard him swear and curse, as something had dropped out of his hands and had slid down the roof, bouncing and clattering the full length and ending up on the ground below. Knowing what a struggle it must have been for him to get up on the roof in the first place, Lucy ran out of the house and went round to the back, where the ladder was positioned against the wall, with Adam still cursing on the roof.

'Sir, are you alright? I don't think you should be up there,' Lucy yelled.

'I've dropped my bloody hammer, and I need another of those two slates.' Adam wobbled and tried to straighten his leg in order to come back down the roof to get what he needed.

'Stay there. I'll bring them up to you and then I'll see you down,' Lucy shouted up to him and grabbed both hammer and slates, tucking them under her arm as she gathered her long skirts up and climbed, rung by rung, up the ladder.

'Mind you don't break your neck. Your father would hang me if you fell, because it would be all my fault.' Adam looked at the determined young lass as she balanced what he needed under her arm and appeared at the edge of the roof, with flushed cheeks.

'You are more likely to break your neck than me. I told you it wasn't a fit job for you to do, with that dicky leg.' Lucy caught her breath and looked up at Adam, forgetting who she was talking to as she passed him the slates. 'Don't worry about me. I've always been a tomboy – I could climb any tree better than my brothers, if it

38

wasn't for these skirts that us women have to wear.' She grinned as Adam took the slates and placed the tiling nails securely between his lips, unable to argue with her, as she waited for him to finish the job in hand. 'It's a grand view up here. You feel like you are on top of the world.' Lucy gazed around her as Adam hammered the nails down, securing the slates into position and making the roof dry.

'I'll just be glad to get back down – never mind the view.' Adam cautiously edged his way back to the ladder, after throwing the hammer down onto the grassy bank at the back of the house. 'Mind out. I'm coming, and my leg feels dead with cramp, so if I don't fall on you, you'll be lucky.' He waited for a second, watching Lucy, who quickly climbed down the ladder out of his way, then stood and watched attentively as he reached for each rung of the ladder with his good leg first, and then his bad one. Eventually he reached the ground, his legs shaking with the effort, and brushed himself down and looked at Lucy. 'Thank you. I don't think I could have done that without your help.'

'Perhaps next time you need to get a fitter man to do the job, sir, or at least someone with two good legs,' Lucy stated as she looked drily at him.

'Perhaps you are right, Lucy. I should know my limitations.' Adam smiled at his straight-talking maid, without whom he'd have still been up on the roof. 'But I'm a stubborn devil and I don't like to admit defeat.'

'No, neither do I, sir, but there are some things I'm not daft enough to do, especially when I could kill myself doing them. Now I'll put the kettle on and go and put my bread in the oven; it should have risen well by now.'

Adam sat at the table and looked across at Lucy. 'You seem to have made yourself at home here already.'

'Well, I know that you are in need of looking after – it's as plain as the nose on my face. It's like my mother says: it's a woman's touch that makes a home, and menfolk are no good at making things pretty about the house.' Lucy grinned as she watched Adam sip his tea, while he glanced at the Welsh dresser with its array of blue-and-white china proudly displayed upon it. 'I'll make the list that you need for when you go into Keighley, after the bread has come out of the oven. You've no polish left and there are not many candles, not to mention flour, eggs and the like. What you have already won't last very long, so I hope that you are not short of brass.'

'No, I think I can manage to pay for what we need. Stocking the house's cupboards is the least of my worries. Next week I'll have to start and look for some stock for the land, but first I'll have to get some better pain relief for this leg of mine. It's letting me down, and I can't be having that, when I need to inspect the boundary walls and perhaps mend and repair them.' Adam sighed. He was beginning to think his idea of living back in his old home had been a foolish fantasy and that he was going to struggle with his new lifestyle.

'You need somebody to help you. Archie Robinson, the lad who brought your limewash, is a good hand at anything. He only works three days a week for my father, and the rest of the time he does odd jobs for people. He looks after his mother, bless him; he lost his father after an accident at the quarry, so his mother depends on him.' Lucy stood back against the window and looked at her master.

'I can guess your plan, Lucy. I noticed that you were sweet on him when he introduced you to me. I don't think your father would be that pleased if I took him on as well as you; and besides, you'd be too busy flirting to get anything done for me.' Adam grinned and looked at Lucy's cheeks flush.

'It's not like that, sir. I just feel sorry for him. Archie never has any time for himself and he works so hard to keep a roof over his own and his mother's head. He used to have dreams, like me, when he was young, but with being the only bread-earner at home, he's worn down. He deserves a bit of luck and he hates working at the flay-pits. I've known him since we were little, so I do tend to wind him up a bit with my cheek, but I never think of him in that way. It's like you say: my father would kill me if I had to marry him. My father has set his head on somebody far more important for me, although I'll marry who I want and he'll not stop me, if I have my way.' Lucy hung her head and then walked to the oven to check on her bread.

'And who does your father think suitable for you then, Lucy? It sounds as if he has somebody in mind.' Adam looked at the flushed young woman, who had ideas of her own when it came to the man she was going to love.

'He thinks I should be fluttering my eyelids at Alex Braithwaite from the quarry, but I'm not having any of it. Or one of the Buck lads, but neither are for me really. I might flirt with them, but I haven't come across the right man yet. Besides, Alex Braithwaite is never out of The Fleece of an evening. It's no good marrying a drinker – my mother told me that and she should know, because my father likes a gill or two and often comes home from The Fleece the worse for wear. It's his usual night for having a gill tonight, and I bet he'll come home in a right stinker this evening, especially if my mam has told him her news. Me and the young ones will keep out of his way and hide under the bedclothes, if he starts ranting. He'll not have taken the news well, and I only hope my mam will be alright.

'He's got a bit of a temper sometimes, although he never raises his hand in anger; just gobs off and frightens everybody with his language. But it's as my mam says: at least she's not like Rebecca Town that lived down in Keighley – she had thirty children before she died at the age of forty-four. Thirty children, and all of them died before they reached five! The poor woman must have died of a broken heart.' Lucy was thankful she couldn't see the response on Adam's face, as she bent down to take the second loaf from the oven. Her father's temper wasn't something she'd told everyone about, but her new employer seemed a kind man and had shown a tender side to him, in the two days she'd worked for him.

'Now I'd never have thought that of your father. He seemed a reasonable man. I've not heard of this Rebecca

Town, but it does not surprise me, in the depravity of Keighley town. It is somewhere I'm not very fond of.' Adam looked concerned at his young maid; it would seem that Bill Bancroft was not what he appeared, and that Lucy had seen fit to talk to him about her father's temper, out of worry.

'My father's just got a lot on his mind, what with the tannery and all of us to feed. It's only when he's had a gill that he lets rip. We all know to keep out of his way then. You'll not say to anyone that I've told you, will you? He doesn't like us to gossip – he'd bray me to within an inch of my life.' Lucy shot a look at Adam and wished she hadn't said anything.

'No, I'll not say anything, Lucy. But if he gets too violent, you come here with your sister and brothers. I'll not have any of you hurt by a man in drink. Even though it's none of my business.' Adam looked across at the blushing young woman and decided to leave it at that, saving her any further blushes. 'I'll go and have a walk around the higher pastures, inspect the walls and see what needs to be done. Can you put me a slice or two of that newly baked bread with a chunk of cheese? That will do me for my dinner, and then I'll return before dusk, for you to go home.' Adam watched as Lucy hurriedly cut into the new loaf and bundled a good slice of Wensleydale cheese into a napkin for him to carry.

'Don't be going too far – think of your leg,' Lucy said, as Adam took the napkin in his hand and put his cap on. 'I'll be making a stew of some sorts, with what we've got, for your return; and I'll tidy that spare bedroom, not that you have a lot of furniture in it.' Lucy wanted to make sure her new master realized that she wouldn't be idle while he was out and about.

'Aye, that's grand. And don't worry – I'll take it easy. It's been a long time since I've walked up the moors around here. I used to love the view. I've had many a tanned backside for being late home, and my parents wondering where I'd been, when I was just a lad.' Adam smiled as Lucy shook her head.

'It's fellas: they never grow up. My mam says that, God knows how many times a day, and she's right.' Lucy watched as her master closed the door behind him, leaving her to worry about what was going on back at home, and whether her mother had plucked up the courage to tell her father about the baby, which was not wanted. Thank God she was out of the way for a while, because there would be hell to pay, for sure.

Adam walked slowly but surely around his acres of land, which he would have covered in an hour or less when he was in his prime, but now the rough moorland and his injured leg made walking that little bit harder, and he rested on one of the limestone walls that were in need of attention. He leaned back and closed his eyes and smelled the rich, clear moorland air, and listened to a skylark singing above his head. It was a million miles away from the roaring cannons of the battlefields of the Crimea, and his experience there made him appreciate every second of the wild moor's silence.

He opened his eyes and smiled as he watched the

moorland grass blowing in the wind. In another few months it would be covered with cotton-grass flowers, like little puffs of white cloud upon the dark peaty bogs. It seemed but yesterday that he had walked these pastures with his father and built and mended the rough limestone walls, complaining that his hands and back hurt, when his father said he was slacking. His father had been right. There was more hurt to be had in life than sore hands and an aching back, but it was too late to tell him, now that he understood. Adam breathed in deeply and followed the contour of the wall, watching it dip down into the next valley, where the village of Haworth tucked itself into the hillside. The cobbled streets were busy with small shops and people going about their business. He'd go and spend a day there shortly, perhaps call in on the vicar at the parsonage, and see the heartbroken old Reverend who lived there. He'd been a rock for Adam after the death of Mary, even after suffering heartbreaking losses in his own family.

Adam took a last look around him and decided to head home, to see what transformations Lucy had made to the old homestead in his absence. So far her employment with him was working well, and he realized that his initial opinion of an empty-headed flirt of a girl had been wrong. Lucy was a good worker and would be an asset to him in the future.

He stood up and made his way back down over the moorland to home, just as the sun was starting to dip in the sky. As he walked down back into the Worth valley he looked down upon Keighley and the industries that meandered along the valley bottom. The Industrial Revolution had arrived in his valley, and wool and cotton factories and ironworks were rising up everywhere. He was glad that he was out living in the wilds, and not part of the mad lifestyle in the valley bottom. He might not be the richest of people, but at least he was his own master.

'Eeh, Master Brooksbank, what have you walked so far for? You look so weary.' Lucy gave him a portion of potato-hash, fresh from a pot that had been simmering over the fire since the time he had left. 'There's no meat in there, but it'll warm you through and I've added some sage that I found in the overgrown garden. Give me another month and I'll have that garden full to the brim with vegetables and herbs. I've added to the shopping list some packets of seeds that I need, if you can remember them. It's exactly the right time of year to be turning the ground and planting things.'

'I'm after buying a horse first, Lucy. Do they still have the horse market in the centre of town? Or has that gone now, like everything else? A horse will save the trudge back and forth into Keighley and I can ride it around my land. It would save my legs.'

'You've missed the main horse sale of the year; it's usually held on Scott Street or Russell Street. You need to go and see Tom Gaine on Fell Lane – he breeds sturdy little fell ponies that will not think twice of carrying you, or anything else, across their backs. Everyone goes to him, he's a right good horseman. My father swears by him, and so do a lot of folk around here, so he must be a good fella.' Lucy looked at Adam as he ate his hash, and thought how good it smelled.

'Have you had any of this?' Adam looked up from his supper and noticed how hungry Lucy looked.

'No, sir, I made it for you.'

'Well, there's enough for two, so pull up a chair and get yourself a plate and join me. I'm not sending you back home with an empty belly. You can join me each evening at supper, if you wish. I'd be glad of the company, and I'm not one for standing on ceremony and keeping my maid at arm's length. We are all God's children, after all.'

'Are you sure, sir? I shouldn't sit at the same table as you, it isn't right. My mother said I'd to mind my manners and not be impudent.' Lucy looked at Adam with concern.

'Go on, help yourself, and then I'll walk you part of the way home. The sun's setting fast, and I wouldn't want you to be accosted by any rogues out there.' Adam watched as she placed a helping of the hash on a plate and sat down at the other side of the table from him, eating it so quickly that he couldn't help but think it had been the only thing she must have eaten all day. 'You eat when I eat, while you are here. I never thought of saying that, when I took my bread and cheese with me this morning. I'll not pay you any less for your meals, so don't be afeared of that. You can't do a day's work on an empty belly.' Adam smiled and looked across at his maid.

'Thank you, sir. I'll not eat you out of house and home. There's no need to walk me home, as your leg's bothering you.' Lucy stood up and cleared the plates, washing them quickly in the stone sink in the back kitchen, before returning with her cloak tied around her.

'I'll walk you home so far, and then I'll watch you the rest of the way. I must admit it's been a long day and my leg feels the worse for it. I'm going to have to realize that I'm not the man I used to be.' Adam rose from his chair and opened the door for them both to walk out into the darkening night. They walked in silence down the dark track to the crossroads, from where Lucy's home could clearly be seen.

'The stars are out tonight, sir, and there's a full moon just beginning to rise. Leave me here – look, my home's in sight now. Watch me run down the hill to home and then go back yourself. There's really no need to walk me back home every night; it's only a five-minute walk.' Lucy realized that Adam's limp was getting worse with every step, and she didn't want him hurting himself further.

'Go on then, it'll save me climbing back up the hill from your home, but I should have walked you a little further.' Adam was thankful for her suggestion, and looked down the hill towards the row of workers' cottages, which were easily seen in the silver of the moonlight. He watched as Lucy, with cloak and skirts billowing, ran down the hill and disappeared into her home. He turned and walked steadily back, leaning heavily on his walking stick, thankful when the lights of his home came into sight. It had been a long day, but one that he had enjoyed, and he was pleased with his choice of maid. He had but one more job to do before retiring to his bed, and that was to write a few words to Ivy Thwaite and tell her that he was home at last, and perhaps she would care to visit him. It would be good to see a friendly face, Adam mused, as he put pen to paper before calling it a night. In his letter he told Ivy of his move and his new employee, and that he had missed his old friend's correspondence.

Sitting on the edge of his bed, Adam sighed. In the dim light of the oil lamp by his bedside, he swallowed the mixture known as Kendal Black Drop and waited for the warmth of the opium, mixed with spices and vinegar, to overcome him. As he looked at the empty bottle that usually contained his preferred pain relief of laudanum, regret for his weakness at his pain filled him. He should have made sure that he had enough laudanum; instead the bottle had been empty since his arrival at Black Moss. Tomorrow he'd visit the chemist in Keighley, as he couldn't manage without the laudanum any longer.

5

'You've had a long day. Does he expect you to work these hours every day? If he does, I hope he's willing to pay you for what you are worth, because I'm missing your help around here.' Dorothy Bancroft lifted her head and scowled at her fresh-faced daughter as she burst into the three-bedroom cottage they considered home. 'Our Bert is teething; Susie is wailing about, because she's lost her doll; and I'm up to my arms in washing and ironing. It's alright your father sending you out to work, but who's going to help me with all our bairns?'

'I'm back now. I'll find Susie's doll – she usually drops it under our bed when she's half-asleep and forgets about it. I'll look for it now.' Lucy looked around her. Although they weren't that poor, you'd never have guessed it, by the state of the house. Unlike Adam Brooksbank, her parents took no pride in their home, as they were too busy working and bringing up all their offspring.

Lucy untied her cloak and hung it behind the kitchen

door and picked up the teething Bert under her arm, as she climbed the wooden stairs to the bedroom she shared with her sister. She placed Bert on the bed as he bawled yet again, his cheeks flushed with pain and his snotty nose mixing with his tears. 'Just be quiet, our Bert – here, chew on this.' Lucy passed the blond-haired, blue-eyed baby a dolly peg that she always carried in her pocket for him to chew on, and to ease the pain in his gums, as she lay down flat on her stomach on the bare floorboards of the bedroom and fished from under the bed a hand-made rag doll that had been handed down by several members of the Bancroft family. 'I knew where it would be. Susie should be old enough to look for it herself, instead of having tantrums and moaning about it,' Lucy said as she looked at her young brother. He was now sobbing and fretting while holding his hands out to be hugged by his older sister, discarding the dolly peg and wanting some closer attention from his substitute mother. 'Black Moss Farm is like heaven compared to this,' Lucy whispered as she picked him up and wiped his snotty face on the edge of her apron. 'Now, let's take Susie her dolly and put something on your swollen gums, and see who else needs my attention.'

'Oh, you've found it – thank God for that! And just look at Bert. I couldn't make him do, and now he's as quiet as a mouse in your arms. Nathan! Stop that this minute, else you can go and sleep in the coal house tonight, out of my sight. Lord knows, you'll probably be safer out there anyway, the state your father will probably come back in this evening.' Dorothy clipped her

51

eldest son around the ear as he boxed and fought with his younger brother, making him cry. 'You are all enough to send me to an early grave, I'll be glad when the summer months are here and I can turn you all out of the house until bedtime and save you from being under my feet. What your father thought he was doing, sending you out to work, our Lucy, when I've all these on my hands, I don't know. If he stopped his visits to The Fleece, we wouldn't need the extra money.'

Lucy placed Bert down on the pegged rug by the fire and passed Susie her doll, as she sat sulking in the chair next to her mother, who was busy ironing.

'Thank you, Lucy, I knew you'd find it. Dolly will have been crying all day without me – she doesn't like to be left alone.' Susie kissed her older sister and grinned. 'I've missed you too, and Mam says we've to get to bed in good time tonight, to get out from under her and Father's feet. I don't want to go to bed without you, and I thought you weren't going to come home when it went dark.' Susie hung onto her sister's neck and wanted Lucy's assurance that all would be well, now that she was home.

Lucy stood up and looked at her mother, after kissing four-year-old Susie. 'So, we are due a new one in our family, and you've told my father? He'll not be pleased.'

'Aye, he'll not be in a good mood when he comes home tonight. But what does he expect? I told him to sleep away from me; that he's only to look at me and I'd be with child again. My mother was the same – we catch on so fast. You'd do well to keep your legs closed until you are wed to a good man, else you'll end up the same

52

as me, with a house full of bairns and no time for nowt.' Dorothy looked at her eldest; if she had lectured her once about the virtues of keeping pure, she must have lectured her a dozen times. She wanted better for her daughter than a life married to a temperamental husband, and a life of drudgery, with children tugging on her apron strings every second of the day, as she had.

'I'm never going to be like you. I don't care if I never have any children. I've seen all too well what it does to a woman. Besides, I'm going to find me a man that will look after me and not keep me chained to housework and bringing up his children.' Lucy smiled at her young sister; she did love her siblings, but when it came to having a family of her own one day, that was a different matter. She'd seen all too well the anguish of bringing up a family on little money, and with little or no help from the breadwinner of the family.

'You'll change your tune when the right man comes along, and catches your eye and corners you with his soft words and loving touches. We've all said the same as you, and before you know it, you are wed with children around your feet and the bloom of youth faded from your cheeks. Now, help me get these children to bed before your father arrives, because aye, he's not pleased and it's best that you are all out of his sight.' Dorothy sighed; she needed to protect her children from her husband's wrath, and the best way to do that was to get them all in their beds and out of earshot of the harsh words that she knew he'd be yelling, if not more.

*

Lucy lay next to her sister in their attic bedroom at the top of the house. Even though she was as high up as the house was tall, she could hear her father's voice bellowing in the kitchen below. She glanced at her sister and was thankful she was fast asleep, and that it was only her who could hear their father's ranting and the plates being smashed on the kitchen floor. Her poor mother. It wasn't only her fault that she was with child yet again; it took two, as anybody knew. Her father should have kept his John Thomas in his pocket, and then every nine months or so neither her nor her parents would have to endure the rage that followed the news of yet another baby to be born within the family. She only hoped that this night Father would not raise his voice any louder at her mother, and that perhaps the amount of ale he'd drunk would make him ready for his bed.

She held her breath and looked up through the attic skylight at the frosty night sky outside. If only she could escape this life of drudgery; of being responsible for her siblings and having to smell the stench of the flay-pits every day. She'd got to the age when she was ashamed of her roots and of her father's profession – a stinking hide-tanner with too many children, and a home that was volatile with worry, although there was still love within it. No wonder none of the more well-to-do young men of the district would give her a second glance. It didn't matter that she was the bonniest lass in the district; she was nothing: no money, no class and a father who was a drunk at least one night of the week.

She bit her lip as she heard her father's footsteps, dull

and heavy, ascending the stairs to his bedroom below, and then heard her mother come up the stairs after him, sobbing. Thank God the row was over for the night, although it would be carried on again more than likely until the next baby was born, dead or alive. It wouldn't be the first time her mother had given birth to a stillborn baby; the first two had been given proper churchyard graves, but the other two were quickly got rid of, buried in the quicklime in a corner of the yard that only her father used. Their soft bodies decomposed over time and were never acknowledged by anybody except her mother, when a wave of depression and grief for her lost children came over her.

Lucy held her breath, not daring to think the worst of her parents, but sometimes she wondered if the babies her mother had borne, and who had been declared dead at birth, had actually been alive; and that between her mother and her father, they had simply agreed to do away with them in the quicklime. It was a dark thought that she kept to herself and didn't want to acknowledge to anyone. It was a thought that was best kept a secret and not breathed to another soul. After all, it was an act of murder, and Lucy didn't dare think that of her parents.

6

Adam woke to the noise of banging on the back door and his name being shouted in desperation. His mind was coddled from the heaviness of the previous night's taking of Black Drop, and it took him a while to realize that he was not lost in one of his illusion dreams. Reaching for his pocket watch, he squinted and focused his eyes as he tried to read the time.

'Mr Brooksbank, sir. Are you alright?' Adam recognized the voice of Lucy, shouting with concern up at his bedroom window, between bouts of hammering on the back door of Black Moss Farm.

Nine o'clock – no wonder she was worried, as he was usually up and about by six. Adam sat on the edge of the bed for a second and then slicked back his hair, pulling on his trousers and braces before going to the window to reassure a worried Lucy.

'I'm fine, Lucy.' Adam leaned out of the window and squinted in the sharpness of the sun's light. 'Sorry, I didn't realize the time. Give me a minute and I'll be down to open the door.'

Lucy looked up at her drowsy employer and sighed with relief. She was beginning to worry that something was wrong and she hadn't known what to do.

Adam quickly freshened his face with cold water from the jug in his bedroom; a shave would have to wait. Then he walked as fast as he could down the stairs to the cold, empty kitchen. His head was swimming with the excesses of his previous night's indulgence in pain relief, as he pulled back the bolt on the front door and let Lucy in.

'Are you alright? I thought you were ill or, even worse, that someone had murdered you in your bed.' Lucy bustled past him. She threw her shawl down and looked at her employer. 'You look ill, sir. Are you sure you are well? Perhaps you did too much yesterday. I'll get the fire lit. By the looks of you, you could do with a drink of tea and something to eat.' She looked hard at her employer and made Adam feel uncomfortable, by the long stare she gave him.

'It's not like me to not realize what time it is. I've had such hard days since I came here – it's just sleep catching up with me. I'd welcome a cup of tea. I'll go back upstairs first and shave quickly.' Adam watched Lucy as she set about riddling the fire's ashes and laying kindling sticks, before relighting the fire and placing the kettle to boil on the newly flickering flames. Lucy said nothing as he left the room and, climbing the stairs to his room, Adam swore quietly under his breath. She could have been right; she might have found him dead in his bed, not from murder, but by his own hand and an overdose of Black Drop as a substitute for his preferred laudanum. Laudanum he could handle; the effects of it might sometimes make him feel drowsy, but not like Black Drop, which made him hallucinate and sleep too hard. Damn the pain in his leg and the pain in his heart! Opium and laudanum were his only release from both, but he'd have to be more careful that they did not rule him.

'Here you go, sir. Some porridge and a warm-up in front of the fire will soon make you feel more like yourself.' Lucy pulled up Adam's chair at the end of the table for him to sit in, as he arrived, clean-shaven and more awake, back in the kitchen. 'It's like you say, sir, you've done a lot of late, and what with your bad leg and all. It will have taken things out of you.'

'Thank you, Lucy. I'm sorry you had to wake me. It'll not happen again. You look tired yourself this morning. Are you alright? I'm not driving you too hard, am I?' Adam looked up at the pale-faced young woman and smiled.

'Oh no, sir. It's just that I didn't sleep well. It was as I had suspected: my father came home in a temper and I heard it all going on downstairs. And I'm always afeared for the young ones when he's like that.' Lucy bowed her head.

'Oh, I see, so the news was not greeted well, I take it?' Adam watched as she stirred the pot of porridge, before pouring some into a dish and passing it to him.

'No, not at all. He'll not be talking to any of us for a day or so now, he'll be in such a mood. God help any of his workers, because they'll not be able to do anything right today, the way he's storming about the yard.' Lucy watched as Adam ate his porridge. 'Are you still going into Keighley today? It's a bit late in the day for you to be making tracks now, sir.'

'No, I must go today, I've urgent business. And besides, the quicker I get a horse bought, the better it is for me. Once I've eaten this porridge I'll be on my way. Could you see to my bedroom? It needs a good clean, as it's not been touched since I moved in, and the spiders seem to think they have free run of the room, the way they are hanging down from the beams in their intricate webs.' Adam sat back and pulled on his boots, leaving half of his breakfast uneaten. He had to get to Keighley, come hell or high water, to visit the apothecary for something less potent than the Black Drop, which he could all too easily become too dependent upon.

'You'll take care, won't you, sir? Have you got my list of what you need? Although if you are to buy a horse today, I can manage without some of the things upon it, as I know old Mr Gaine will natter you to death. He can talk for England, folk say.' Lucy watched as Adam put on his jerkin and headed for the door.

'I'll be back before dusk, Lucy, hopefully with a four-legged friend and whatever provisions you have requested. Will you be alright until I get back?'

Lucy stood at the farm's doorway and looked up at Adam. 'I'm sure I'll manage. Those spiders will have had to find new homes by the time you are back. Take care, sir, and watch your wallet – there's a lot of light-fingered pickpockets down there, who would rob you of your last penny.' She smiled.

'Don't you worry about me. I can hold my own. I didn't serve in the Queen's army for nothing.' Adam looked down at Lucy, who looked a little wan and worried. 'Now, make sure you get something to eat while I'm away, and I'll be back for my supper.'

Adam watched as she closed the door, feeling concerned that he was leaving her on her own and that she seemed beset with worries. Although he hardly knew her, he still couldn't stop himself worrying about her, as the life at home that she had disclosed to him was not a happy one and Lucy seemed obsessed with the fact that her mother was with child again. It was probably as she said – her mother and father falling out over the unwanted baby, and nothing more.

He walked briskly down the cobbled road from Denholme, leaving the wild bleak moors, making his way down the Halifax road into the busy town of Keighley. He stopped only to rest his aching leg outside a row of smoke-blackened mill cottages called Hermit Hole, and looked down the steep sides of the Aire valley towards the town of Keighley. Along the busy River Aire's banks stood worsted mills and ironworks, and between the mills and works were cottages filled with wool-combers working in their own bedrooms, making a meagre living. In the far distance he could hear the whistle of a steam engine from the recently built railway station that now connected Keighley to other industrial towns of Yorkshire.

His mind went back to the days when he was a young

man, full of dreams and hope for the future, and when he had patrolled the dark, dank wool town as a young peeler. How stupid he had been, judging people by the way they lived their lives. He hadn't realized how cruel life's hand could be, and that not everyone had a decent home to go to, with food on the table. All that had changed with the death of Mary. His life had been left in tatters by the worthless pickpocket that fateful afternoon, spiralling into an abyss of self-loathing and hate, filling his emptiness and sleeplessness by taking laudanum nearly every day, even before his injury. Until, in an effort to put himself out of his misery, he'd accepted his old friend Captain Linton Simmons's offer of a position in the godforsaken Crimea. He'd gone partly with the hope that some brutal Russian in the Balkans would put him out of his misery and kill him. But when he had looked death in the face, he had fought for his life, and now he knew that life was a most precious gift.

The reason for his trip today called Adam back to his senses. He hated his dependence on laudanum, but it brought relief from his pain, and a drop of a night helped him sleep and was not as strong as the Black Drop. Along with his need for a horse, he had to visit Keighley now, whether he was feeling like it or not.

He patted his pocket, making sure his letter to his dear friend Ivy was still safely inside it. Ivy Thwaite had been Mary's and his own closest friend, and she was a link between him and Mary in the world that lay between them. Ivy gave him the hope of everlasting life and showed him that one day he would be with Mary again, through the seances that she held with him, before he went to do his duty in the Crimea. He'd written asking that Ivy come and visit him and reignite their friendship, so that he could speak to Mary through Ivy and tell her of his new life back home. Although he knew that plenty of people thought of seances as a fanciful notion, and one that no sensible person would give the time of day to, sensible people had not seen or dreamed the things that he had, after the death of his beloved Mary. He was convinced that there was more to life than the one on earth, and heaven and hell. Ivy was the connection between the shrouded, misty world where souls tried, in desperation, to contact their loved ones, and he needed her services.

A rag-and-bone man passed him, shouting loudly his requirements, his old horse, its head down, pulling the heavy, dirt-ridden cart up the steep hill. 'Rag and Bownes!' His voice ran around the small terraced houses, as he waited for women with their cast-offs to run to him and haggle a price. Adam quickly came to his senses and watched the filthy man and his beast, before carrying on his way. The man would be the first of many traders that he'd meet, once he was down in Keighley. The potato blight in Ireland had seen an influx of Irish, who were eking out a living from knife-sharpening, shoe-cleaning, tinkering and any other trade that they could turn their hands to. If Keighley had been a poor town before their arrival, then it was even poorer now, with families in up to the teens living in two-bedroom houses, and open gutters running with human and animal waste. Those who had money had started businesses along East Street, and above the shop doorways were names that depicted their Irish roots: Murphy's and O'Haggan the butcher's being just a couple.

Reaching the centre of Keighley, Adam made his way to the corner of College Street and deposited his letter, to be sent to Ivy in Kendal by the daily mail-coach. The new postal building and service were a lot more professional than when they were run from the parlour of the Hare and Hounds by old Mrs Martha Cooke, who had scrutinized every letter sent or received, before passing them through a hinged pane in the window. Perhaps Keighley was progressing. The Mechanics' Institute and the Court House on North Street showed progress, Adam thought, as he stood and summoned up the courage to enter the apothecary's shop.

Adam recognized it well, from when he had patrolled his beat, and knew the chemist would perhaps recognize him, despite the fact that he had aged in his time away from the area. He looked around the shop at the various coloured jars of poisons, drugs and concoctions. People were obsessed with their health and would buy anything that promised a fix for their ills. A display of Dr Airey's Celebrated Indian Pills, Fox's Anti-Cholera Mixture and Fox's Never-Failing Cure for Thick Necks adorned the polished wooden counter, leading people to think they would cure whatever complaint they had.

'Can I help you?' The chemist turned round from measuring out some dark, vile-looking mixture and glanced at Adam.

'Some laudanum, please.' Adam spoke in a low voice; even though laudanum was a common everyday drug, he knew the chemist would know its properties, and that he had been at one time a regular visitor for the drug.

'Pills or drops?' The chemist stared at him.

'Drops, please,' Adam answered quickly.

'It's a penny for twenty-four drops – will that be enough?' The chemist looked harder at him. 'I seem to recognize you from somewhere.' He measured the drops out into a bottle and passed it over to Adam.

'Perhaps you've mistaken me for someone else.' Adam exchanged his penny with the chemist and placed the bottle and its contents safely into his pocket.

'They say people experience pain because of their sins. Do you think that is correct?' the chemist quizzed. He'd realized who his customer was: older now and not as cocksure, but it was definitely Adam Brooksbank.

'I wouldn't know, sir, as my pain came from a Russian's sword. Thank you for your service.' Adam turned and made for the door, knowing the old man would not stop there.

'That's physical pain, but your pain must be deeper, my friend.' The chemist leaned over the counter and watched as his shop's door slammed shut, leaving the doorbell above it ringing. So Adam Brooksbank was back and was still hurting; hurting so much that he had to find relief in laudanum.

Adam stood for a minute and pondered whether to go back into the apothecary's shop and tell the chemist that the years he had been away from his home town had changed him; that now the drugs were definitely for his sword wound, and not to ease his heartache. But then he thought better of it, for the old man would think what he wanted, no matter what Adam said. Folk did that, hearing only what they wanted, most of the time. He should by now be used to gossip, and should ignore any that he heard or that was of his making. At least he had his laudanum now, and a few good nights of sleep, free of pain, would make all the difference.

He put his hand in his pocket and fished out Lucy's list of storeroom ingredients; all the items she had requested were available from the shops along North Street. Adam decided to leave her list with Harrison's, the main supplier of provisions on North Street, for them to get ready for his return, after seeing Tom Gaine with regards to his need for a horse. What Harrison's couldn't supply, he'd pick up elsewhere on his way home, and would strap it all to the horse's back. He quickly walked the few yards to Harrison's, giving them the list to put together, before making his way across to the other side of town towards Fell Lane, seeking directions from a woman who was peddling her goods at the crossroads that led out of Keighley up to the wild moorland.

Standing on the doorstep of Daisy Cottage, Adam looked around him. But for the row of cottages and an inn, appropriately called The Three Horses, this part of Keighley had not yet been touched by the ongoing Industrial Revolution. Instead it was surrounded by grassy scrubland and fields, where Tom Gaine's love of horses was obvious to all, as numerous beasts stood and grazed in the surrounding fields.

'Aye, what can I do for you?' A small, wiry-built man answered his knock. His face was wrinkled and tanned and he had a look of a travelling Gypsy about him.

'I'm told you are the man I need to see about a horse. I'm in need of a steady, strong mount that'll carry my weight and is not too headstrong. I'm not bothered about the breed, just as long as it's not an old nag that you sell me.' Adam looked at the old man and waited.

'I'm not into selling old nags – they go to the knacker's yard. My horses are the fittest you'll find; all broken in by my own hand, and I know all their temperaments. Now, is it for pleasure or work? And more to the point, have you the money to pay for it?' Tom Gaine looked at the well-dressed fella and tried to work out who he had standing on his doorstep.

'Aye, I've got brass, and I know horses, as my father always had at least one up home. Young Lucy Robinson, from the flay-pits at Denholme, told me you were the one to come to, if that makes a difference. She said you were the best horseman for miles around.' Adam realized that to get anywhere with Tom he had to state his business, else he'd be getting nowhere fast.

'She did, did she? She's a fair lass, is that one. She'll make a good catch for someone some day. Full of cheek, mind. So how do you ken her?' Tom grinned.

'I've taken her on as my maid at my farm at Black Moss, up above Denholme. She is a good lass, as you say.' Adam looked at the old man as he closed his door behind him and made his way to the field gate next to his house.

'You must be Len Brooksbank's lad. I thought you'd been killed in the Crimea? Yet here you are, standing in front of me, as large as life. Your father was a good sort. You know you broke his heart, when you left him and turned your back on farming? Still, you are back now. We all get wiser with age and realize what we once had was worth holding onto.' Tom looked Adam up and down, then led him into the small pasture with ponies and horses grazing contentedly within it. 'You are limping, lad. Have you got something wrong with your leg?'

'You knew my father! And yes, you are right, I've come to my senses and returned home. I might not have got killed in the Crimea, but I felt Russian steel through my leg. That, along with a need to get around my land, is why I need a horse.' Adam looked around him at the various horses in the field and spotted a beautifully marked piebald horse, at least seventeen hands tall. 'That's a grand horse. How much is he, and how old is he?'

'You want nowt with him, lad. He's my prize stallion, but doesn't he know it! He's got that much temperament that there's only me can handle him. But I'll give you something – you've got a good eye for a horse. Now, this is the lass for you: she's gentle-natured, built to carry any load you care to put on her, and is as sound as a pound. She's happen not the bonniest, but she'll serve you well and is just the right height if you have a dicky leg. She's broken in, and as kind as you like, when you are on her

67

back. Here, look at her teeth and feel her fetlocks – she's a grand li'l horse.' Tom ran his hand down a small, dark fell-pony's neck and pulled on her mane to lead her to Adam. 'She's one of my favourites and she needs a good home – not carting goods back and forward on these turnpike roads, with a switch across her backside every five minutes.'

Adam looked at the dark-eyed fell-pony, which was no more than fourteen hands tall. She was a drab looker, but when he stared into her eyes and inspected her teeth and hooves, he knew that Tom was right. He needed nothing with the flash stallion that had a mind of its own. 'How much do you want for her?' He stood back and looked at her shape.

'Fifteen guineas, and she's worth every penny of that.' Tom looked at Adam and held out his hand to shake.

'Nay, I think fourteen's enough, and I expect a saddle and harness thrown in, even at that.' Adam stroked the little horse's mane.

'Fourteen and a half. And aye, I'll be daft enough to throw in a saddle and harness. I sometimes wonder how folk thinks I make a living.' Tom held his hand out once more and smiled.

'Go on then, we've got a deal. She does look right for me and, as you say, she's placid.' Adam shook Tom's hand, as he spat on it to seal the deal, and watched as he walked to the ramshackle hut in the corner of the field that held all the horse tackle, appearing with a saddle and harness.

'You'll not regret buying her. She'll give you foals, if

nothing else, if you don't want to ride her,' Tom shouted as he put on the reins and saddle.

'Nay, I need her for my legs. I'll not be keeping her in foal every year.' Adam put his hand through the little horse's mane and pulled on her reins, as Tom opened the field gate for them both to leave. Passing him the money from his top pocket, he watched as Tom quickly put it in his own.

'What the missus doesn't see, she won't grieve about. I aim to keep a bob or two of this for myself – there's nothing better than a gill or two at The Three Horses of a night.' Tom smiled. 'It's better than drinking water, from what I can make out. The poor buggers at Haworth were dropping like flies because of the water there. It's a good job the parson got involved a few years back, else they would still be drinking water that ran off the churchyard, and getting ill from the stinking midden-steads that were everywhere. He's a good man is the parson; it's a pity he lost all his family, with one thing and another. Those lasses, I believe, could write a right good tale – not like their brother, who must have been a disappointment to his father.' Tom stood on his doorstep as Adam climbed the mounting block next to his door and bestrode the little black mare, who did not flinch an inch. 'See, I told you she was golden.'

Adam sat back in the saddle, holding the reins tightly, and felt the horse beneath him. 'I used to know all the family very well. The Reverend has had his fill of grief over the years. When I've time, I must go and see him.'

'I hope you had nowt to do with that son of his. He was as wild as a mountain hare, always in bother with somebody or someone. Anyway, because of his father addressing Haworth's problems, Keighley Waterworks are sorting out the water down in Keighley itself. It's been announced that reservoirs are to be built at Ponden, Watersheddles and Blackhill. You'll not find me saying anything against them – we need 'em – but folk from them parts are moaning. The stench down in Keighley is enough to knock you over some days. God only knows what the water tastes like down there. I've my own spring, so I never drink anything when in town. You want to go and see Haworth; it's cleaned up just grand, and there's plenty of fresh water pumps now. Well, I'd better get back to my old lass, she'll want to know what I'm about. Take care of my horse and if there's anything else you want, let me know.'

Tom turned his back on Adam and his horse and went inside, leaving Adam pondering whether a visit to his old friend, the parson at Haworth, was in order. He used to knock regularly on the parsonage door when he was a peeler, to tell the Reverend that his errant son was in bother once more, and had always been graciously accepted.

Adam reached home as dusk was descending. Tom had been right about his four-legged purchase, and the sturdy animal had not quaked once at the uphill journey back to Black Moss, even though she carried the weight of Adam and all the supplies that he had bought while in

Keighley. He was thankful to see the oil lamp lightening his window and a cloud of smoke rising from the chimney, as he dismounted from the pony for the last few yards up the wild, overgrown path to his home.

'You are home, sir. I was beginning to worry that you were not going to make it before nightfall.' Lucy greeted him at the porch doorway and helped him in with the supplies.

Although he had not been living there long, the house already felt like home, with the fire blazing and the smell of a good stew simmering in the pot, Adam thought, as he helped her with his goods.

'My brother Nathan came by with a brace of rabbits, so I put them in the pot along with an onion and some tatties. So you've got a warm meal waiting for you, and I've not been idle – I've sorted and cleaned your bedroom. There'll be no spiders tonight, sir.' Lucy grinned as she carried the loaded hessian sacks into the kitchen. 'You've got a horse, then?' she asked on her return, eyeing the dark-haired creature that stood at the garden gate.

'Aye, she's a good 'un, just like Tom Gaine said. She's not flinched once, and has done everything asked of her, so she deserves a night's rest. I'll unsaddle her and take her into the small paddock behind the house. At least she can't go far in there, for the walls are sturdy enough. And then I'll sit down and have my supper.' Adam grabbed the reins of the small, sturdy pony and went to unsaddle her, hanging the saddle up in the ramshackle stone hut that his father and his grandfather before him had used for horse harnesses. He stood at the paddock gate and watched as the small mare trotted around her new home and then rolled in the middle of the field, flailing her legs in the air and snorting and whinnying, as if she knew that she had come to a good home and was going to make the best of it.

Adam smiled to himself as he walked back to the kitchen. He'd got himself a horse, his house was looking like a home and he couldn't wish for any better maid than Lucy. For once in his life he was content, although he couldn't help but worry how long it would last.

After a while he sat back and licked his lips. It had been a long time since he'd eaten rabbit stew that good. The sprigs of mountain thyme that Lucy had placed in the stew had made it more than simply palatable, and he thanked her as she took his plate away into the back kitchen to be washed. Suddenly there was a sharp knock on the door, and Lucy rushed back into the room to greet the visitor.

'I hope you don't mind, sir, but this will be Archie – Archie Robinson. I asked him to call this evening to talk to you about your need for someone to help you with your boundary walls and fences. I happened to see him as I left home this morn.' Lucy blushed and wondered if she had been too forward in asking Archie, and if she should show such enthusiasm at answering the door.

'Well, you'd better let him in then. It could have waited a while yet, but spring will soon be upon us and I'll soon be needing to put the stock on the land, so you've done right.' Adam sat back in his chair next to the fire and reached for his pipe, lighting it with a spill from the fire, as Lucy opened the door and bade Archie remove his cap and stand in front of him.

'So, Lucy tells me she's talked to you about my need for a drystone waller? Would you be interested, lad, and can you lay hedges as well as a drystone wall? My boundaries are a mixture of both in places, and none of them have been touched for a good few years now.' Adam drew on his pipe as the young lad played nervously with his cap between his hands.

'I can, sir. I've worked for various folk roundabouts. You can ask them what they think of my work – I don't think they have any cause for complaint.'

'Of course they don't, Archie, you know they don't. Stop doing yourself down,' Lucy butted in.

Archie gave her a dismissive look, wishing that she'd mind her own business and leave it to him.

'Well, I could do with someone perhaps two days a week. Lucy's already told me that would fit in with your work at the flay-pits. I'd pay you reasonably and you'd get fed, but in return I expect you to graft and not complain. There are a few miles of boundary to be seen to, and it will take all summer.' Adam looked at the expression on Archie's face and knew that he was grateful to have been asked.

'I'd work hard, sir, you'll not regret taking me on. Besides, the sooner you get your boundary walls up, the better. You've not got the best neighbours, with the Baxters farming next to you. They let their stock stray and are not averse to stealing the odd sheep or two. My mother says they always will – it's in their blood. "Bloody Border reavers," she calls them. If you'll beg my pardon, sir.' Archie hung his head.

'I've not come across them yet, lad. They must have come since I used to live here, because we all used to rely on one another when I was a lad, and there was none of that stealing. Now, when can you start, and what days are you to be mine?' Adam looked at Archie and noticed Lucy listening in at the doorway of the back kitchen, where she was hiding away.

'Will next week – Thursday and Friday – be soon enough for you?' Archie looked hopeful.

'Yes, that'll do. We can manage that. I expect you here as soon as it's sunrise, and the days will be long ones, until we get all done. And then we will see where we go from there.' Adam saw the look of worry vanish from the young lad's face.

'I'll work hard, you'll not regret taking me on. I'll not let you down. My mother will be so glad that I've got secure work for the summer. Thank you, sir.' Archie glanced across at Lucy, who was smiling at the good news.

'I tell you what: start your work with me tonight, and walk Lucy back down home – save these legs of mine. Lucy, leave those pots to wash and get yourself home with Archie, and then I know you are safe.' Adam tried to keep his face straight as Lucy protested, from the depths of the kitchen, that she would rather be washing the pots than walking home with Archie.

'Get yourselves gone. The dishes will still be there in the morning,' Adam shouted.

'Yes, sir; if you say so, sir.' Lucy reached for her cloak and hat from behind the door and grinned at Archie.

'I'll see you in the morning, Lucy, and I'll see you on Thursday, Archie.' Adam rose from his chair and patted Archie on the back, as he opened the door for them both to leave into the darkness of the evening. He stood for a while and watched the couple for as long as he could, as they disappeared down the farm track, listening to the giggles of a flirting Lucy as she egged poor Archie on.

How he wished he was young Archie, with his life spread out in front of him to do as he wanted, and with Lucy his for the taking. She'd make him a good wife, if Archie did but know it. How come life was wasted on youth? Why hadn't he made the most of his own youth? And why did he feel just a hint of jealousy creeping in as he watched the lively Lucy disappear into the darkness of the night?

7

'Don't you be fluttering your eyelashes at that simpleton of an Archie Robinson – he's worth nowt. Not a brain cell in his head, nor a penny in the bank. I need you to do better than that.' Bill Bancroft spat out a mouthful of saliva and growled as he watched his eldest daughter going out of the family home, full of spirits, to her work at Black Moss Farm, knowing that Archie was to start work there.

'Don't worry, Father, I just like his company. I aim to marry someone who's got money and can look after me, and will not have me scrubbing floors and washing dishes all my life.' Lucy tied her straw bonnet on tightly and grinned.

'If you can't win over Alex Braithwaite with your looks, then you could start to set your sights on Edward Buck. He's plenty of brass, and his family owns more land and houses than anyone else in the area. And don't you be flirting with Thomas Farrington; he might be a good worker, but he drinks his pay every week,' Bill yelled at her.

'I'll choose who I want. And as for Thomas Farrington, well, he looks at me in a way that no man should look at a woman. He frightens me. You'll not get me flirting, and definitely not wedding him, so don't worry about that,' Lucy answered back, before looking at her mother, who said nothing in her defence.

'You'll marry who I bloody well say you do. Happiness doesn't enter into it; all that matters is security and money. So you can bloody well do as you are told,' Bill growled as the youngest of his family started to wail and his wife, Dorothy, looked at him anxiously. He was fed up of constantly having children at his feet and headstrong women nagging him – the worst being his eldest, Lucy, who was proving to have a mind of her own when it came to finding a suitable husband.

Bill sighed and swore at his wife, as Lucy banged the kitchen door behind her and made her baby brother cry even more, sensing the atmosphere in the room. 'It's you, woman, that's made her like this. She thinks herself better than a lass from the flay-pits. It's time she was lined up with a man. I've seen how everybody looks at her when she struts about the place. And this last week or two, since she went to work for that Adam Brooksbank, she's put on right airs and graces,' Bill growled.

'Well, you've only yourself to blame for that. You got her the position. I told you I needed her at home, but you wouldn't listen. You should be proud of her. She's the bonniest lass in the district, and she could turn many a man's eye. Don't you be giving her away to just anybody. And she's right in what she says about Thomas Farrington – he isn't right in the head. Alex Braithwaite or one of the Bucks would be suitable. I could see myself, all dressed up on her wedding day and being talked about in society. Nobody would look down their noses at us then.' Dorothy smiled and thought about a lifestyle that she could only dream of.

'Lucy's a working-class lass, a maid on a farm. It was all talk on my part, and well you know it. But the sooner she gets wed, the better. It'll be one less under my roof, and one less noise of a morning. For God's sake, woman, shut that brat up before I lift my hand to quieten it!' Bill jumped to his feet and glowered at the baby in Dorothy's arms. 'I'm off to work, I get more sense out of the men than I do in this madhouse.' He pulled on his leather jerkin and slammed the door behind him.

'Nothing's ever your father's fault, is it, little 'un? Happen if he kept his todger in his pocket, his house would not be as noisy. But our Lucy has a mind of her own, and she'll not listen to him and his plotting. The right fella will come along for her one day. And for now, I'm happy that she is still at home.' Dorothy sighed.

Lucy walked with intent up the track to her work. She wiped away a tear that was falling down her cheek and breathed in deeply, in order to set aside her fears about her father wanting her to marry. Why Thomas Farrington had been mentioned in the conversation, she didn't know. She hated him and she was scared of him; he'd be the last person on God's earth that she would want to spend her life with. She could not understand why her father had not got rid of him, from both his job and the cottage that he rented from them. She longed to be away from the small community on Providence Row and the stench of the flay-pits. She was better than all of that, and she would prove it, if given the chance.

Her feet carried her, like magic, up the winding moorside and into the yard of Black Moss, her head so full of thoughts that the usual drag up the hillside went unnoticed. It was still early morning and there was dew on the grass and a chill in the air as she opened the gate into the yard. She was taken aback by the sight of a short-horned roan cow standing in the centre of the yard, with a halter around its head. It looked at her with large, soulful brown eyes and then carried on with the business of eating the docks that grew wild around the edge of the yard.

'Ah, Lucy, so you've met my latest buy.' Adam came from round the back of the house and walked towards the cow, grabbing its halter and leading it with a switch across its back to what used to be the old cowshed. 'Ted Leeming brought her up for me from Denholme before it was light this morning. I told him last week I was in need of a cow of my own, when I went to buy some milk from him, and he was good enough to sell me Daisy here. She needs milking. Have you ever milked a cow before, or do I have to show you?' Adam tied up the cow to one of the wooden stalls that used to hold up to three cows when he was a child, then stood back, looking at his

79

latest piece of livestock as Daisy munched contentedly on some hay that Ted Leeming had also brought that morning.

'Me, milk a cow! I've never done that in my life. I know where it comes from, but I've never been that close to a cow before, let alone milk it.' Lucy looked at him in horror.

'Oh, well, I'll have to show you then. I'd hoped that you already knew, but it won't take long to learn. I'll expect you to milk her every morning, and make butter from the excess milk we have left over, as we will have plenty of that for a while – that is, until I buy myself a pig or two. They'll soon drink and eat anything that's going to waste.' Adam stood back with his hands on his hips and looked at Lucy's face. 'I might as well show you now. Archie hasn't appeared yet, but once he does, we will be away up the moor to look at what needs doing. Here, grab the stool from that corner, and here's a bucket. Now, watch me and see how it is done.'

Lucy passed Adam the three-legged woodworm-eaten milking stool, which had been in the corner of the cow-shed since Adam was a lad, and stood back and watched. She hadn't realized that part of her daily task was going to involve milking a cow, and she didn't relish the experience.

'She's a quiet enough lass, so don't worry – she's used to being milked.' Adam rubbed his hands together, warming them, then sat down next to the back-end of the cow, his feet wedging the bucket between them, placed underneath the teats. 'Look, you get two teats at a time between your thumb and forefinger and gently pull down, squeezing the length of the teat. It takes some strength in your fingers, but you'll soon get used to it.' He put his head on the cow's haunches and pulled gently on the teats, filling the bucket with warm, foaming milk. He carried on for a while, then stopped and stood up. 'Here, you have a go. Take the two teats I haven't touched; she's nearly milked out in the others. You can tell because her udder's gone all wrinkled on that side. Now, sit down quietly and rest your head on her side and pull as I did – you'll soon get into a rhythm.'

Lucy sat down on the small stool, her skirts touching the dirty cowshed floor, as she hesitantly placed the bucket of milk between her legs, ready for squirting the milk into. She looked at the cow's hind legs and flinched slightly when Daisy lifted one of her legs up, as Lucy's cold hands felt her warm, smooth teats, nearly knocking over the bucket of milk.

'You forgot to warm your hands. She's like any woman – she likes warm hands on her and a little coax-ing.' Adam laughed, then concentrated on watching Lucy try to milk her.

'It's hard work and I'm not getting anything out of her, as you did. My fingers ache,' Lucy whined as she squeezed and pulled on each teat.

'Just pull and squeeze with one hand and then the other. Get into a rhythm, as I did. It will become easier each time you milk.' Adam stood back and turned as he heard the footsteps of Archie coming into the cowshed. The lad stood in the doorway and smirked at the sight of Lucy trying to milk the cow, and fell about laughing as the beast whipped her across her face with her tail.

'Bloody animal!' Lucy swore. 'And you can shut up, Archie Robinson. I bet you've never milked a cow before.'

'I have, and when I did, it wasn't half as slow as you. It's going to be evening before she's milked. Put her tail under your head and on her side, then she can't swish you with it – that's what I always do.' Archie stopped laughing as Adam gave him a look.

'Aye, do that. And I'll take Archie into the yard while you finish milking, as the last thing you want is an audience.' Adam patted Archie on the back and led him out of the shadows of the cowshed.

Lucy hesitantly picked up the tail of the patient cow; it was filthy and smelled of urine, as she wedged it between herself and the cow's side, then went about trying to do her best milking the poor animal. Her fingers ached along with her back, but eventually – as Adam had said – she got into the swing of it, and sat back with a smile of satisfaction as the last drop of milk was squeezed from the cow's udder. She'd learned to milk a cow, something she had never done in her life before.

She got up from her stool and patted the cow on her hindquarters. 'I promise tomorrow I'll be better, and I'll warm my hands,' Lucy said as she picked up the bucket of frothy milk. At least there was no shortage of milk today and it was fresh; not like the watered-down stuff that was delivered to the townsfolk down in Keighley. She looked around her; she quite liked the smell and warmth of the cow, and the contented noise it made as it digested the hay it had been given. Although her fingers ached, they would get stronger each day, and she could see herself enjoying her time as a milkmaid. It was, after all, a million miles away from being a tannery owner's daughter who had the threat of an unwanted marriage hanging over her head. For a short while, her thoughts had been on the matter in hand and not on thoughts of the marriage that her father seemed to think was for her. How she wished that her home and her father were far away, and that she could spend her life on the moorside as a simple farm girl. But come nightfall, Lucy knew she would have to return home and face her father's wrath, no matter what the day ahead held.

'So, you managed it then.' Adam smiled as Lucy made her way across the yard with her bucket of warm milk. 'I thought you would, once you had got the hang of it.'

Archie grinned and put his head down. He remembered the first time he had been asked to milk a cow; he'd been only eight or nine years old and had shown no fear or worries, after watching his grandfather do the same job for many a year.

'Yes, to be honest, I quite enjoyed the task. It was, as you say, soothing. And I don't mind doing the job every morning, once my fingers get used to the work.' Lucy put her bucket down. 'I'd better get on and make you some breakfast. You'll need it before you go up on the moor to attend to the walling that you have planned.'

'I've had mine, Lucy. I got up with the lark this

morning, as my leg is not giving me as much pain, and I knew it was going to be a busy day. Archie, have you eaten? You'll need something in you, for lifting the stones in place as we go along today. Although now I've got myself a cow, we will start with repairing the lower pasture wall, and then I can turn her out into it when the frosty nights have ceased.' Adam looked at the young lad.

'Aye, I've had my breakfast. My mother wouldn't let me out of the house until I'd something in my belly. She's always fussing over me.' Archie blushed.

'That's what mothers do, lad. Don't be upset with her for it. She's showing that she loves you. Now if we are all fed and watered, let's make a start on the day. Lucy, you see to the house. When that milk cools, skim the cream off the top and put it to one side for making into butter; the rest you can do with as you please. Come on then, lad, let's make a start – there's a lot of work to be done here before next winter. I aim, with your help, to pipe water into the house from the stream that already feeds the trough here in the yard, so that will be a job and a half for us both.'

Adam picked up the stone hammer that he'd placed by his side and stepped outside, leaving Lucy to go about her duties in the house. He wanted to make a good start on securing the lower pasture's boundaries, and he had no idea how fast young Archie could put up the limestone wall, which had been neglected for so many years. 'I take it that your father learned you to wall?' Adam talked to Archie as they made their way up the track behind the house that led to the lower pasture.

'Aye. Although he worked in the quarry, we had a few acres of land and I used to help him with all the jobs, even though I was more of a nuisance than a help. He learned me all that I know.' Archie sighed and went quiet.

'Lucy told me he had died. You must miss him?' Adam looked at the young lad.

'I do – me and my mother. Times have been hard since he died. We had to sell what land we had, and folk took advantage of knowing that we would be grateful for any money we could raise. We hardly had enough money to bury him, until the Baxters came along with their so-called "good offer". But they were only taking advantage of our bad luck, and we should have asked for more. I hate that Robert Baxter: he's trouble, and everyone knows he is.'

'Aye, well, we'll try and keep away from him and his kin. I try not to fall out with anyone – life's too short to hold grudges.' Adam patted Archie on the back and stopped short of the dilapidated drystone wall that was in need of their attention. 'Just look at it. There are a few yards in need of our attention, and this isn't as bad as some of the walls up on the tops. We've got our work cut out, lad. I hope that your back's strong and your arms have plenty of muscle.'

Both men looked at the bleached white stones of the wall, which had more gaps than a colander, and thought that the day was going to be a long one.

'Sooner we start, the better. It is not going to go away and at least the fallen stones are still in place. It's only a matter of putting them back and making the wall strong again.' Archie rolled up his sleeves.

'Ah, the optimism of youth. I remember those days, when nothing daunted me. Come on then, lad, let's make a start. You have this stretch and I'll begin higher up.' Adam shook his head and left Archie looking at where to start his part of the wall.

Archie stood back and decided to take the wall back to its foundations, so that it would be strong, and to make it easier to fill the gap between each side of the wall with the stones that he had. He carefully handled each stone, finding just the right shape and position to make the wall straight and sturdy. And filling the middle of the wall up with smaller stones and rubble, which he called 'fillers', and occasionally placing a long, thick, strong piece of limestone the full width of the wall, called a 'through', to make all the stones fit and bind together. It was a job that not many people had been taught, and it was a skilled task to build a wall with no mortar, but only the stone and rocks that nature had provided. It was also a slow, back-breaking process, and even a good drystone waller could only be expected to build a yard and a half per day. The size of the gap that he was working on would take him to the end of the week – that was, if the weather held. However, once it was done, with the large top-stones in place, he would be proud of his achievement and so, he hoped, would Adam Brooksbank, because he preferred to be working on a farm rather than down in the flay-pits.

'Are you alright, lad?' Archie heard Adam shout, as he stood back and looked at the work he had done so far.

'Aye, I'm fine. It's a grand day and I'm doing something I enjoy. What more can I ask for?' Archie nodded his head and reached for another stone. Not only that, he thought, but he had Lucy Bancroft out of the reach of her father and the leering Thomas Farrington, and she was near him and would be for two days a week from now on. Now was the time to pick up the courage and ask her to walk out with him on a Sunday, if he dared do so. The trouble was, he knew he wasn't good enough for Lucy, and that she simply teased and flirted with him because she could. Besides, her father hated him, and he'd never agree to Lucy walking out with him. So, for now Archie would just have to be content with Lucy flirting, and himself looking at her like a love-struck fool. His hard life since his father died had worn him down, and gone was the optimism of his youth; he'd no money, and nobody with any sense would look twice at him. He looked down at the white sharp-edged stones and decided to get on with the job in hand. At least it gave him satisfaction, and some money to take home to his mother. She loved him, if no one else did.

8

It was Sunday, and Adam sat back in his chair by the fire, content with his lot in life. Things were going to plan, he thought, as he listened to the sound of the church bells being carried up from the church at Denholme upon the wind. He had no time in his world for religion, but realized that some people needed its comfort and the hope of everlasting life, and that there was something much greater that they yearned for than the miserable lives they had on earth.

He leaned forward and stoked the fire. There was no Lucy to keep him in order today, as he had arranged that each Sunday she would stay with her family and not bother seeing to his needs. He smiled as he remembered the shocked look on her face when she had been asked to milk the cow, and how angry she had got with herself when she tried the first time or two to squeeze the teats, only for no milk to appear. Now, a few days on, she was managing well and had made her first batch of butter, which he had enjoyed spreading on the toast that he had made himself, by placing a slice of bread on a brass toasting fork and holding it close to the fire's embers until it turned a golden brown. It was something his mother had done many a morning, and he still loved the smell and taste of newly toasted bread with creamy butter on it. Sunday he still respected as a day of rest, a day to write letters, sit and contemplate the week just gone and the week ahead of him, or to visit friends and neighbours, and that was what he planned to do with his day. He'd milked the cow and there was nothing more to do, so he had decided as he banked the fire up to visit Haworth and spend a little time with the elderly parson at the parsonage, and now made to saddle his newly acquired horse.

The cobbled streets of Haworth were quiet as he rode up the slight incline to the parsonage and church, where he knew he could find the ageing parson. An abundance of shops, selling anything from sweets to everyday essentials, lined the street sides, and Adam noted the sight of new water pumps and drinking troughs. The village was more pleasant than Keighley, set on the moorside with the view over the other side of the valley clear to see, and the houses were more of a cottage style than some of the slum-like dwellings in neighbouring Keighley, although the soot and smoke from nearby woollen mills and forges had blackened their stone exteriors, giving them an aged, dirty look.

Adam made his way up to the church and church-yard, tethering his horse outside the wall that surrounded the long Georgian parsonage. It was one of the grandest houses in Haworth, showing how much respect was shown to the clergy of the area. He looked across to the church of St Michael and thought about the family of his dear friend, all buried there in the vault deep below: the rector's wife, Maria, and his four daughters, along with their wild and wilful brother. Only the youngest daughter had chosen to die and be buried in a place she loved, by the sea in Scarborough, when the family curse of consumption had taken her. How could anyone still keep their faith, after losing so many loved ones, Adam wondered. He himself struggled most days with the thought of the death of his beloved Mary, but the parson had lost everyone dear to him. His family had been struck down one by one – the death of his five daughters being the cruellest blow, as three of them had just found fame in the literary world before their individual deaths, brought about by the dreaded consumption.

He breathed in deeply and opened the metal gate, then followed the flagstone path that led to the steps up to the grand front door. He'd stood there many times previously in his policing times, when he had to come and inform the good parson that his son was the worse for drink and laudanum, and had got himself into a spot of bother with the locals. The parson had always taken it in his stride, while his sisters beseeched their sibling to stop his wicked ways and become the brother they craved. His shocking mop of auburn hair had always made him stand out in the crowd, and he was easily spotted and named when any trouble erupted. He'd been a wild one, that was for sure, and not the kind of man a parson would want as a son.

Adam lifted the heavy brass knocker and waited for a reply. It was a little after one; dinner should have finished being served, and there would not be another church service until that evening, so he expected the parson to be in as he waited for a response. Sure enough, he heard footsteps coming to answer the door as he stood with his hat in his hand and waited for the door to open.

'Yes, how may I help you?' A tall dark-haired man with fierce, bushy sideburns answered the door, dressed in clerical robes, and looked down upon him, his voice still betraying his Irish roots with a slight lilt.

Adam recognized him as the curate who had earlier been married to the parson's middle daughter until her death. Indeed, people blamed the curate for her untimely death, after making her take a walk in the pouring rain, and it was rumoured that he had not cared, or shown his wife any love.

'I'd like to see the Reverend.' Adam held out his hand to be shaken. 'It's Arthur, isn't it?' Adam watched as the curate tried to remember the face in front of him.

'Yes, do I know you? I'm afraid I don't recognize your face?' The curate looked down at Adam and scrutinized him.

'I'm Adam Brooksbank, you probably don't remember me. I've been away for some time now and, to be honest, we only met perhaps once or twice, under difficult circumstances, if you recall. The Reverend knows me well.'

'Oh yes, I remember, you were a peeler. You used to help Branwell, and you lost your wife in tragic circumstances and then you left the district. Such a sad affair – the good Lord does not show any mercy to our feelings sometimes. I'll just see if the Reverend is available. Please do come in and wait in the hall. He's in the study. I'll check if he's awake, as he usually has a nap nowadays after his dinner,' Arthur said, leaving Adam in the hallway.

Adam looked around the entrance hall, which was sparsely furnished but homely, and had always drawn the parson's family back between its walls from whatever lives they had been living elsewhere.

'Ah, Adam, so you have returned to us. Like all prodigal sons do. No matter where you go, the place of your birth will always draw you back – my girls all knew that.' The ageing parson held out his hand to shake and urged Adam to join him in his study, as Arthur left them to catch up on old times.

'I have indeed, sir. Perhaps I should have returned earlier. I regret not being there when my father and mother passed away. But Her Majesty's army and the fighting in the Crimea got in the way.' Adam smiled at the old man as he urged him to sit down opposite him in the chair next to the fire.

'A dreadful war, from what I hear. Man's inhumanity to man I still cannot understand. Still, you have survived and are back with us now. I hope you plan to stay?' The parson looked at the man who had been always understanding when his son had driven him to despair, and watched as Adam looked down at his feet, noting the regret of his past life's decisions.

'I am. I've returned to Black Moss and I'm rebuilding what nature has done to my old home over the last few years. I should have known that hiding away from hurt and sorrow does not work, and that self-pity only leads to self-loathing. I cannot bring my Mary back, but I can lead a good life and try to be there for others now.' Adam looked across at the old man, who had experienced more than his fair share of pain in life, but despite that he had not lost his faith and still helped the people around him.

'God moves in mysterious ways. Here am I, without any of my family alive, all of them dying from consumption. An illness that made me look at how my parishioners lived, and made me fight for their right to have clean water and sanitation. The vapours that were being breathed in by one and all have killed a good many, but it took the death of my dear daughters to make me realize that. Now, with the help of Benjamin Babbage and the good Lord, I have saved many a soul, through losing the ones that I loved. There is a purpose to life, Adam. Never despair, you will eventually find peace with yourself.' The Reverend reached out to Adam and patted his hand. He knew what pain Adam had felt when he lost his wife, and how he blamed himself, but it was time for him to put that behind him and enjoy his life now, back in his home, where he had always belonged.

'I'm trying, sir. I'm no longer the headstrong youth I used to be,' Adam whispered.

93

'Good, then you will find happiness. Now, enough of these worries. Let us enjoy a cup of tea and perhaps a scone? My cook makes the most wonderful scones, and even though I have just had my dinner, I can find room for one, if you'll join me.' Patrick smiled.

'That would be most agreeable sir,' Adam replied.

'Then tea and scones it is, and you must tell me about your travels.' The parson sounded the small silver bell by his side, and no sooner had it rung than a maid in a mob cap came and quickly asked what he required. 'Some tea and scones for my good friend here. And perhaps, Alice, you'd be kind enough to fill the coal scuttle while you are here.'

'Yes, sir.' Alice bobbed and took the brass coal scuttle to be filled, returning within seconds and adding some coal to the fire, as both men talked about days gone by and their hopes and dreams for the future, while sharing a pot of tea together. They had both loved and lost, but neither was without hope as they looked into the future.

Adam arrived home at dusk and, after turning his horse out into the now-secure paddock, went and settled down in his chair by the still-lit fire and thought about the conversation he had shared with his old friend, the parson at Haworth. The Reverend had listened to his woes and troubles without judgement or bias, even though he had been through hell and back himself, after losing his own beloved family. He'd urged Adam to embrace life before it was too late; perhaps to take another wife, even though his heart still ached for Mary.

Perhaps the ageing parson was right. Perhaps he should find himself a wife, but his heart told Adam otherwise – it would always be Mary's, and hers alone.

He sat back in his chair, watching the newly stoked fire's flames cast shadows on the whitewashed walls. It would be good to have someone to talk to of an evening; some company to listen to his ambitions for the farm, and to give advice and encouragement when he needed it. But where to find such a woman, Adam didn't know, and he didn't care to think about it, either. His heart had been broken, and he cared not to socialize with the fairer sex. Even his lifelong friend Ivy Thwaite had not replied to his letter of yet; perhaps she too had turned her back upon him since his time in the Crimea. There were no deep feelings between them, but he did crave her company, for old times' sake. What would be would be, he thought, as the darkness descended outside and night came to the farm. Tomorrow Lucy would be with him again, with her caring ways and hard work. She would suffice as company for now; indeed, she brought just the right amount of pleasant company into his life.

He felt content with his lot and now that the laudanum drops had eased the pain in his leg, he was starting to enjoy life slightly again. Tomorrow he would go and start walling the gaps between his fields and those of his neighbours, the Baxters, whom he had not yet seen or met, although Archie did not have a good word to say about them. However, until he had met them, Adam would not judge them, and he would take them to be decent people until he found differently. People were too quick to judge, he thought, remembering his own encounters with other people's thoughts.

As for today, it was nearly done and bed awaited him, with the help of the laudanum. Morning would soon be upon him, and he would have to see what the following day brought with it. He'd leave the house shortly after daybreak, take his dinner with him and leave Lucy a list of errands that needed doing for that day. A full day alone on the moor would do him good, building up the limestone walls and listening to the skylark's song. He was at peace on his well-trod piece of land.

9

Dorothy Bancroft sat on the edge of the bed and rocked her body and sobbed as she looked down at the blood-stained sheets and the body of the not-yet-formed baby that Bill was quickly wrapping in sacking, not even letting her look at the baby that had been growing within her body for the last few months. This was the fifth child she had lost, all badly deformed but through no fault of her own, and each time it hurt a little bit more. She sobbed and cried as Bill stood up and cast aside the small, imperfect body onto a chair and then moved to bring the jug and bowl filled with water next to her, to cleanse her of the bloodied clothes she sat in.

'Aye, lass, it didn't suffer. It wasn't right, you couldn't have called it a baby. Now hold your noise else you'll wake the rest of the house, and it's best they don't know that we've lost another, under the circumstances.' He bent down and kissed Dorothy on the head, before gently washing her private parts and making her stand to change her nightdress and the sheet beneath her. 'It wasn't wanted anyway. We've enough bairns without another under our feet. I'll keep myself to myself from now on. You've had enough heartache, losing all these babies. Something must go wrong with your insides sometime, and I'd be best not asking you for any favours.' Bill looked at his wife as she sobbed and shook on the newly cleaned bed edge, then he threw the soiled nightwear and bedding into a darkened corner of the room. 'We've enough bairns. Bert's only a year old. Look after the ones we have got and don't mourn over the ones we've lost.'

'Was it a boy or a girl this time?' Dorothy whispered.

'I can't tell. Besides, it's best you don't know. I'll take it out into the yard and put it in the quicklime pit, along with the others. It's the best end to it. There's no need for a burial, or that condescending parson to be involved. He'd only want to christen it, and then he'd be shocked at the sight of such a baby. It'll soon disintegrate, like the rest that I buried there, and nobody will ever know our loss. The first two we lost were nearly perfect – it was right we buried them in the churchyard. But not this one; this one isn't right again. Besides, the church would only charge and they don't like burying chrisoms; they think every baby, no matter what, should be christened.'

'Don't call it a chrisom. It might not have been baptized, but I would have loved it and would have had it christened, if it had lived and had been normal. I can't bear to walk past that part of the yard, knowing what is hidden in the pit. I have to live with my guilt every day, and I can't help but cry for my babies' souls.' Dorothy lay back in bed and buried her head in her pillow and cried.

'And you think I don't care? I'm the one that buries them there. Thank God nobody knows what is lying there, else they would take both you and me to the cells. You've not told anybody you were expecting, have you? After all, you weren't that far gone and you only told me the other week.' Bill looked at his wife and, even by the light of the candle, he could tell that she hesitated in her answer.

'Our Lucy knows. She's not daft; she knows the signs nowadays. She's seen me being sick of a morning, and she's been more caring than usual when it comes to looking after the li'l 'uns. So I had to tell her.' Dorothy glanced at her husband as he scowled at the news of Lucy knowing her mother's condition.

'I'll talk to her in the morning – tell her that you've lost the bairn and she's not to say anything. She can stop at home tomorrow, wash this bedding and look after her siblings. Adam Brooksbank will have to do without her for one day. It isn't as if he's got a manor house to look after. It's only a scratty bit of land on the edge of the moor.' Bill sighed and looked across at the remains of the baby that he had to dispose of.

'You'll not tell her what you've done with the baby? She'd not understand that you are embarrassed by the deformity of the ones we lose. I wish she'd not noticed that I was expecting, but she's of an age where she misses nothing.' Dorothy pulled on Bill's sleeve and begged him

99

not to say anything about the burial of this baby, and the other babies that had been born and had died with hideous deformities.

'I'll not say owt. It's an embarrassment to both of us. What makes them like that, I don't know, but both you and I know we couldn't have them buried in the churchyard and all the world know about them. God takes them away before they are fully formed, thank heavens, and the lime pit is the best spot for them.' Bill stood up. 'I'll take this 'un and bury it now, before it's light and folk are stirring. You lie down and stay in bed this morning. Lucy can look after everything, once I've had a word with her.' Bill looked down at his pale-faced wife and smiled. 'It'll be alright, lass. It's best got rid of.'

He walked over and picked up the bundle, then stopped just for a second as Dorothy whispered, 'You'll say a prayer over it, won't you, Bill?'

'Aye, I will, lass. Now get some sleep and leave me to my work.' Bill walked quietly out of the house and across the yard to a part where nobody else went. He looked around him as he placed the bundle on the cobbled yard and started digging in the back of the quicklime pit, which nobody else but him touched. His heart filled with pain as he placed the small body from the sack that he'd wrapped it in and buried it quickly under the quicklime, leaving it to be dissolved in the flesh-eating substance. Nobody must know his secret. He didn't know why his wife kept having these deformed babies, but he suspected it was something to do with the chemicals and potions that he worked with in the yard. If he wanted to keep his workforce, he'd have to keep the babies' deaths and his suspicions to himself or risk everything he'd ever worked for.

He glanced around him and looked towards the east as the first glimmers of daybreak crossed the sky. He'd have to face the world as if nothing had happened, and talk to Lucy, telling her that her mother had lost the baby after carrying it just a few weeks, not months. That would make her think that nothing was wrong, for many a woman miscarried in the first few weeks, leaving nothing to show but blood-stained sheets, which he would ask her to wash in the copper that morning. No doubt she'd complain that she couldn't go to work at her new place of employment, but family came first and he was sure Adam Brooksbank would understand, once told the circumstances. The main thing was that Lucy never learned about his own and Dorothy's secret or, knowing Lucy, she would talk and tell someone about the dark corner of the flay-pits where the decomposing bodies of her kin were buried.

Thomas Farrington yawned and stretched, then pulled back the tattered bedroom curtains of his window, which overlooked the yard of the flay-pits. In the dim morning light he watched as Bill Bancroft stood for a second with a shovel in his hand, his head bowed as if he was praying.

It wasn't the first time he'd seen his boss digging there at a strange time of day. What was he doing there? What was he burying there, and why would he not let anyone use the lime from that particular pit? Was Bill burying money? Surely the lime would dissolve it in time, for the lime burned and dissolved everything it touched, including his own skin, which was blistered and sore from the constant splashes of undiluted lime that splattered on his body. Whatever it was, he was going to find out, Thomas decided. He too would dig in the lime pit and discover exactly what was hiding there.

Lucy sat on the edge of her bed, still half-asleep and trying in vain not to wake her young sister, Susie, with whom she shared her bed. She'd been awakened by her father urging her to get dressed and join him in the kitchen, as he whispered to her from around the corner of her bedroom door.

She shivered in the cold morning light as she pulled on her bodice and underskirts and plaited her long blonde hair, in readiness for her day at Black Moss. She'd have a wash once she had heard what her father had to say; whatever it was it must be urgent, as he never ventured into their bedroom. Not like her mother, who usually stirred Lucy from her sleep if she had overslept. She'd have to get a move on anyway; she had to get to work, milk the cow and see what Adam Brooksbank wished her to do that day. As she ventured down the stairs she noticed that her parents' bedroom door was still closed. It was usually open to the world, and her mother could normally be heard stoking the fire and seeing that everyone was fed before going about their work or getting ready for school, in the case of her two younger brothers. She feared the worst as she walked down the creaking wooden stairs into the kitchen.

Bill stood at the kitchen window looking out into the yard, where his workers were already starting on the day's toil. He watched as a cartload of new animal skins was delivered and Thomas Farrington directed the men where to put them. Bill was thinking to himself that Thomas was a good worker and it was a pity he was not blessed with the most pleasant of natures, and that some people even thought he was not quite right in the head. He turned as he heard Lucy come into the room. He'd been dreading having to tell her the news, as it wasn't something that a man talked about with his daughter.

'Now then, our Lucy. Your mother's had a bad night. I don't know if you'd realized, but we were going to be expecting another one into our family. But the good Lord decided against it and she miscarried it, early on this morning. It's a blessing that she was only a few weeks with child, so there's no harm come to your mother, but she'll need a day or so in bed. You'll have to stay at home today and look after your brothers and sisters, instead of tending to What's-his-name up at Black Moss.' Bill looked at his eldest daughter and saw a look of doubt and concern come across her face.

'Is Mother alright? And what about the baby?' Lucy gasped.

'Your mother's alright; give her a day of peace and she'll be right as rain. There was no baby, or nothing that looked like a baby. She was only a few weeks gone – more blood than anything,' Bill lied. 'Her bedding is in

103

the corner over there. It'll need washing, and I dare say a cup of tea would be welcomed by her, once you've lit the fire and seen to the rest of them's needs. I'm off out to the yard; there's a delivery come and I'll have to sort the men out.' Bill looked at the doubt on Lucy's face and knew that she realized he was lying.

'I'll see to the fire and put a brew on. I'll bring you one out to the yard, along with some bread and dripping for your breakfast. I'll send our Nathan on his way to school to tell Adam Brooksbank what has happened, and that I'll be back with him as soon as I can. I'm sure he will understand.' Lucy bowed her head and thought about her mother recovering upstairs from yet another lost baby.

'Aye, well, he can please himself what he thinks. Your mother and your family come first and, just this once, you are needed at home. Make sure that Nathan doesn't go into what ails your mother.' Bill scowled as he closed the kitchen door. The fewer people who knew about the business, the better. Besides, it was women's business and not to be shared with the likes of Adam Brooksbank.

Lucy sat down on one of the kitchen chairs and looked around her. So it had happened again – another baby lost, and no tears from her father and no explanation of what had happened to the poor lost soul's body. Her mother had been more than a few weeks pregnant. Her father was a fool if he thought he could get away with that lie. She'd seen her mother being sick, so she was definitely more than a few weeks gone. Lucy didn't want to think the worst of her parents, but couldn't help but think that perhaps they were killing the babies on purpose. She'd heard that in Keighley there were women who got rid of babies that were unwanted, and her mother had visited Keighley only the previous day. What if she had visited one of these women and got a potion or suchlike? It didn't bear thinking about.

'Now then, our lass. Where's our mother? The fire's not lit, and my breakfast's not ready. What's going on?' Nathan pulled his braces over his twill shirt and slumped down in the chair next to Lucy.

'Mam's not well. You'll have to wait until I get the fire lit, then I'll make you a brew. Go into the pantry and bring me a loaf out. You and William can make do with bread and dripping this morning, else you won't have time to do what I'm going to ask you to do before school.' Lucy stood up and riddled the embers in the hearth and opened the door of the side-oven, where a handful of sticks had been drying overnight for use as kindling that morning. She screwed up a sheet or two of newspaper from next to her father's chair and placed it and the kindling sticks on the still-warm ashes, adding a lump or two of coal from the scuttle in the hearth, before wiping her hands on her apron as the flames leaped and caught hold.

'I don't want to bloody well go and see your fancy fella and tell him you're not going to work today. It's a right trail up to that spot, and I promised I'd meet Stanley Hodgson and we were going to look for some frogspawn in Ing Beck. William can go – he runs faster than me,' Nathan moaned.

'Do you want me to lose my job? I won't hear you moaning when I give you and William a ha'penny each for a barley sugar, next time we are at the shops. Now, you can both go and tell him. The frogspawn will still be there tomorrow. Besides, it's a bit too early for it yet.' Lucy looked at her brother as he pulled a face, then she filled up the kettle from the shared water pump with the yard, just outside the kitchen door. 'Go on, get the bread. William's coming down the stairs and if he wakens Susie and our Bert I'll not have time for either of you, and you'll be going to school with nothing in your bellies and no snap tins for your dinner under your arms.'

Nathan got up and went to the pantry, scowling at his younger brother as he placed the loaf of bread on the table in front of Lucy.

'Where's Mam?' William looked up at his older sister and then noticed the dark mood his brother was in.

'She's not well, and instead Miss Bossy Boots here is running the house. The sooner we get to school, the better.' Nathan picked up his slice of bread with butter and dripping adorning it and bit into it. 'Just get me a drink of milk, our Lucy. I'll not wait on the kettle boiling, and then I've more time to do what you want me to. Our Will here will have the same. Won't you? Then we can get away.' Nathan winked at his younger brother as Lucy made them jam sandwiches for their snap tins to take to school.

'But I like—' William started to say, only for his brother to kick him under the table to shut him up.

'Alright then. Here, drink it all, mind. I'm not having

that prim Miss Procter saying that you were sent to school unfed and unwatered. You've both washed this morning, haven't you? I'm not sending you to school mucky, either.' Lucy looked at both brothers as they quickly ate their bread and dripping, followed by a glass of milk, before both grabbed their now-full snap tins and headed out of the kitchen door. 'You'll not forget to go to Black Moss, will you?' Lucy yelled after both brothers.

'Nah! We'll go,' Nathan yelled back, pulling his younger brother with him as they ran across the flay-pit yard as fast as their legs would carry them.

'What are we going all the way up to Black Moss for?' William asked his brother.

'We're not. Miss Bossy Boots can think again. We are off to meet Stanley Hodgson, like we agreed yesterday, and bugger our Lucy! Frogspawn's far more important than trailing up to Black Moss.' Nathan grinned as he and his younger brother passed the turnoff for Black Moss Farm, with no intention of giving Lucy's message to Adam Brooksbank.

'Are you alright, Mam?' Lucy picked baby Bert out of his cot and stopped him crying, which had wakened her mother from an uneasy sleep. She looked at how pale her mother was; her greying hair, unbrushed and tangled around her on the pillow, made her look older than usual.

'I'll be fine, now don't you fret. I just need a day in bed, and then I'll be up and going in the morning. You'll manage all the jobs, won't you? There's no need to bake any bread, as I made plenty yesterday. And you'll find

107

some cooked ox tongue in the pantry for your father's dinner. That'll do him, and I know you'll feed the children and see to them alright.' Dorothy looked at her daughter, with her youngest balanced on her hip, and noted the concern on her face.

'I'll be fine, Mam, as long as you are alright. Can I bring you anything? Do you need a drink or something to eat?' Lucy juggled baby Bert as he started to whine yet again. He was hungry, and his nappy was full and in need of her attention.

'No, you've enough on. Leave me to sleep, and then I'll be up and going again in the morning. Will Adam Brooksbank be alright with you missing a day? He'll wonder where you are at,' Dorothy said, nearly in a whisper, as she closed her eyes.

'Nathan went to tell him before school that I'd not be with him today, so don't worry on his part. He'll understand.' Lucy stood in the doorway and watched her mother drop off to sleep, then she gently closed the door behind her and gave her attention to her youngest brother, who wailed loudly as she carried him downstairs into the kitchen and the warmth of the fire. Once in front of the fire, with a full belly of bread porridge inside him and a clean nappy on, Bert was content to crawl and stand on unsteady legs around the kitchen table, as his sister Susie sat up at the table and ate her breakfast. Susie was unconcerned that it was Lucy seeing to her needs and not her mother, and she watched Lucy fill the copper boiler in the corner of the kitchen with water, ready to wash the soiled bedclothes from her mother's bed.

Lucy picked up the soiled bedding and dropped it all into the almost-boiling copper, adding soda crystals to the wash to get rid of any stains, before she turned her attention back to her two young siblings. This was not the kind of life she wanted – beholden to bringing up squabbling children all her life, washing and cleaning, with no thanks for the long days of toil. If she was to marry, she had to be careful not to become pregnant, although she knew it would take more than good luck not to, as children were an inevitable part of a marriage.

She sighed and thought about Adam Brooksbank. There was something about him; although he was quite a bit older than her and more worldly-wise, she quite liked him. He was handsome and, if it wasn't for the limp he had, he'd be physically attractive. More so than poor, shy Archie; he'd always be just a friend, much loved but nothing more. Although even Archie was better than the scowling, moody Thomas Farrington. God forbid that she ever had to marry him; he was getting more and more odd by the day, and the lads in the yard had warned her that he was fixated upon her, which she knew to be true, as she often caught him looking at her in a strange way. It was better that she set her sights on Alex Braithwaite, the son of the owner of the quarry, no matter what her father thought of her chances. But in the meantime she'd work hard for Adam Brooksbank, when her family allowed. She could dream for now, but dreaming was all it would be, as she set about tidying the kitchen table and pacifying both of her young siblings.

*

That evening Adam made his way down from the moorside. He ached all over and was tired after drystone walling for the best part of ten hours. He was looking forward to seeing the welcoming face of Lucy, and to warming up by the fire that he knew she would have lit, along with eating whatever she had concocted for his supper. She might not have been with him long, but he already valued her company and the running of his small household. He stopped short of the yard gate and noticed that there was no smoke rising from the chimney of the farmhouse, and the cow in the bier was making a fearful noise.

Where was Lucy? He shouted her name as he entered the house he'd left early that morning. The fire was unlit and nothing had been touched since his departure, so she'd not been at her work today. No wonder the cow was sounding distraught; she was in need of being milked, and she would be in pain. Adam swore as he pulled his knapsack off his shoulder and looked around him, before storming out of the house. Damn the girl – had she left him high and dry, just as he was beginning to enjoy her company and appreciate the work she did for him?

He stomped across the yard and opened the cowshed door, pulling up the milking stool as he placed the wooden bucket underneath the wild-eyed cow, then he relieved the pressure from the over-full udder by milking her. 'Shush now, lass. I don't know what's become of the maid, but she's let both me and you down, and I'll want to know why in the morn.' Adam put his head on the side of the cow and milked her steadily, leaving her fed and content as dusk fell over the farmyard. Tomorrow, if Lucy did not appear, he'd go and pay a visit to Providence Row and the flay-pits and see what had kept her. He stood outside the long, low farmhouse and watched as lit candles and oil lamps started to appear in the windows of the houses in the valley below, twinkling and shining like magic along the moor and valley sides. He found himself wishing, and hoping, that nothing had befallen Lucy Bancroft. It was not in her character to let him down, of that he was sure. Something must be wrong, and if she did not show her face first thing in the morning, he'd find out what, and why she had not worked for him that day.

10

The morning broke dark and sullen, with rain coming down so hard that Adam had to run from the shelter of the cowshed to the warmth of the farmhouse kitchen. Once again Lucy had let him down and he had to light his own fire, make breakfast and milk the cow, without a word coming from either her or any of her family. It was out of character, he thought, as he hung his oilcloth coat up behind the kitchen door and went to make himself warm again next to the fire.

He looked out of the window as he warmed his hands next to the flames. It was a sod of a day, that was for sure – typical spring weather, just what always came about the week before Easter and during the festive period itself, or so it would seem. Nevertheless, it would not bother him; he could keep himself dry and not be worried by the rain for the next day or two. And he could always find young Archie an inside job, mending the hayloft in the adjoining barn, or whitewashing and mending one of the old, derelict outhouses ready for a pig, which he aimed to rear and fatten for bacon later in the year. He would, however, dress for the weather once again and go down to Providence Row and the flay-pits and call on the Bancrofts. If Lucy had decided against working for him, then he'd need a new maid. He'd have thought better of her if she had told him herself that she no longer wished to be in employment, instead of having to go and find out for himself.

He swore quietly under his breath and decided that rather than get wet again later in the day, he would visit Lucy now. He'd give her a piece of his mind; the least she could have done was be civil with him and tell him, if she no longer wished to work for him. Adam grabbed his still-dripping coat and set out to walk down the rutted track. There was no joy sitting astride a drenched horse in this weather; better that he walked the half-mile or so down to Lucy's home.

The wind and rain blew across the valley, making the moorland rushes and grasses bend in the strength of the powerful gusts. Adam swore yet again, as water seeped down his neck, getting his shirt and body wet. Damn the maid; he must be mad chasing after her in this weather. Perhaps it would be better if he advertised his need for a new one. After all, Lucy was quick to give her opinion and often spoke out, not knowing her place. But those were the things that he knew he liked about her: she wasn't afraid to say what she thought. Besides, she had been just the right tonic for his new life back home – full of life, a good cook and bonny with it, too.

113

He reached the flay-pits still in two minds, as he wandered into the yard to find Bill Bancroft. Then, if he had no explanation, he would visit Lucy at home in the row of terraced houses that backed onto the yard. Although the weather was as wild as you could get, the men of the yard were still working. The flay-pits were filled to the brim with smelly mixtures of toxins, softening the leather, and the piles of skins were heaped high, ready to be scraped and made supple before reselling. The stench was terrible and the excess water, mixed with lime and whatever else was in it, ran down the yard into a drain behind the row of houses. Adam looked around, trying to stop himself from retching.

'You – is Bill Bancroft here?' Adam shouted to a dark, moody-looking man who was pulling treated leather out of one of the pits. The weather was not making any difference to him, as he was used to being wet most days; it was part of his life and, if the heavens opened, it just meant that his head was wet, along with everything else.

'Nay, he'll be in his home. There's nobbut us fools that work for him getting sodden this morning. Besides, his wife is badly – he's with her.' Thomas Farrington scowled and looked at the stranger in his midst. His dark hair stuck to his head like rats' tails, and the many layers of protection from the rain made him look bigger than he actually was. 'Third door down over there, that's where you'll find him.' Thomas motioned to the back door of the row of cottages and sniggered, as Adam looked down at the pool of filthy water that lay all around him.

Adam walked over to the door that was indicated and wondered how anybody could put up with the everyday smell from the pits and the filth. His home was like heaven compared to this, although it was out in the wilds and remote. Most days he smelled just the wild moorland air and had grassland under his feet. He stopped at the back door of the terraced house and stood next to the water pump for the whole row. The drained water from the yard rushed down a ginnel beside the row of houses and bubbled down a drain next to it, and Adam looked down at the putrid water, hoping that both drinking water and the filthy water from the yard were not one and the same. He knocked heavily on the door and waited as he heard children's voices from within, and the sound of a man shouting to let the visitor in.

'Mr Brooksbank! What are you doing here, in this weather?' Lucy opened the door and looked shocked. 'It's terrible out there – come in and get dry. Have you come to see how my mother is? That's terribly kind.'

Adam took his sodden cap off his head and shook it free of the excess water, before stepping over the cottage's threshold. 'On the contrary, I've come to see what ails you, and why you have not shown your face at work,' he growled and then looked around him at the cramped living conditions. Bill Bancroft was sitting by the fire while the baby sat next to him, and a small blonde-haired girl was sitting at the scrubbed kitchen table, playing with two carved wooden dolls.

'Did you not get my message? Did Nathan not call and tell you that my mother has lost the baby, and that

I was needed here to mind the family?' Lucy looked at Adam and then quickly glanced at her father. She knew that he did not want to make their grief public.

'No, I've not heard so much as a by-your-leave from any of your family. But now that I know why, I am more at ease with the situation.' Adam looked at Lucy and then at Bill Bancroft, who sat and said nothing, not even turning to acknowledge him standing there. 'You have my sympathies, Mr Bancroft. Is your wife recovering? It is heartbreaking to lose a child,' Adam said, playing with his cap, as he felt he had judged Lucy wrongly and should have known that something was amiss.

'I told Nathan to tell you, on his way to school yesterday. Wait until I get hold of him – I'll scalp his backside,' Lucy muttered as she went to the aid of Bert, who had pulled himself up to his full height and then fallen hard on the stone flags of the kitchen floor and was about to cry.

'I thank you for your kind words,' Bill said. 'Dorothy is mending; she will be up and about tomorrow. You'll have my lass back with you in the morn. But save your sympathies. I doubt you know the pain we are feeling. Although we are blessed with a decent-sized family, the Lord's decided that we must lose as many bairns as we already have. Dorothy's heart breaks a little bit more, each time we lose one. I shouldn't be telling you this, but my heart is also heavy today, as my wife is weak and the weather is dark, and I am beside myself with anguish, as I feel that we are being punished by the good Lord himself.' Bill held his head in his hands. Dorothy was taking

116

her time to recover from her loss this time, and every time he walked into the yard he thought about the not-yet-formed bodies of the babies that he had buried in the unused pit.

'I too have known grief. I lost both my wife and my unborn child when I was younger, so I can understand a little of your pain. Has your wife seen a doctor? Is there a reason for her miscarriages?' Adam sat down across from Lucy, his coat still dripping with the rain, but now his concern was for the man who sat across from him and the pain he was suffering.

'Nay, a doctor will not do anything. Every woman loses babies – it's a fact of life, and nowt can be done about it. I should have the sense to keep myself to myself and save her the heartache, instead of having my lustful way.' Bill glanced quickly at Lucy and caught her blushes as her father talked so openly with her employer. 'Besides, we've been blessed with five fit 'uns; that's more than enough to feed and educate. And doctors cost money – something I have very little of, by the time I've paid the men their wages.' Bill sighed. 'We'll just have to make the best of it. Dot is recovering now and, hopefully, this will be the last one we lose. Neither of us is getting any younger. Perhaps that's what's wrong this time.'

'Well, now I know the reason for you not being with me, Lucy, I can fully understand. You stay at home until your mother's strong enough to run her house and look after your siblings. Children come first. I am used to looking after myself, and a few days more will not hurt me.' Adam looked across at Lucy, who seemed to be out

117

of place in the dire conditions of the tannery owner's humble home. Although the house was spotless, it was sparsely furnished, with the minimum of frills and pottery. Indeed, from the outside the whole row of houses looked dilapidated and in need of urgent repair. Perhaps the tannery was not doing so well and the Bancroft family was struggling. However, now he understood why Lucy had been fascinated by the story of Rebecca Town and the number of children she had borne and lost. It was true that life was cheap in the society they lived in, but Bill Bancroft was sitting across from him, grieving, and Adam felt for the man and his family.

'I'll be away now. If there's anything I can do, you know where I am at.' Adam stood up and looked down at the man, who could not be bothered to raise his head to acknowledge his departure. 'Lucy, there's no rush back. Look after your mother and these little ones.' Adam smiled down at baby Bert, whose cheeks were bright red and whose nose was running with snot.

'Sorry, sir, he's teething. It's his birthday tomorrow – he'll be one, although he's a lazy one, he's not even walking properly yet. Susie and I were walking a long time before that. It's lads that are always slow. Still are, seeing that my brother never delivered my message to you. Just wait until he gets home – I'll give him what for.' Lucy shook her head.

'No, leave him be. He'll have had better things to do. I remember what it was like to be his age, and life was full of more important things than running errands for big sisters.' Adam laughed.

118

'I thank you, sir, for being so understanding,' a weak voice from the bottom of the stairs whispered, as Dorothy stood, still in her nightdress, holding the bottom of the stair rail. 'Lucy will be back with you tomorrow. I aim to be back on my feet then.'

'Mother, go back to bed – you are still unsteady on your feet.' Lucy went to her mother's aid as Dorothy walked hesitantly to sit on the chair next to her youngest daughter. She smiled as Susie looked at her and carried on playing with her dolls.

'I heard voices, and I knew that you would be sitting blaming yourself, Bill. Now, I'm on the mend. I'm not about to leave this earth just yet, so we'll have none of this gloom. There's enough of that outside, with the weather. Bill, come on now – your men need you. And I thank you, Mr Brooksbank, for showing your concern. We've lost a baby, but it happens every day. My mother lost one or two, of that I'm sure.' Dorothy gave a wan smile.

'Aye, lass, go back to bed. I'll stir my shanks and get back out there, now I know that you are looking a bit livelier.' Bill stood up and looked still dark in mood, but knew that he had to do as his wife said, else his yard would not be running smoothly, despite his faith in Thomas Farrington. 'I'll walk out with Mr Brooksbank here, although I'll be drenched to the skin within minutes, as the weather shows no kindness towards us, either.'

'Come, we will walk out together. Now, Lucy, you take care of your mother, and return only when she is fit and well enough to leave. You are needed here more than with me. Besides, the weather means I can't be out on my land, so I can keep my own house until this weather lifts.' Adam walked out behind Bill, who glanced backwards at his wife and family before closing the kitchen door behind them both.

'Bill, I noticed when I walked down your yard that all the water and waste are running down this ginnel and nearly into the same place as you draw your water from. You don't think there's something in the water you are all drinking that causes your wife to keep miscarrying? I only say this because over in Haworth they have had a lot of deaths and disease, and that was because of their water supply being contaminated. There must be plenty of unpleasant substances in those hides and in the lime that you use. If it's seeping into your water, it could be poisoning you and your family.' Adam stood and looked at the filth and water running down the yard and disappearing just short of the row's water supply.

'We'd all be ill, if that was the case. All the row uses the same water supply. Sometimes we do get belly gripes, but not that bad.' Bill took offence at the suspected uncleanliness of his yard, and that it could be his fault that his wife could not bear children.

'But have any other women on this row lost babies? It could affect just that part of a woman.' Adam had listened with interest when the parson at Haworth had informed him, on the day of their tea together, that some women had lost babies because of contamination in the water, especially near the ironworks.

'There are no other women down here, except my family. No woman in her right mind would live down here and breathe this stench every day, and all the houses are in need of attention. My old lass and all mine complain about the yard most days. But that's what you've got to put up with, if you are in my line of business,' Adam grunted.

'Then perhaps you should think about moving your family away from here, to protect them. Or at least channel the waste away from the house and water supply, because I bet that's where your problems lie.' Adam pulled up the collar of his coat and looked at the dawning on Bill Bancroft's face that his words might carry some weight. 'It's worked in Haworth – the mortality rate for babies has nearly halved.' The rain dripped down over his face and he hoped that Bill would take his words seriously, as he looked around him.

'I'll think about it – you might be right. But it'll cost too much to move, and it'll cost a lot to make drains for all the pits. I'm not made of money, not like some.' Bill scowled at Adam and thought long and hard about his words. The drains of the yard needed his attention, and in wet weather like the current day, the pits did find their own drainage, running down the yard into the nearest drain near his back door.

'You think about it. If you need help, I'll give you a hand. It's what neighbours are for.' Adam patted Bill on the back and saw him giving time to his words, before setting off on his way home.

Bill stood in the yard and watched Adam walk back

up to his home high on the moorland. Perhaps he was right: it could be his fault for not keeping on top of the yard's drains. There were all sorts of chemicals and pollutants in the hides, not to mention the lime that burned skin and irritated eyes. If it stopped the worry of his Dorothy losing babies, then he would have to do something about it, whether money was short or not. He was thankful that Adam had not asked what had become of the baby. His secret was safe for now at least, and that was how he'd like to keep it.

Thomas Farrington looked around: the pits were silent, everybody was in their beds and the moon shone down ghost-like, throwing a haunting light over the flay-pits and the heaps of hides yet to be processed. All was quiet except for the squeaking of the rats that inhabited the yard, and the owls that flew silently down to catch them as their prey. He lifted his shovel and put his oil lamp down beside the lime pit that everyone who worked in the yard was forbidden to go near, by the outspoken Bill Bancroft. This was where he'd find the bastard's money, Thomas thought as he dug deep into the pit. He'd worked hard for Bill all his life and had never been shown any respect by him or his family. Now was the time to pay; the time for him to grab the box of money that Bill obviously hid in the heap of lime, else why had he been digging in it in the early hours of the other morning?

He dug his shovel into the lime, where he had seen Bill digging. Suddenly his shovel hit something, but it wasn't hard; it was soft, and Thomas bent down to throw it to one side to make way for the box of money he hoped was hidden underneath it. He pulled on the sacking, displaying the contents enclosed within it onto the lime pile. He felt his stomach churn and held his hand against his mouth to stop him vomiting. There in front of him were the skull and limbs of a baby. But not a normal babe; its limbs were not yet formed, and likewise its face and features. It was obvious to him that the child had been born too early and would not have survived even if it had been born full-term, by the look of its features. So this was Bill Bancroft's secret: there was no hidden money, just a dead baby.

But it wasn't the first time that Thomas had seen Bill digging there, so as he wrapped the deformed shape up, he decided to dig deeper, only to reveal the badly decomposed skulls of a further two babies, before placing the sack and its contents back into its white, acid-eating grave. The lime pile was a burial place for miscarriages, and he had witnessed the disposal of the latest one. They couldn't be Lucy's babies, for she was as thin as a lathe, so they must be those of Dorothy Bancroft. And Bill was flouting the law by hiding them in the lime pit without a decent burial; whether they were full term or not, they still had to be accounted for. Now what to do with his discovery, he didn't quite know, as he hurriedly buried the deformed body back in the lime pit. But he knew he could use Bill Bancroft's dark secret against him and would take great delight in doing so.

11

Lucy had been back working for Adam for the last three days. Her mother was recovering nicely and was managing to look after her youngest two, while her father went about his business as usual. The weather had improved and the warmth of a spring day shone down on Black Moss. The lower fields of the farm were beginning to be filled with the smiling faces of white daisies and golden-coloured celandines, while underneath the more sheltered hedges, primroses and violets were starting to flower.

'I love this part of the year. Summer is coming and everything is starting to look fresh and green.' Lucy stood on the front step of the farmhouse, after shaking the tablecloth free of crumbs when Adam had finished his dinner. 'Just smell that fresh air. I wish it smelled like that down home. Sometimes my stomach retches with the stink. I'll be glad I'm working up here this summer, because the smell gets worse with the heat.'

'I told your father to move – it would be better for all of you, in my eyes.' Adam looked across at the young lass who had taken his home to heart.

'He'll never do that; it'd cost too much. Although I have heard him muttering about digging some new drains down into the river, so that the yard isn't such a puddle. So your words have not fallen entirely on deaf ears.' Lucy sighed. 'I'd love to live away from the flay-pits, somewhere like this. Although I've noticed that when the wind is blowing a certain way, you can still smell them, even as far up the moor as here.' She walked into the kitchen and folded the tablecloth, then placed it in the kitchen table's drawer.

'He'll pollute the river then. But I suppose it would be better for all of you. Now, I'll away and see how Archie is getting on. He's made a start on some of the gaps in the walls in the top pastures. I'll soon be able to get some sheep and their followers in another month or two, and then my work will have started and I'll no longer be the man of leisure that I feel I am now.' Adam pulled on his jacket.

'You are not a man of leisure – you are forever busy. The difference to this place is unbelievable, since you arrived. It's a true home now. There's always something being done to improve somewhere, sir.' Lucy knew that her master worked hard and was proud of his home.

Adam smiled. He'd have to start to earn some money with his stock and his land, as his army savings wouldn't last forever and his father did not leave him that large a fortune, although he was richer than most of his neighbours. The sooner the old place was in shape, the better. He aimed to go to the spring fair at Denholme to buy himself a flock of sheep with lambs, to earn him some income in the autumn.

'I'm going to see your friend "Old Moffat" later today. He's got some chickens for sale. So we will soon have hens in the yard in the morning. It's apt that it's Easter tomorrow and that I'm bringing chicks onto the farm. I'm going to place them in the coop that I made while it was pouring down last week. Now on Sunday you don't usually work for me, but tomorrow being Good Friday, I'd expect you still to come, although I'm willing to let you have Easter Monday off. I'm not a religious man, but I do respect other people's beliefs, and perhaps you need to be with your family on that day.' Adam stood in the doorway.

'Chickens at Easter will be lovely. Susie would love to see them,' Lucy exclaimed. 'Thank you for giving me Monday off, sir. I'll be able to do something with my brothers and sisters and take some pressure off my mother. She says that she's alright, but I know she's just saying that; she looks really weary.'

'She'll have to look after herself and take care not to overreach herself with tasks. Why don't you bring your sister and the baby to see the chickens? I'll be here. I'm not going anywhere, and it seems that I am not to have any visitors. I was hoping a dear friend, Ivy Thwaite, might have written to me, replying to my letter I sent her quite a few weeks ago, but it seems that she has not had time yet.' Adam's face clouded over. He was hoping that

126

Ivy was alright, and was more than a little concerned at not receiving news from her.

'She'll write soon, I'm sure, sir. I would like to bring the two youngest to see the chicks – it's very kind of you to ask us. And thank you for giving me both the Sunday and Monday off. My mother will want us to go to on Sunday. Although I hate going, it's expected of us.' Lucy pulled a face; she loathed attending and walking up the hill to the church at Denholme in her finest. And the Sunday service was so long, when she could be doing so much else with her time. The only good thing was that she could smile and flirt over the pews with Alex Braithwaite from the quarry, or perhaps the youngest son of the Bucks, if they were in residence at their home in Denholme, and not in Wales.

'No, you won't be getting me to church, either. I'll go and tell the Lord my sins up on the moor. Now I must go. Poor Archie is all on his own, and he'll be thinking I've deserted him.' Adam walked out of the farmhouse and into the paddock where his horse was grazing, lifting its head and trotting towards him on his approach. 'Aye, come on, lass. Four legs are better than two, when I've this moor to walk up. But we'll not saddle you; now that you've got used to me, we'll dare going bareback today.' He ran his hands over the little faithful horse and led it through the gateway and into the yard, pulling on its mane to guide it to the mounting block in the corner of the yard. 'Now, hold still. It's been a long time since I rode bareback and without reins, but we've got to know one another, and both of us will prefer being without restrictions.'

127

Adam held tightly to the horse's mane and then threw his left leg over the sturdy little mount, which flinched not an inch. 'Now then, let's see – if I give pressure with my knees and a bit of encouragement from my heels, we should go where I want to go, and not where you want to go.' He grinned as the horse started to step out up the steep hillside to the moor. He patted it on its neck and pulled on one of its ears, as it made its way higher up the hillside. 'I never did like saddles. I always rode bareback when I was a lad and now, thirty years on, I'm back doing it. My father will be laughing, if he can see me, and thinking what an idiot I've been, wasting my life in other men's service when this could have been mine all along,' Adam whispered, and then halted the mare as they reached the top of the moor. He would never tire of the view from his land; it was his home, the place he loved, but it had taken him half his life to realize it. What an idiot he had been.

Lucy swept the hearth tidy and then went into the dairy to skim the cream off the top of the day's milk, before putting it into the butter churn. She filled the large glass jar halfway up, then screwed the lid on it. The lid was attached to a handle and gears, which turned two large wooden paddles that hung down in the creamy milk; when the handle was turned, it agitated the milk, making it separate into butter and buttermilk after a good length of time.

However, today it took no time at all, in Lucy's eyes. She was too busy wondering who Ivy Thwaite was, and what had she to do with Adam Brooksbank. Were they just good friends or more than that? Perhaps they were lovers? Was Ivy beautiful or a plain, ordinary woman? Whoever she was, Lucy hoped that she would never visit, because another woman in the house would only bring worry, in her view. She enjoyed running the house at Black Moss and she didn't want any interventions in her perfect position of maid and companion to Adam Brooksbank, especially if it came from another woman. She was beginning to look at her master in a different light. He was kind, witty and, for a man his age, quite attractive. What's more, he was a man of means, and Lucy found herself wanting his company when she was not at Black Moss, even though she only worked for him.

Lucy looked at herself in the wardrobe mirror in her bedroom. She viewed herself from all sides and pinched her cheeks to give them a little colour. If she was to be made to go to church, then she might as well have something to enjoy doing, rather than listening to the vicar bestow his views of religion on one and all. Dressed in her finest blue dress edged with lace, and with her hair tied back and plaited, she aimed to catch the eye of Alex Braithwaite and flirt with him over the pews to alleviate the boredom of the church service.

She smiled as she looked at herself. If Alex could resist her advances, then he was better than half the local lads, who were forever yelling their comments at her, and whom she usually looked upon with disdain. She had higher ideas about who she was going to marry, and it wasn't going to be any Tom, Dick or Harry with hardly a penny to his name. It had to be someone who offered her security, and at the moment she wasn't showing commitment to anyone. She was simply going to enjoy herself and flirt with them all.

Sitting in church with her mother and siblings, Lucy looked across the pews at the blond-haired, red-cheeked Alex Braithwaite. He was sitting in his family pew and his father kept looking sternly at him, as Alex kept turning his head to look at her.

'Stop it, our Lucy – behave yourself! You are in the Lord's house now, so stop your flirting with Alex Braithwaite,' Dorothy whispered to her daughter. But secretly she smiled to herself. She knew that her daughter took many a man's eye, and secretly hoped that Lucy would end up with the quarry owner's son.

'Sorry, Mother, but he keeps looking at me, and what am I to do?' Lucy smirked and put her head down to avoid Alex's gaze.

'You can ignore him until we are out of the church,' her mother whispered. 'He should have more respect – just like you.'

Lucy looked up and blushed as Alex winked at her, and the vicar stared from his pulpit at the flirting that was undermining his service. She hoped that she would be able to talk to Alex, but she knew his father would have other plans once the service was over, and that his carriage would be waiting to take them back home to celebrate Easter Sunday in his luxurious home at Rockfield Hall. She would never be good enough for the owner of the quarry, who expected his son to marry into money, and not a lass from the flay-pits.

On Easter Monday, Susie and Lucy had been busy. They had wrapped hens' eggs in onion skins, encasing ferns and leaves next to the onion skins, before dropping them into a pan of boiling water. There was a drop of cochineal in another pan of water, to die some extra-hard-boiled eggs – called 'pace eggs' – bright red, ready for rolling down the hillside at Black Moss Farm; the holder of the last egg to crack would be declared the winner, a tradition that was as old as religion itself. Susie had also decided to make Adam Brooksbank an Easter Garden, in thanks for his invitation to see the chicks that he had penned up in the yard, along with their mother hen.

'Do you think Mr Brooksbank will like my garden?' Susie enquired of Lucy, putting her head to one side and resting it on her hand as she looked at her Easter Garden from every angle.

'I'm sure he will love it. It's the most beautiful Easter Garden I've ever seen.' Lucy smiled at her young sister. They had scoured the wall tops along the lanes around their home for the moss that grew on the limestone walls, along with sprigs of white blackthorn blossom, violets and daises, to be placed like a carpet on the metal lid of an old biscuit tin, making it look like a garden with a pond, with the aid of a piece of broken mirror in the centre of the delicate affair. Lucy was in the process of tying two blackthorn twigs together to make a cross shape, to be placed on part of the garden that they had built up high with layers of extra moss to make it look like a hill. She pushed it in firmly to the layer of moss and hoped it would stand upright, and not topple over with the first bit of movement. 'There now, it's complete with the cross that Jesus was placed on, to save our souls.' She sighed and looked at her little sister. All Susie was worried about was that she had made a beautiful garden, and she didn't care about the fact that it signified Christ's resurrection and that it had a deep meaning at Easter time.

'I don't think I want to give it to Mr Brooksbank. I want to keep it. It's too pretty to give away.' Susie pulled a long face and looked up at her older sister.

'Then you keep it. We've got some pace eggs boiling, so you can give him one of those, and we will pick a bunch of primroses on our way to his farm. I noticed some growing in the bankside when I walked down home the other night. They will look nice on his kitchen table.' Lucy smiled at her young sister.

'I think I'll give it to my mam. She's been poorly and it will make her feel better.' Susie beamed. 'And Mr Brooksbank is a bit posh, and I don't know him.'

'He's not that posh – he's a good man. I enjoy working for him, he's very kind.' Lucy thought about her master and felt her cheeks flush as she considered the man she was employed by, and had found herself growing fond of. 'Now, let's get these eggs out of the pans and see what they look like. I always like peeling the layers of onion skins off the eggs, to see the pattern it has made on them.' She reached for the two pans filled with a dozen eggs that had boiled on the fire for the last twenty minutes, then poured the excess water from them, to reveal nicely coloured red eggs in one pan, and six eggs still wrapped in onion skins with a string holding them in place in the other.

'Woo! Look, pink eggs – I like those.' Susie clapped her hands.

'Just you wait until we have taken the skins off these eggs; they should have lovely patterns on them. Heavens, they are hot.' Lucy juggled the onion-skinned hard-boiled eggs in her hands as she untied the string and peeled back the layer of onion skins and ferns. 'Now, isn't that beautiful? Look, the eggs have turned a yel-lowy-brown and where the fern's been, it's left its pattern.' Lucy looked at the delight on her sister's face as she passed it across to her.

'It's like magic,' Susie whispered.

'We will give Mr Brooksbank that one, because it's perfect and it would be a shame to smash it, when we roll it down the hill. Besides, we have another five to unpeel yet, so there's more than enough to go round.' Lucy placed the egg to one side and helped Susie peel the remaining five, each one having a different pattern from the others.

'Well, you two have made a good job of those.' Dorothy glanced at the decorated eggs as she came in from the yard with baby Bert on her hip. 'It's a pity they

133

will end up smashed, broken and eaten. I don't know what's got into your father, Lucy. He's digging up half the yard, and poor Thomas Farrington is helping him. It might be Easter Monday, but he's making him work. It must be something important that he's up to – he's even got Nathan helping, so he'll not be joining you on your visit to Adam Brooksbank, as his father says he needs him.' Dorothy sat down in the chair next to the fire and put Bert down on the pegged rug next to her. 'Don't take this one with you, either. He's nothing but a moaner this morning; his back teeth must be coming through. Besides, I'm feeling a lot better now and I can manage him.'

'You still look a bit pale to me. Are you sure that you are alright, Mam?' Lucy asked with concern.

'I'm right, lass. Now you, Susie and Will get your-selves gone to Black Moss. It will suit them seeing some young chickens and rolling the pace eggs. Bert and I might have half an hour on the bed, if I can get him to sleep. It will do us both good.' Dorothy sat back and looked at Susie. 'Are you taking Mr Brooksbank the garden you've made? It looks lovely.'

'No, Mam, it's for you. I don't love Mr Brooksbank, but I do love you.' Susie got down off her chair and went and kissed her mother.

'I love you too, my little angel. Now you go and have a lovely afternoon with Lucy, and don't show her up. Mr Brooksbank is her boss, and we don't want him to think we have no manners, no matter where we live.' Dorothy kissed Susie's blonde hair and picked up baby Bert, who was beginning to cry yet again. 'I'll get his dummy and lie on the bed with him – he'll soon drop off. Now get yourselves gone. It'll be dark before you know it, although the days are beginning to draw out a little now. Spring should be here: it's April after all.'

Lucy tied Susie's cape around her and put the dyed eggs into a basket, before pulling her own shawl around her. 'You sure you will be alright, Mam?' she said as she opened the kitchen door into the yard.

'Yes – get yourself gone. Will's waiting for you both. Your father will be glad to get him out from under his feet. He's too young to help and is only hindering the job he's trying to do.' Dorothy stood up and walked to the bottom of the stairs with Bert in her arms and watched as her two daughters left the house. She'd be glad for a bit of peace, once Bert had dropped off to sleep. An hour or two without anyone else in the house but her and her youngest would be a welcome respite from the usual bustle of her family and its noise.

'What are you up to, Father?' Lucy looked around her as Nathan and Thomas Farrington dug deep into the earth of the yard.

'I'm making drainage from that pit to the beck. Every time it rains, that pit overruns and flows down the yard nearly to the back door. It needed doing. So I thought I'd do it while we haven't many men at work. Tom here's being a good help; he said he'd nothing else to do with his time, so he might as well earn some brass. And Nathan's not at school today.' Bill stood with his hands on his shovel and wiped the sweat from his brow as he looked at Thomas Farrington and his son digging out a small trench, which he aimed to fill with some second-hand drainpipes that he'd managed to find, and which would cover just the first drain of many that he now knew he had to dig. He'd no intention of telling anyone about the conversation that had taken place between himself and Adam Brooksbank. 'I hope you are taking Will with you up to Black Moss. He's hindering us something terrible, and he'll get the rough side of my tongue, if he doesn't bugger off.'

'Yes, I'll take him. He'll enjoy the walk and it'll get him out of your way.' Lucy glanced up and noticed Thomas Farrington looking at her, as he shovelled dirt to one side of the trench. She turned and shouted at Will to stop hindering Nathan and to join her and Susie.

'Can I bring my jam jar? I might find some frogspawn or tadpoles up where we are going. I've never looked in those streams up there,' Will yelled, as he ran for his jam jar from behind the kitchen door, with a piece of string tied around it for a handle.

'Hurry up then.' Lucy set off walking with Susie out of the yard. The sooner she was out of Thomas Farrington's gaze, the better, as he looked darker than ever in mood and manner.

Thomas leaned back on his spade and looked at the lass that he was besotted with. He'd watched her growing up into a good-looking young woman, and with every day he admired and needed her more. The trouble was that she never looked at the side he was on, preferring to wind up Archie Robinson with her flirting. If Lucy flirted with him like that, he'd show her what sort of man he was. She'd have no need to look at any other man ever again. She didn't know it yet, but she was going to be his – he was going to make sure of that. He'd longed for her for too long, and now he was going to make Lucy his, before any other man sullied her.

'Stop your bloody gawping at our Lucy, and put your back into it,' Bill shouted at Thomas, as he caught him watching Lucy disappear from the yard.

'Yes, boss. I was just having a rest,' Thomas replied, as he swore under his breath. He was going to show the bastard; he'd plans for Bill's daughter and for his yard. Bill would not be boss for ever, not if he had his way.

Adam raised his head from the job in hand, as he heard the sound of young voices approaching his yard. He'd decided, since the sun had started to show its strength, to turn over the much-neglected garden, which had always been so neatly planted in his youth. Now it was a mass of dock leaves and nettles and was taking longer than he had anticipated to clear. The packets of seeds that Lucy had requested on his first visit to Keighley still stood on the mantelpiece in the kitchen, where he had placed them after showing her the selection he had bought her; but that had not been followed up by digging the plot over. Now, with it being Easter Monday, he'd been reminded of his father saying that early potatoes and broad beans should be planted at Easter, and had decided that if he needed to be self-sufficient in the coming months, he would be best getting on with digging the plot over. With only half the garden already cleared and the soil turned over, he was glad of the distraction of his young visitors, for his leg was aching and he was ready for a break.

'Good afternoon. I see I've got visitors.' Adam smiled and shoved his spade into the earth of the garden and brushed his hands on the side of his breeches.

'Yes, I hope we've not disturbed you. Susie was anxious to see your chickens, and Will wonders if you could tell him if you have any likely spots for frogspawn or tadpoles in a stream or pond near you?' Lucy looked at her employer. He was wearing a white shirt with the sleeves rolled up and was partly showing his chest as he walked towards them. She couldn't help but think that, with his black collar-length hair and muscled body, he could pass for a much younger man – a very attractive man.

'I can oblige with both.' Adam tussled Will's hair. 'Frogspawn can be found just down there, in that gully, if I remember rightly. There's a small wet spot down by those rushes, and I'm sure it will still have frogs breeding there. Your jam jar will soon be filled, if you are lucky. But I hope that you'll free the tadpoles, once they've grown too large for your jar, else you'll end up with one large tadpole, as they are carnivorous and eat one another, you know.' Adam smiled at his visitors.

'Can I go, Lucy? I can't wait to show Nathan, if I get my jam jar full – he'll be so jealous. He's been looking for some for weeks.' Will looked up at his sister, seeking her permission, before thanking Adam.

'Yes, but take care you don't fall into any water, else you'll be wet until you get home. Go on. Susie and I will stay here until you get back and will look at the chickens, which is what we really came for.' Lucy watched as her brother ran down the length of the field, his jam jar down by his side in readiness for his catch.

'And you, young lady, would like to look at my chickens, I believe?' Adam bent down on his knees and looked at Susie. 'They are growing fast. I've only had them a few days and already they are walking around the pen and worrying their mother to death. Just like your mother worries about you, I bet.'

Susie pulled a face and retorted, 'My Mam never worries about me, but Lucy says I'm nothing but a pest and a worry. She's always moaning at me.'

'Does she now. Well, you come with me and we will give her five minutes free of worry as we look at the chickens. Then I see that you've brought a basket full of pace eggs. We will have to see whose eggs crack first, when we roll them down the hill in the back field when your brother returns.' Adam held out his hand for four-year-old Susie to take, which she did without a minute's hesitation.

Lucy watched from the garden wall as Adam and Susie walked across the farmyard to where the hen and her chicks were living in the newly made coop. She smiled as she listened to the conversation between her employer and her young sister, and to the giggles and

139

laughter as Adam placed one of the few-days-old chicks in Susie's hands.

'Lucy! Lucy, come and look. Come and see: I'm holding this baby chick. It's so fluffy and it's crying for its mummy.' Susie turned with a big smile on her face, holding desperately onto the fluffy chick while its poor, distraught mother clucked about and tried to control her brood, in the hope that she would not be losing another one to the hands of the child.

'It is lovely, darling, but its mother would really like it back with her. She's full of panic for her baby – she thinks you've pinched it.' Lucy walked over to where Adam and Susie stood. 'Let's put it back with its mother, and perhaps Mr Brooksbank will let you feed them with some meal, and then you can watch them eat.' Lucy took the chick from Susie's hands and stroked the chirping bird, as Adam opened the coop's lid. 'There, we will put it back with its mother, where it belongs.' Lucy bent down next to Adam and placed the little chick back with its brothers and sisters and its mother. As she stood up she nearly brushed cheeks with Adam, and she caught her breath and looked into his eyes.

Adam, noticing her blush, closed the lid quickly and turned to talk to Susie. 'Come with me and we will get some cornmeal for their dinner and feed them, like your sister Lucy says, until your brother returns. They may only be small, but they are always hungry.' He took Susie's hand and walked across the yard, leaving Lucy looking out across the valley.

Her heart was beating fast and she could feel the

colour rising in her cheeks. How stupid she was to feel this way about her employer. He was a good few years older than her, and he'd never shown an ounce of interest in her, and yet here she was looking at him and going weak at the knees, when they touched briefly. It wasn't right. He was the master of Black Moss and she was just the lass from the flay-pits. She shouldn't even be thinking that way, and couldn't understand what had come over her.

Lucy lay in her bed, with her young sister fast asleep by her side. She had enjoyed one of the best afternoons that she could ever remember.

Susie had loved the attention that Adam Brooksbank had shown her, and Will had been bragging all evening about his catch of tadpoles, making his older brother mad and envious of his day at play, while he had been busy in work with his father. Lucy smiled as she remembered Adam and her brother and sister chasing the hard-boiled pace eggs as they rolled down the steep hillside of Black Moss's fields, then eating them once they had cracked open wide – all done in remembrance of the breaking open of the Lord's tomb in the garden of Gethsemane. None of them were religious, but they enjoyed the fun that the Easter festivities brought. But most of all, Lucy had enjoyed being next to Adam and not being in his employment for that one day. 'Adam Brooksbank,' she whispered to herself and visualized his face and his smell, as she clutched her pillow close to herself. She was trying not to think or dream of him, but she could not keep the man out of her thoughts, no matter how hard she tried. He was the first man she had ever felt this way about, and her heart fluttered like a trapped butterfly as she lay in bed trying to sleep.

12

Thomas Farrington hid in the shadows of the hedge that ran on either side of the path from Black Moss Farm to the road that led to Providence Row and the flay-pits, waiting for Lucy to return home from work. He paced back and forth, thinking over the plan that he had hatched in his head since the discovery of Bill Bancroft's secret. He'd lusted over Lucy Bancroft for so long and knew she was the key to inheriting the flay-pits after her father's day, if he was to marry her. He spat out a mouthful of saliva as he thought about her disdain for him and how little respect she had shown him, even though he was her father's right-hand man. Well, that was going to change as from today. She would do as he wished, else it would be the worse for her family.

He stood still as he heard Lucy coming down the road and then stepped out in front of her, his plan clear in his head. Today was the day he would become top dog and she would respect him.

'For Lord's sake, you frightened me to death!' Lucy exclaimed and then walked on past him. She wasn't going to stop and be alone with a man she always thought not quite right in the head, and of whom she was frightened. She wondered whether to break into a run, but knew that in her long skirts he would easily catch her.

Thomas followed her every step and caught hold of her arm tightly and made Lucy stop in her tracks, pulling her round to look at him. 'That'll be the last time you look down your nose at me, if you've any sense. Or it will be the worse for you and yours,' he snarled as he held her tight.

'Let me go, you idiot! I'll tell my father, and then it'll be the worse for you!' Lucy pulled on her arm and tried to free herself, while Thomas caught her other arm and pulled her tightly to him.

'No you don't. You listen to me, Miss Flighty, you'll do as I say.' Thomas held her closely, his foul breath making Lucy feel nauseous as he held his face just inches from hers. 'I know your father and mother's little secret, and I'm not about to hold my tongue unless you do as I demand.'

'I don't know what you are on about. Now let me go – you are mad in the head and need locking up,' Lucy yelled and struggled.

'Mad in the head, am I? It's not me that's buried all those babies in the lime pit in the yard. That could be classed as murder or, if not murder, then your father could be jailed by the authorities for not notifying them of their deaths. Even that would give your father at least two years in jail for each baby buried there. Time enough for your own family to be put out on the street, and for the slander that would follow to ruin you all. So what are you going to say now, Miss High-and-Mighty?' Thomas held her even more tightly. 'Now that I know your dirty family secret.'

'Let me go! I don't know what you are on about. What babies?' Lucy struggled, her heart pounding as Thomas put his face next to hers. The stench of the flay-pits was on his clothes, for unlike her father, Thomas never bathed and he stank.

'You know – you can't help but know. And now I'll tell you what you can do to stop me from opening my gob to the peelers in Denholme. You wouldn't want to see your mother and father took away and both your brothers and your sister left parentless. That would be a terrible shame.'

Thomas kissed her cheek and Lucy squealed and tried to kick him and free herself.

'Now that's no way to treat your husband-to-be – because that's what I am, unless you want the world to know about your father and mother's secret. You'll marry me to keep your family's shame hidden.' Thomas sneered and tried to kiss Lucy as she protested, shaking her head.

'Never! You can do your worst,' Lucy screamed.

'Then I will and you'll lose everything, and that will include your nice clean job with your high-and-mighty Mr Brooksbank, I'll see to that.' He pushed Lucy back into the thorn bush at the side of the road and attempted

145

to kiss her again, before loosening one of her hands from his grip in order to feel her breasts.

'Never! I'll never marry you.' Lucy slapped his face with her free hand and managed to push him off her body, as the thorn bush pierced her clothes. She kicked Thomas hard and tried to shake him off her, as he kept his grip of her arm.

'You will, and you will start by walking out with me. You'll meet me here on Saturday night – else Sunday morning I will be walking into Denholme and having words with the sergeant there.' Thomas held her arm tightly and pushed her back into the thorn bush.

'I'll never do that. Me walk out with you – I'd rather die! You are a filthy, despicable man and I don't know why my father employs you. I hate you. I'll never marry you,' Lucy yelled at him.

'Oh yes, you will, or else everything your father has worked for will disappear in the blink of an eye. And you will be so desperate that the prospect of marrying me will seem like heaven. Don't think of saying anything about this to your father, either, else I'll make more problems in that yard of his and he'll soon find out who the real boss is. And it's not him. Those men that work for him look up to me, not him.' Thomas forced another kiss from Lucy and then pushed her further into the thorn bush. 'Saturday evening, six o'clock, here – else it will be the worse for you.' He threw Lucy to the ground and stood over her. 'And I expect more than a kiss. After all, you've promised more to every man you've flirted with, so now it's time to show me what you've got.'

Thomas leered over her and then spat next to her. He would have her, if not by fair means, then by foul. It had been a good night when he had seen Bill burying the family shame, and Bill had played straight into his hands. He swaggered off down the lane back home to satisfy himself, before going for a drink at The Fleece.

Lucy lay, distressed and crying, in the roadside, thankful that she had not been raped or worse, as she watched her filthy attacker walking down the road towards the flay-pits. What was she to do? Thomas Farrington knew everything, and he could ruin her family with just a few words to the police down in Denholme. She'd no option but to meet him on Saturday night, but she'd no intention of ever marrying the manipulative, horrible bastard. For now, she would keep out of his way and not say anything to anyone about the attack. Come Saturday night, she would be more prepared. And if Thomas thought he was going to lay a finger on her, he could think again, because she might flirt with men, but she would never lift her skirts for any man – especially a man like Thomas Farrington.

'Are you alright, Lucy? You seem quiet this morning.' Dorothy looked at her normally chatty daughter, as she buttoned up her boots before setting out to walk up to Black Moss.

'I'm fine, Mother, just a little tired. I didn't sleep well last night.' Lucy looked up at her mother and wanted to tell her about Thomas Farrington's threat, but didn't wish to give her more worry.

'Don't you work too hard for that Adam Brooksbank. You'll get no thanks off that sort, and you never do. They take everything for granted.' Dorothy looked at the white face of her daughter as she stirred the porridge for everyone's breakfast.

'He's not like that, Mam. He looks after me well and never asks too much of me.' Lucy quickly defended her boss.

'Aye, well, you can sit down and have some breakfast before you go up there. You look pale and if you get any thinner, there will be nowt left of you. It's alright watching your figure, but you need something inside you in order to work.' Dorothy shoved a bowl of steaming porridge in front of Lucy and watched as she pulled a face at the breakfast being thrust under her nose.

'I'm not hungry, Mam, and I'm going to be late. Give it to our Nathan.'

Lucy grabbed her shawl, not giving her mother the chance to reply as, out of character, she left her home by the front door, rather than walk out of the back door and through the yard, where she knew Thomas Farrington would already be at work. She didn't want to set eyes on the man. She hated him and the more she thought about meeting him on the coming Saturday, the more she realized that she could not do it, no matter what his threat. He'd have to carry out his threat; or perhaps she could move what was left of the poor babies buried under the lime without anybody knowing. Both thoughts filled her with fear as she climbed up the lane that led to Black Moss Farm, passing the hedge where Thomas had attacked her. The scratches of the thorn tree were still sore on her back, and her blouse had been torn by his aggression. And she was filled with terror as she remembered the look in his eyes and the way he had treated her. There was no way she would ever marry a man like that and ruin her life. No good would come of such a union, so she had to think of a way to thwart his threats. And she would rather die than lie next to him every night of her life.

The morning was warm, but it made no difference to Lucy as she walked up the road to the farmhouse. The weather could have been doing anything and she would not have noticed, she was so lost in her worries. Walking through the farmyard, she was thankful for the refuge of Black Moss – she was safe there. Thomas Farrington would not dare bother her there, and Adam Brooksbank would defend her, if ever he dared to. She could relax and go about her business until it was time for her to walk home again. And with today being Thursday, she would ask Archie to wait for her and would walk back home with him. Archie would never even think of doing the things Thomas Farrington had done to her, with his filthy hands groping her breasts. How dare he, she thought, as she stepped into the porch of the farmhouse and opened the heavy oak door into the homely kitchen.

'Morning, Lucy. I've just finished chopping the kindling sticks. I can lay the fire, if you wish?' Adam looked up at his maid and smiled.

'No, it's alright, sir. I'll do it.' Lucy knelt down next to the fire and riddled the still-glowing embers from the

149

previous evening, laying the newly chopped sticks on the warm coals and blowing gently for them to catch fire, before adding coal to the blaze.

'I've filled the kettle and got the bread out of the pantry. A slice of bread and butter with some cheese will suffice for my breakfast. I want to be out in that garden as soon as I can. The day promises to be a good one, so hopefully I'll get the rest of the soil turned over and then you can help me set it with whatever seeds we have.' Adam sat back in his chair, with his jacket not yet on and his braces hanging down by his side, instead of being pulled over his white chambray shirt.

Lucy looked at her boss. He was better than any other man she had ever known. Who else would do the things he had done, when it was expected of a maid.

'Thank you, sir. I'll brew your tea and butter the bread, and then I'll go and milk the cow. It does look like a good day – spring is here, by the looks of it. It will soon be summer and the swallows will be returning to nest under the eaves of the buildings. They always tell me that summer is not far away,' Lucy said as she put the kettle on to boil. 'Archie is due to be here today, isn't he?' she enquired, hoping that he had not changed his mind about the day's work.

'Yes, he's going to be up on the moor. He's going to make a start on the top pastures, now that all is straight in these bottom fields. I can let the cow out in another few weeks, so she won't have to be fed, once the odd sneaky frost has disappeared, so that will be a job less. Next I'll go to the May Fair and buy myself some sheep

150

and perhaps a piglet, and then I'm fully stocked and can quite happily feed myself and sell the surplus for a little profit down in Keighley. To think I turned my back on all this, all those years ago. I didn't know what I was giving away.' Adam sighed.

'Perhaps it was not the right time for you, sir, but now you appreciate it more. You sometimes don't realize what you've got until it's threatened.' Lucy passed Adam a slice of bread and cheese rather than have him leave the warmth of the fire, and poured him his tea when the kettle had boiled.

'You have got a wise head on your young shoulders, Lucy. I wish I had been blessed with as much sense when I was your age. Instead I was headstrong and selfish.' Adam looked into the fire and thought about the past.

'I'm sure you did what you thought was right at the time. Sometimes you have to do things that you regret, but hopefully things always right themselves.'

Lucy stood up straight and looked at her master. He had regrets, but none of his regrets would touch hers, if she got blackmailed into marrying Thomas Farrington. She couldn't do it; she wouldn't do it; and she would not be walking out with him on Saturday night.

13

Adam stood back and looked at his handiwork: the garden was free of weeds and the ground was dug over and planted with potatoes, broad beans, beetroot and cabbages. And Lucy had planted a row of peas, with sticks foraged from nearby hedges already in place, for the young shoots to grow up. It had been a good day, but now he was in need of a slice of the bacon-and-egg pie that Lucy had left him for his supper, and a drink.

The days were drawing out and the sun had not yet set, when he decided to sit outside with his supper and ponder the day. He bit into his cold pie and looked around him. No wonder his parents had been so content to live here, for there was nothing more to be desired in life. He'd enjoyed his day, getting his hands dirty with the earth's good soil and Lucy keeping him company. Although saying that, she had not been her usual sparky self today, it seemed, and she'd asked if she might walk home early with Archie, even though she didn't seem to be flirting with him in her usual manner. In fact, the more he thought about it, Lucy had definitely been a little reserved in her ways the whole day. He must remember to ask her if she was troubled by anything, and if her mother and family were alright? It was usually her family that she was bothering about, when she had not a lot to say for herself.

He took another bite out of his pie and followed it by a drink of tea, then thought how good a gill of ale would be, after a day of toil in the garden. In fact he'd been meaning to pay a visit to The Fleece for some time. Perhaps this evening was as good as any, he thought, as he collected his cup and empty plate from beside him and went inside, to change his shirt and wash before he walked the half-mile to where the inn stood by the roadside, at the crossroads between Halifax, Keighley, Cullingworth and Denholme.

The Fleece was the local hostelry for those who worked at the flay-pits and the quarry. It was Thursday evening, so nobody should be intent on drinking themselves into a stupor, as all would have work the following morning. Thursday night would be as good as any, he decided, as he pulled on his waistcoat, added his fob watch and drew on his jacket, picking up his walking stick as he left the house and starting down the lane with a whistle. A gill of the finest Yorkshire bitter would be a welcome reward for all the effort he had put into the garden, and it was time he met some of the locals and made himself known to them.

A soft spring breeze was blowing, the smell of the

153

surrounding peaty moorland filled the air and the sky-
larks that were busy nesting flew up above his head,
flitting and singing, as Adam made his way down the
path and onto the main road, stopping finally outside
The Fleece's main doors. When he had passed it on the
night of his arrival home, the inn had looked foreboding
and dark, but now, in the light of the setting evening sun,
the old drinking hole looked welcoming as Adam walked
up the three steps into the entrance of the centuries-old
inn.

'Good evening, sir. What would you like to drink on
this fine spring evening?' The jovial barman, with his red
cheeks and a balding head, but sporting a fine pair of
greying sideburns, leaned on the bar and looked at the
gent who was new to his inn.

'A gill of your best dark ale, please.' Adam stood at
the bar and looked down the low-beamed room, with
tankards hanging from the beams and whitewashed
walls covered with paintings of local scenes. It had been
a while since he had last drunk in the old place, and it
had obviously changed hands in his absence. He looked
around for a place to sit, once he had found the correct
payment for the tankard of frothy ale that the landlord
put in front of him. On the other side of the bar, in the
main room of the inn, a group of young men stood
together. All were drinking fairly heavily, and were laughing and making enough noise to wake the dead.

'I'd stop in the snug end, if you don't mind me saying
so, sir. Alex Braithwaite and his cronies are in, and they've
been drinking since they arrived just after dinner. His

father will have something to say to him in the morning.' The barman winked and nodded to the tall blond-haired lad who was entertaining all the well-dressed men that stood around him, with his tales of derring-do. 'They get a bit ripe with their language and then, if some of the lads from the flay-pits come in and all, they usually get to arguing.' The barman nodded to the small oak table in the corner of the room next to the fire, which had just been lit. It was the best seat in the small snug, and Adam could still hear and see all that was going on in the main bar, but without getting involved.

'I think you are right, although I don't mind the freshness of youth and I've not been that sheltered. I doubt they will say anything that I've not already heard.' Adam smiled. 'I've spent many an hour doing the same myself in my younger days, doing the exact same thing in the same spot, so who am I to judge?' He took a sip from his gill and winked at the barman.

'So you are from around here? I don't think I've had the pleasure of serving you before?' The barman looked at him and shook his head as a roar went up from the other side of the bar. 'Bugger it, now we are in for fun – some of the lads from the flay-pits have come in through the back door. I'll have all on to keep the peace, as they hate one another. I'm Ernest Shepherd, but these are not my flock. If I weren't making money out of them, I'd kick their arses home, the whole lot of them.' He threw his not-too-clean towel over his shoulder and turned to serve his new customers.

'I'm Adam Brooksbank, and I live up at Black Moss.

I've been there a few weeks now,' Adam shouted across the bar, but his voice was lost in the noise and hullabaloo from the other room. He glanced at all the faces of the men who had just come in from the flay-pits, remembering especially the dark, foreboding face of Thomas Farrington, who stood at the back, next to another fireplace that was the main feature of the room. The large sandstone open fireplace had a fire burning brightly in it, and a gleaming copper kettle stood on the side of the hearth, with a pair wrought-iron firedogs, with a poker and shovel balanced upon them. The room was divided: on one side were the flay-pit lads, and on the other stood the lads from the quarry, and neither gave one another the time of day.

Adam went and sat in his corner with his gill. What he had thought was going to be a quiet drink was promising to be anything but, as the banter between the groups started.

'God, there's a stink in here! Have you noticed it? For God's sake, Ernest, why do you serve rabble like that?' one of the lads from the quarry shouted, loud and clear, for everyone to hear.

'Now then, hold your tongue. You lot are not much better yourselves, and I can throw the lot of you out, if I have a mind,' Ernest said drily, watching both sets of men as they settled down.

Adam observed both groups and noticed that Thomas Farrington sat on his own, drinking tots of gin, unlike his colleagues who sat and discussed the day's affairs and played a round of dominoes while enjoying their gills of bitter. He was a surly one, a loner – a man that it would seem no one trusted, Adam thought, as he went to the bar and got himself another ale.

'There's always fun and games when I have these lots in. The mouthy ones are not too bad, but that bugger in the corner, sitting by himself, he's got a nasty temper on him and his liking of gin doesn't help him,' Ernest said, nodding his head in the direction of Thomas as he poured Adam his gill from a jug that he kept under the counter.

'Yes, he looks black in mood, scowling away at the lads near the bar,' Adam said as he handed Ernest his tuppence for his gill.

'Aye, the trouble is they take great delight in winding him up, the silly buggers. It often ends in a fight and I've to throw the lot of them out.' Ernest grinned and went and leaned on the opposite bar to keep an eye on his over-zealous customers.

'Hey, Alex, I saw that lass from the flay-pits making eyes at you on Sunday in church. She's yours for the taking, I'd say, by the looks of her,' one of the lads from the quarry said loudly to his best friend and slapped him on the back, while the rest of the group laughed and jibed at Alex's expense.

'I could have her any day. Just imagine her lying on a bed, whispering for me to satisfy her, that long blonde hair and those blue eyes begging me to do what I've been wanting to do for weeks now.' Alex swigged his ale back and looked at all his mates, and saw how envious they were of his imaginary conquest.

157

Thomas Farrington looked over at the group and scowled. It was the drink that was talking, but they were talking about his Lucy. They'd no right to talk about her in such a way. He felt his blood boiling as he jumped to his feet and walked to the bar. He'd wanted her for so long, and didn't they know that she was to be his, no matter who she flirted with.

'You shut your mouth, do you hear? I'll not have Lucy talked about like that in here. Besides, she's to marry me, so you needn't even look at her, you bastard,' Thomas yelled at Alex and stood just a few inches from his face. 'You get your hands off her – she's to be mine.'

'Give over, she'd never marry you – look at you. You are filthier than the rats that scuttle around that yard you work in. Now piss off and go back to your corner.' Alex turned his back on Thomas and looked at his group of friends, who slapped him on his back and jeered.

Thomas wasn't having any of it. Lucy Bancroft was his, and he'd prove it. He reached for his inside pocket, where his knife for skinning hides was, and pulled it out and stood his ground. He'd make Alex Braithwaite not fit to look at, by the time he'd used his skills with his knife.

'Alex, he's got a knife – the bastard's pulled a knife on you.' His friends stepped back and watched as Alex turned and looked at the man who had taken his jibes all too seriously.

'Put that down, you idiot. You can punch me, but I'm not fighting you with a knife in your hand.' Alex looked at the wild-eyed man who stood in front of him.

158

'Aye, put the knife down, lad. We'll have none of that in my pub.' Ernest Shepherd lifted the bar hatch and stood next to Alex, while Adam put his gill down on the table and walked round to the next room, standing in the doorway.

'No, you've insulted me one too many times, and I'll not have Lucy talked about in that way. She's mine, do you hear? And you are going to pay for your words.' Thomas lunged forward, his hand outstretched, with the knife pointing at Alex. But Ernest was too quick for him and pushed Thomas hard to one side, making him fall and lose his balance. His body fell heavily onto the flagged floor of the inn, and his head hit the firedog and the sandstone hearth of the fireside, spilling blood onto the sandy-coloured stone and making everyone gasp as the pool of blood trickled around the lifeless form, and the knife lay a few inches from his hand.

'Is he dead?' Alex Braithwaite whispered as Ernest stood over the body.

'I don't know. I just wanted to stop him – I didn't mean to kill him.' Ernest looked fear-stricken.

Adam pushed his way through both sets of young men and bent down to feel the pulse on Thomas's body. He looked up at the worried faces and shook his head, as he wiped his fingers clear of the blood upon them. 'Aye, I dare say he's gone. One of you go for the peeler down in Cullingworth. They'll need to be informed about what's gone on here tonight.' He stood up and looked around him. 'Nobody was to blame – he pulled the knife. I saw it all, and I used to serve in the police

159

around here, so there should be no repercussions.' Adam looked at the innkeeper, whose face was ashen. In his head Adam replayed the words said by the now-dead Thomas; why had he said he was to marry Lucy? She hated the man and she'd probably rejoice at the news of his death, her loathing and fear of him had been that deep. There was more to this than met the eye.

'I didn't mean to kill the bugger, just stop him!' Ernest muttered. 'He always was a bad lot, but I never saw that coming. What possessed him, and what made Thomas think he was to wed that lass of Bancroft's? She'd not look the side he was on, if she had any sense.' He shook his head and sat down on one of the chairs, as everyone muttered and whispered and patted him on the back, knowing that if Thomas had not been stopped, it could have led to Alex Braithwaite lying dead – and perhaps more besides.

'Don't worry, Ernest, we all know Thomas was off his head. You saved Alex here and, as this good gentleman says, it wasn't your fault – you were simply defending your customers. He's had it coming to him for a long time, has the bastard; nobody could abide him down at the flay-pits.' One of the lads from the flay-pits slapped Ernest on the back. 'You shouldn't speak ill of the dead, but he was a right Nickey. We were all winding one another up; it's part of the banter between us lads, but there was no need to pull out a knife.'

Alex Braithwaite walked over to Ernest. 'You saved my life. I'll tell the copper that it was either Thomas or me. And that Thomas cracking his head open was an accident. I wish I'd never egged him on about Lucy Bancroft, else this would have never happened.' He bowed his head.

Adam looked around him at all the worried faces. He had meant to have a quiet drink and enjoy his evening, but now he was a witness to the death of Thomas Farrington. But perhaps it was no loss. He knew for sure that one person would not be mourning over his death, and that was his supposed bride-to-be.

14

It was just six-thirty in the morning when Bill Bancroft saw the peeler coming in through his yard gates. He felt panic and looked quickly at the lime pit where the bodies of the babies were hidden, hoping that no one had told the policeman of his crimes. He sighed deeply in relief as he heard, with some disbelief, the real reason why he was visiting, and couldn't quite take in the words that the peeler was telling him.

'Nay, you must have got it wrong. Thomas Farrington can't be dead – don't talk daft. You're talking about the wrong man. He'll be coming out of his back door and starting work any minute now, along with the rest of them.'

'I'm afraid he won't be, sir. He's cold to the touch on the mortuary slab. He got himself into a bit of bother last night at The Fleece, where the landlord had to protect one of his valued customers from being attacked. Unfortunately it ended up with Thomas's demise, when he fell and cracked his skull open on the hearth. It was an accident – we have reliable witnesses to prove it. By all accounts, your Thomas Farrington was a nasty bit of stuff, if riled, and that was what had happened, when somebody was bragging about catching the eye of your daughter. And Thomas lost his rag, because he said he was to marry her. In fact I need to talk to your daughter to tell her the news, if they were to wed.' The constable looked at the open-mouthed pit owner and saw a smile come onto his face.

'Now I know you've got the wrong man. Our Lucy would never marry Thomas. She thinks him thick in the head, and I've never heard a wedding mentioned, or even his name uttered by her in my house. In fact she plays hell with me, whenever I mention the lad's name.' Bill laughed.

'No, it's right, boss. I was there when Thomas died. And it was all through him getting it into his head that he was to marry your lass,' Ted Briggs, who had just entered the yard and overheard the conversation, butted in. 'Thomas went mad when Alex Braithwaite was jibing him about her. He pulled a knife on Alex, so he did.'

'Well, I don't know what to make of it. The poor bugger – Thomas might not have been the full shilling, but he was a bloody good worker. You'd better come into the house and see our lass, before she sets off to work. I'm sure she'll put you right, Officer, that there was no such marriage planned and it was all in his head.'

Bill walked across the yard and into the kitchen,

which was busy with his children wanting their breakfasts and Lucy getting ready to go to Black Moss Farm.

'This lad has come with bad news this morning, and he wants to get something straight with you, our Lucy.' Bill looked at the faces of his family as they realized that a peeler had entered their house.

'I'm sorry to disturb you. I can see that you are busy. But it's like Mr Bancroft says: I'm here with bad news, especially for you, Miss Bancroft.' The peeler hesitated for a moment, watching an expression of puzzlement on Lucy's face. 'I'm afraid there was an incident at The Fleece last night and your husband-to-be died in a terrible accident.' He dropped his eyes and heard gasps all round the room.

'What's he on about, Bill? Our Lucy isn't promised to anyone.' Dorothy wiped her hands on her apron and looked at her eldest daughter.

'I don't know what you mean. I'm not wedding anyone. Who's dead? And why am I involved?' Lucy stood up and felt her legs shaking. This news could only mean one thing: that Thomas Farrington had died. But she didn't know just how much the peeler knew. And she had no intention of telling him about his blackmail unless she had to.

'That's not what Thomas Farrington thought,' Bill said to his daughter. 'He'd got into his head that he was marrying you, and he pulled out a knife on Alex Braithwaite, the stupid bugger. But old Ernest came between them and pushed him to one side, only for Thomas to hit his head on the fire hearth. This lad says

164

he's laid out in the mortuary in Keighley, dead as they come.' He shook his head. 'He always was a hot-headed devil, but why he decided he was to marry you, lass, I don't know.'

'Tuppence short of a full shilling, that's what he was – always had been. His mother, when she was alive, worried about him and was thankful he found work with you, our Bill. Perhaps we should never have kept him on, as he was a dark soul.' Dorothy sighed. 'Are you alright, Lucy? You'd better get a move on. Adam Brooksbank at Black Moss will be waiting for you, because I can't see you shedding any tears over the news that's been given. You hated him more than you loved him, the stupid bugger.'

'So Thomas was not to wed. He'd imagined it, and his death was over nothing.' The peeler looked around him, especially at Lucy.

'It would be a cold day in hell, Officer, the day I married Thomas. He was the lowest of the low and, personally, I'm glad he's gone to his grave. Now if you'll excuse me, I'll be on my way to Black Moss.' Lucy felt shaky, but at the same time she was jubilant over the news of the death of Thomas. Her secret, and that of her family, was safe, as Thomas Farrington would be taking it to his grave.

'So you work for Adam Brooksbank? He was one of the witnesses who gave a statement on behalf of the landlord. I'd never come across him before, but the sergeant down at Keighley had. He told me Brooksbank was an ex-peeler, but lost his way when his wife and unborn child were killed. He seems like a decent man.' The peeler looked at Lucy as she threw her shawl around her.

'He is a good man. I've no complaints. Now if you'll excuse me, I'll be on my way.' Lucy looked around at her family: the oldest of her siblings were not daring to stir, with a peeler's presence in the kitchen, and her mother and father were shaking their heads at the news.

'No, you get away. I'll not keep you any more,' the peeler said and then turned to Bill. 'Do you think we could have a look around his home? I understand he rented it from you? Just to see what state of mind he was in when he picked his fight with young Braithwaite.'

Lucy made for the kitchen door and caught her breath, hoping against hope that there was nothing in Thomas's home to contradict her saying that her marriage to him was simply a fabrication, made up by his unstable mind. She said a silent prayer also that nothing would be found that would incriminate her father; with the babies buried in the lime pit, she hadn't had time to move them, and had not relished the idea of digging for the poor lost souls or known what to do with them if she did find them. She glanced at the flay-pit workers, who all watched her as she walked across the yard.

'We all know Thomas was fucked in the head; we all know he was lying. We didn't believe for one minute that you were going to wed him. Nobody in their right mind would even look at him,' Ted Briggs shouted to Lucy, as she put her head down and made for the pathway and the sanctuary of Black Moss Farm.

Lucy did not reply. She didn't know what to say in reply to the curious workers.

Bill and the peeler stood in the bedroom of Thomas Farrington and looked at the possessions and sketches carefully arranged on the set of drawers.

'These are our Lucy's buttons and ribbons. She kept saying she was losing things off her clothes, when they had been hung out to dry, but none of us took any notice. The carts and animals push back the washing, and the clothes could easily become snagged. The weird bugger has been collecting things of hers. And look at these pictures he's drawn – now that's not normal.' Bill rubbed his head and looked at the peeler.

'He's obviously been obsessed with your daughter and perhaps you should be thankful that he's died, for there could be no knowing what he'd have done over time.' The peeler looked around him. 'How could anybody live like this? He's got a two-bedroom house to himself, yet it's like a pigsty inside.' Both men inspected the room, which was covered in filth and dirt and still had the same curtains hanging at the window that had been there since his mother had died, when Thomas was just in his early days. 'Now what do I do with his body? Are you willing to pay for him to be buried?'

'I am not. Seeing this around me, Thomas can rot in hell, because that's where he looks to have been living for quite a few years. He's nowt to do with me, and definitely nowt to do with our Lucy.' Bill spat out a mouthful of saliva and looked at the peeler.

'Pauper's burial then, unless he's left some brass to bury himself with,' the peeler said.

'I doubt you'll find a farthing. He spent all his money at The Fleece and never had two pennies to rub together. I've been bloody blind. All I saw was how hard Thomas worked, but now I know differently; he was a filthy, weird bugger who could have harmed my lass. As I say, he can rot in hell, as far as our family is concerned.' Bill shook his head at the state of Thomas's home, along with the state of his mind.

'If you don't mind, sir, I'll have a quick look round – see if I can find anything that might lead us to a family member who might help with his funeral costs, or any savings that he might have stashed away.' The policeman looked around him again, not wanting to stay too long in the foul-smelling place. How anybody could make their home on Providence Row, he didn't know, but this house was worse than anything he had ever seen. He could see that it was infested with vermin, and that Thomas Farrington had been anything but house-proud.

'Aye, do what you want. I've never known him to have visitors, nor known of any relations. Nobody ever crossed his doorstep, and now I can see why. It'll take my old lass and me some work to get this anything like inhabitable, and I dread telling her. I can't believe that all this was going on, under my own nose. I've been blind to how the mucky bugger was living,' Bill growled and looked at the room again in disbelief, before going down the stairs and out into the flay-pit yard.

'Are you alright, Mr Bancroft?' Ted Briggs yelled across to his boss and the owner of the yard.

'Aye, lad, but we will be better off without the likes of him, now that I've seen what he's about. I'd have killed the bastard myself, if I'd have known how his mind was working.' Bill looked at all his workers – who had always shunned Thomas Farrington, and now he knew why – before glancing at the lime pit where his secret lay buried.

Lucy stopped halfway up the moorland path to Black Moss. She leaned over a gate at the side of the path and looked down to the valley below. She could just make out Providence Row and the flay-pits as she wiped a tear away from her eyes. 'Please let the secret be buried along with Thomas Farrington,' she whispered. She could never have married him and would never have agreed, if it hadn't have been for his threat of blackmail. Yet even when he was dead, he'd brought the police to their door, and perhaps the danger of them knowing the truth.

Her heart pounded and Lucy felt sick as she started out on the latter half of her walk to work. She'd have to lie to Adam Brooksbank, if he questioned her about the so-called marriage to Thomas – something she didn't like doing, seeing as she respected him and enjoyed his employment. Hopefully not a lot would be said about the matter, and she could make light of it. It would soon be forgotten and then life could return to normal. And although Thomas had died, she could not feel an ounce of grief; only relief at being saved from a life that would have caused her sorrow and pain.

She knew instantly, on arriving in the farmyard, that Adam was up and about, for the farmhouse door was wide open and the chickens and hen were busy eating their morning ration of meal mixed with hot water. She glanced at them before entering the house.

'Ah, Lucy, so you are with us then, this morning. Have you heard the news?' Adam looked suspiciously at her and noticed that she looked as if she had been crying. He started to regret his bluster over Thomas's death. Perhaps after all there had been something in what Thomas had said.

'I have, sir, and it's good riddance to bad rubbish. Nobody's going to miss Thomas, except happen my father, for his work. He was a bad lot. I'm only sorry that I heard you had to get involved in it. I suppose Thomas was the worse for drink, like he always was, and coming out with a load of rubbish about me marrying him. I hated him – that's more like it.' Lucy recalled Thomas's threat to her, and how he had pushed her into the thorn hedge and felt her breasts, and knew she could never have walked out with him on Saturday.

'And there was I, thinking you'd be heartbroken and grieving at the loss of your beau!' Adam grinned. 'Still, I shouldn't make light of it. He lost his life and your name was upon his lips when he died. He must have felt something for you.' Adam looked seriously at Lucy. 'Perhaps you had flirted with him in the past? Alex Braithwaite thinks that you are a tease, so perhaps it would be better if you weren't quite so open with your attentions.' Adam put his head to one side and noticed his maid blushing.

'I never flirted with Thomas Farrington – not once. And as for Alex Braithwaite, he thinks all the girls in the Worth valley are after him. I bet he was saying all sorts to his little crowd of followers. If his John Thomas was as big as his mouth, he'd be worth flirting with.' Lucy's dander rose; she knew she was a flirt, but not to that extent.

Adam laughed. 'How do you know his John Thomas – as you call it – isn't as big as his mouth, if he's not had the liberty?' He smiled at the blushes on Lucy's cheeks.

'I beg your pardon, sir. I don't. Nor will I ever, but from what I've seen, I'm better off without any man about me. Of late they've only caused me trouble. Now if you don't mind, sir, I'll get on with your breakfast and milk the cow. I get more sense out of it than out of any man I've talked to.' Lucy walked into the pantry and brought out the milk and butter.

'Aye, well, the man's dead now. Perhaps for the best, from what I saw of him. He'd a hell of a temper and looked bewitched.' Adam pulled up his chair as Lucy sliced the bread.

'That's what he was, sir – bewitched. Evil as they come, and hopefully the devil has dragged him down to hell with him,' Lucy said and then looked out of the window. 'Archie is late this morning. He's usually here by now.'

'He's here already. He was here at first light, and he's on top of the moor repairing the walls. I met him when

171

I fed the hen and her chicks. I told him the news about Thomas. Archie didn't believe for one minute that you were about to wed him. But he did tell me that you had been especially frightened of Thomas last night, and that is why you asked him to walk home with you. Are you sure nothing had happened between the pair of you, Lucy? It seems strange that Thomas was so set on thinking he was to marry you.' Adam looked at Lucy and noticed a slight hesitation in her answer.

'No, sir, nothing happened. I just made that excuse so that I could walk home with Archie. Like you say, I shouldn't be such a flirt. I'll tell Archie the next time I see him that I was having him on and was only flirting. Now, that cow will be wanting my attention, and we could do with some fresh milk to start the day off.' Lucy put her head down and didn't dare look at Adam. He might no longer be a policeman, but he'd definitely not lost a peeler's instincts. She only hoped that her cover of flirting would be accepted, and that the whole thing would never be mentioned again.

15

The month of April was a fine one, and Archie and Adam were busy every day repairing and restoring the drystone walls that formed the boundaries to Black Moss Farm. It had been hard work, but finally, just in time for the May sheep sale down in Keighley, their job was done.

'I'll have to see to that piece of bog next to the boundary wall. It'd pull a sheep down into it with ease, if it got stuck in it.' Adam stood next to Archie and looked around him at his now-secure kingdom.

'They've more sense than to go anywhere near it, but I can put a fence around it, if you want, to be sure.' Archie looked at his master, whom he enjoyed working for, and he didn't want to run out of work with him.

'I've never known my father lose any of his flock due to the bog, but there's always a first time. It must be what the farm's called after, because the darkness of the moss there warns you that there's something that will suck you down into its depths. Perhaps I'll leave it for now, but I wouldn't want a lamb to get stuck in it. They've no sense and, with a bit of luck, I'll have a flock of sheep and their followers up here in another week or two.' Adam leaned against the newly repaired wall. 'It's beginning to take shape now. My father would be happy to see it back to what it was. I should never have turned my back on it and let it get into such a state.'

'Aye, it's a grand farm. I could do with something like this, instead of working down in the flay-pits. It's not a job for any self-respecting man – it's that mucky. There's nothing better than working on the land.' Archie sighed and looked down over the adjoining land. He spotted the figure of the youngest of the Baxter family walking up the moorside in their direction. 'Bugger, here comes trouble – it's Jacob Baxter, he's the youngest and wildest. I wondered how long it would be before one of them showed their faces,' Archie muttered and walked away from the wall. He didn't want to have to communicate with Jacob, if he didn't have to.

'Morning. Now is this not a grand spring day?' Adam shouted to the young lad with vibrant ginger hair and a beard to match, who walked up and stood at the other side of the wall from him.

'It's alright. You've finally got around to mending your boundaries, then. My father's been swearing about them for years. We couldn't stop our sheep from straying, because of the state of your walls. We can happen turn our newly lambed ewes onto the moor again now.' Jacob scowled and stared at Archie. He didn't know the new owner, but he did know Archie Robinson and he didn't like him.

Archie shook his head, but said nothing.

'Yes, we are all in order now. I'm sorry if it's caused your father concern, in my absence. I've only just come back into the country and decided to return home and farm what's always been our land. I'm Adam Brooksbank. I hope to be a good neighbour.' Adam held out his hand to be shaken by the lad, who looked angrily at him and his friendly gesture was ignored.

'Aye, well, we are the Baxters. We bother no one, if no one bothers us. We keep ourselves to ourselves and would expect folk to respect our ways. I'll tell my father that the boundary is back up, and that you are farming here. Now I'll be on my way. There's plenty to be done at this time of year. We've more sheep and their followers than we know what to do with, and we haven't time for idle gossip.' Jacob glanced at both men, then left as fast as he'd appeared, and Archie came back to Adam's side.

'He's a man of few words,' Adam said to Archie.

'He'll be mad that you are back. I bet half his flock has been making use of the gaps in your walls and grazing your land. I've kept coming across signs of sheep being on the moor, even though nothing should have been on it since your father's death.' Archie watched as Jacob Baxter disappeared over the moorside.

'Aye, well, there's nothing that can get through them now, and nothing can get out, so he can go and tell his father that. I'll not have him making me out to be a bad farmer, when my family has been here for centuries. I'm back in charge now, whether he likes it or not.' Adam looked around him, then smiled at Archie. 'I may be a quiet man, but they'll find that I stand my ground, if pushed. So don't you fret, Archie.'

Adam stood in the doorway of his farmhouse and watched as the first swallow of the year circled and twittered over his head. Its chatter was a welcome sound, heralding summer to the farm. Soon the swallows would be nesting under the eaves, swooping back and forth all summer, feeding and rearing their young, only to abandon all they had built in late autumn.

'The swallows are here! I love their sound. They are so graceful and pretty, swooping around the place.' Lucy gazed up towards the sky as she entered the farmyard for her usual day's work, turning to look at Adam, who stood with a cup of tea in his hand. 'Have you been waiting on me? I'll get a move on, sir. I'm sorry if I'm late.'

'I have been waiting for you, but not because you are late. However, Lucy, I thought you might like a change. I wondered if you would like to accompany me into Keighley. It's the May sheep sales and I am going to buy myself the sheep I need, and I thought you might like to get provisions from various shops. I've also ordered a small donkey-cart from the carter. I'm sure Rosa will be able to pull it, and it will make life easier when it comes to putting purchases – and us – across her back. You may have to walk half the way there, but you'll be returning in luxury.' Adam looked at the surprise on Lucy's face.

'But the house, sir – and the cow!' Lucy gasped.

'The house is tidy, the cow is milked, and I think we both deserve a day in town.' Adam grinned.

'But I'm not dressed fine enough, and I've no money on me. But I would like to go.' Lucy looked down at her skirts.

'You look fine enough to me – better than most of the women in Keighley. And don't you worry about money, as the treat is on me. You've done a lot for me of late, and have helped so much with my return home.' Adam saw the smile that glowed on Lucy's face and knew she couldn't decline his invitation. She was a bonny-looking girl, and he couldn't help but feel a swelling of pride at having such a beautiful young woman by his side as he went around to the stable where Rosa, his faithful little pony, stood, leaving Lucy standing in the yard. He put his hand through the pony's mane and pulled its bridle on, and patted the animal as he placed the saddle on its back. 'Now, Rosa, you've got a rival today – you've to look after Lucy as well as me. I know it's wrong, but I think that flirting smile of hers is beginning to rob me of my senses. No wonder younger men fight over her. And she's the bonniest lass for miles around.'

'You ride on Rosa, sir. I'll walk – there's nothing wrong with my legs.' Lucy watched as Adam brought the pony into the yard and stopped in front of her.

'My leg, if you haven't noticed, has got considerably stronger of late. I'm not in as much pain, and I don't mind walking for a while. Just stand here and I'll lift you up onto Rosa's back. We can change around, if I get tired.'

Adam stood the pony next to Lucy and watched as she worried about lifting her skirts to mount the little horse.

'I'll not look at your ankles, don't worry, although I do have a rough idea what goes on underneath a woman's skirts.' Adam grinned. 'Here, put your foot into my cupped hands and then I'll hoist you up. Pull on Rosa's mane to hang on, and to help you balance.'

He watched as Lucy blushed and lifted her foot into his cupped hands, then quickly slung her skirts and leg over the back of the horse and sat up straight in the saddle.

'Alright? Are you comfortable?' Adam held the pony's reins and checked that she was alright before they set off out of the yard.

'Yes, I've ridden before. But I shouldn't be sitting on her back; she's your horse. I'm the maid, and it should be me who's walking.' Lucy looked down at Adam and felt awkward at seeing her master take the reins while she rode on the horse's back.

'If she had been a little bigger, I would have climbed up with you, but that would be asking too much of Rosa. And besides, I'd be no gentleman if you were walking while I rode. Never mind that you are my maid, I don't believe in keeping people in their place. We are all the same when we come into the world, and we will all be the same when we depart it. It's right that I walk. And besides, look at the day – it's a good day for a stroll down into the town to do business and then return in style.' Adam pulled on the reins and urged Rosa to walk on and leave the farmyard, and to walk the five miles into Keighley steadily.

The road that led from Halifax to Keighley was busy with travellers, packhorses laden with various goods, and people going about their everyday business. Nobody gave the couple making their way into Keighley a second glance, or worried for one moment that it was strange to see a woman on horseback while the man walked by her side. That didn't stop Lucy from feeling that it was wrong, though.

'I'd rather you were up here. Your leg must be hurting by now,' Lucy said to Adam as they stopped for a breather and took in the view of the industrial town of Keighley, which they would soon be reaching.

'Will you stop worrying? I'm not too bad. Besides, we are nearly there. This is Ingrow – it's all downhill from now on.' Adam looked up at Lucy and tried to smile and not show any pain.

'You men are all the same: you never let on when you are beat. Here, pass me your hand and I'll climb down, for you to get on Rosa. As you say, we are nearly there now – another mile and we will be in the centre.' Lucy held her hand out for Adam to help her dismount, but he wouldn't take it.

'Move up nearer Rosa's neck, and I'll get in the saddle behind you. It's downhill for her now, and she won't mind taking us both the last mile. I must admit, the pain is beginning to tell slightly.' Adam led Rosa, with Lucy still astride her, to some mounting steps next to a working worsted mill. The noise of the weaving machines from within the tall four-storey mill was deafening, as Adam made his way up the steps and eased himself snuggly into the saddle behind Lucy.

Lucy breathed in and felt her heart flutter, as Adam placed his arms around her to take the reins. She could feel his breath on the back of her neck, and could smell the soap that he had used to wash and shave in that morning. It was a comforting smell, and a million miles away from the smell of the flay-pits men. His strong arms wrapped themselves around her, and she felt his knees squeeze the side of Rosa, to make her walk on.

'We should be thankful we are not at work, like the poor buggers in that mill. Just look at the dust flying out of the windows. God knows what it would be like in there, working on those looms all day. There's something to be said for being your own man,' Adam said, trying to make Lucy feel more comfortable with being so close to him, as she sat rigidly in front of him.

Lucy looked up at the blue sky, at the mill windows that were open above them, and at the fluff flying up into the air like fairy wishes. She bent her head backwards and nearly put her head on Adam's shoulder in doing so. She'd never been so close to a man before, and she quickly sat forward after looking into his deep-brown eyes and seeing mischief in them, at the thought of her being so familiar with her master.

'I don't bite, you know,' Adam said as she quickly apologized. 'Don't worry, we will soon be in Keighley and then the journey back will be more acceptable to you. Perhaps you'd have been happier staying at home?'

'Oh no, I'm enjoying my day away. I just didn't want you to think I was flirting. After all, you did lecture me about it the other day,' Lucy said quickly.

'I think you know better than to flirt with me, Lucy, so don't you worry about that,' Adam whispered in her ear. It had been a long time since he'd been so close to a woman himself, and he'd forgotten how good it felt and secretly wished she would flirt with him.

Lucy smiled to herself and enjoyed the rest of the ride into Keighley. She knew she shouldn't even think about flirting with Adam, but her feelings were beginning to get the better of her, when it came to the perfect gentleman seated next to her. Although she knew that Adam being a gentleman was something she should be grateful for, many gentlemen still took advantage of their maids, but Adam was different and had never looked and treated her in that way. All too soon, in Lucy's eyes, the small horse took them onto the bustling streets of Keighley and Adam pulled on the reins to stop Rosa in her tracks at the head of Church Green. The tall tower of the parish church stood at one end of the street, while down its cobbled streets were various traders and shops, selling whatever goods were required.

Adam slid down off the horse and offered Lucy his arms to help her dismount. She looked down at him and put her hands on his shoulders, as he held her by her waist just for the briefest of seconds, before quickly gathering his senses and noticing her blush.

'Right, to business! Here's some money – there should be enough for you to buy whatever we need for the house. You'll have a better idea than me, and I can be a bit staid in what I eat, so you buy something for a change that you think I'll enjoy. There will not be a lot of money left, after you've done that and bought this list of staples that I wrote down, but what there is, you should keep for yourself. Treat yourself to one of those fancy cream cakes and a cup of tea.' Adam nodded in the direction of the tea-room, where people were sipping their drink elegantly in the window, while the rest of the world walked by, impoverished. He passed her a list and some money for the things that were needed.

'That's a bit too posh for me. They'd not look the side I'm on, if I walked in there, but thank you, sir,' Lucy said and looked up into his face, then put the money and list in her pocket.

'They bloody well should, because you are just as good as any of them, as far as I can tell.' Adam looked awkward. 'Well, I'm off to the stables and carter's first and then I'm walking down Russell Street – it's where the sheep fair is held. You'll find me there within an hour's time. Do you want to meet me there, and then we will collect the goods for home on our return journey in the new donkey-cart?'

'Yes, I can do that. I'll find you, won't I? I don't like to think that I'll be left in Keighley on my own,' Lucy shouted, and stood for a second watching Adam as he set off down the cobbled street.

'Yes, I'll be there. I'll not go anywhere without you,'

Adam shouted back and then went on his way, leading Rosa to the carter's, before quickly paying another visit – hopefully his last – to the pharmacist. The pain in his leg was healing, along with the hurt in his heart. Perhaps it was because he was home and content, or perhaps it was because he'd found somebody he was growing quite fond of. Whatever, he would hold his feelings at bay. He didn't dare love again, and then be hurt when it all went wrong. Besides, Lucy was still young and was his maid; it was a scandal even to think about it, so it was best forgotten.

Lucy looked around her. She rarely visited Keighley, and she didn't care for it. The people were different; even though she lived only a few miles away, you could tell they were from the town. People might be poor where she lived, but they had pride and you could tell that by the way they kept themselves clean and tidy. In Keighley a lot of people were dressed in rags and were begging on the streets. There was poverty knocking on most doors and the workhouse was always threatening. Back home was more rural, with folk eking out a living from the land, spinning and carding wool in their rooms when the weather stopped them from working outside, and making ends meet by growing whatever they needed to survive. Keighley town was not a friendly place to a country girl, so she would make her purchases and then find Adam. Even the temptation of some money to spend could not persuade Lucy to stay.

She looked at the list and at the money that Adam had put in her hand, and decided to walk down Church

Street to Chatburn's, a shop where she knew she could buy most of the items on Adam's list. And then she would visit the butcher next door and wend her way down the street, turning off at the corner of Russell Street to where the sheep fair was being held. Standing outside Chatburn's, she looked in the window at the advertisements and goods displayed there, smiling at the advertisement that said, 'Brides' cakes and funeral biscuits made here on the shortest notice.' One minute you could be getting married and the next dead, just like Thomas Farrington, she mused. And then she got back to the job in hand.

The shop was filled to the rafters with jars containing pickles and jams, spices, sugars and flour, and the air smelled of freshly ground coffee beans from an elaborate, gleaming brass-and-red coffee-grinding machine that stood on the counter top, with a notice on it declaring it the best coffee in Yorkshire. Lucy waited for the woman in front of her to be served, then stepped forward and gave the rotund moustached man in a white apron her list and watched as he read through it. Her eyes were taking in the counter at the other side of the shop, where cakes and biscuits were displayed so beautifully that it would be hard for her to resist their temptation, if she was to wander over to that side of the shop.

'Aye, we have all that's on your list. Do you want it now, or will you be calling back for it?' The shopkeeper looked at her and could see Lucy's fascination with the coffee beans in the glass dome of the coffee-grinder.

'I'll be calling back for it later in the day. Can you tell

me now how much I owe you?' she asked, and waited while the man totted up the totals.

'That'll be two shillings and threepence. Are you paying now or when you pick it up?'

'I'll pay now, but can you add an ounce of your freshly ground coffee to the order as well, as I've never drunk it before?' Lucy enquired.

'It's not on your list. Will you not get into bother for adding it?' The man looked at her.

'No, Mr Brooksbank said I could treat myself, so that's my treat.' Lucy grinned. She had never drunk coffee, and she could share it with Adam the next day.

'Well, as long as you'll not be in any bother. That will be another tuppence on top.' The shopkeeper held out his hand to be paid and shook his head as he passed her the change. These young maids, they'd take the shirt off your back, if they thought they could get away with it. No wonder his well-to-do customers were always moaning about their thieving servants, he thought as he watched Lucy go out of the shop, without a care in the world.

The butcher's next door had a newly slaughtered pig hanging by its splayed back legs beside the shop's entrance, its ribs open to the world and blood running down its snout into the gore-filled gutter below. It was a smell of death and blood that Lucy was used to at the flay-pits, where they were constantly moving animal hides. She walked past it and entered the butcher's shop and looked around her for the coming week's meat supply. With not much money left, she'd have to be careful, so she opted for some pig's liver, calves' feet, tripe,

185

sausage and a good portion of shin of beef with some kidney. She'd make Adam a nice steak-and-kidney pie, which she thought would feed him two days and would be a real treat. She paid the butcher and made the same arrangement to pick the meat up later in the day.

With her shopping now done, Lucy wandered down the line of shops, stopping to admire the shoes in W. Town's shoe shop, which were advertised as the latest style in American overshoes; and looking at the window in the next shop, J. Naylor and Son, which advertised, 'Teeth extracted in between selling cigars and snuff' – along with various other new inventions and needs that the good people of Keighley required, on her way to meet up with Adam. Her mood was light and she hummed a tune while she walked amongst the townsfolk, with her shawl around her shoulders and her head filled with the return journey home with Adam, in his new donkey-cart. She was foolish, she knew, even to think about her master in that way, but her heart was beginning to rule her head and even the slightest glance or touch from Adam made her heart beat wildly. An afternoon in Keighley would be heaven – as long as she could be near him and watch him, without Adam knowing how she was beginning to feel about him – she thought, as she turned the corner into Russell Street.

Both ends of Russell Street were fenced off from the general public, and the street was full of sheep, lambs and goats, despite people living on either side of the busy, noisy affair. Drovers and farmers leaned over their flocks and talked to one another while deals were done, as animals were sold and bid over. The country had come to the middle of the town, and deals were being shaken on and honoured by most sellers.

Adam Brooksbank strode between the backs of greasy-woolled sheep. Those that had already lambed had their young offspring around their feet, and they bleated in alarm at being in strange surroundings with men walking amongst them, frightened that they would lose their babies. Every so often he would stop at a sheep and examine its teeth and feel down its back, to see how stout it was under the thick wool coat, holding a sheep beneath him as he looked at its markings and guessed its age. There was a flock of twenty, all still to have their lambs, that had caught his eye and he made his way over to the young lad who was selling them.

'You've some fine sheep here. But why are you selling? Your profits are yet to be made for the year, as they are all, by the look of it, near to lambing.' Adam leaned back and looked at the young lad, who was humbly dressed and seemed as if he could do with a good meal in him.

'We can't afford the rent on our lump of land. The landlord increased our rent and we've to be out of our home upon High Moor by the end of the month, if I don't sell these today. I have to sell them, along with another twenty back home. We need the money now and can't wait until autumn, when I should be selling them, to see what lambs they are carrying. But that doesn't mean I'm a pushover. I expect a decent price for them, so don't insult me with a low offer. I'd rather walk my lasses home than see them go for next to nothing.' The lad looked up from under his flat cap and stared at Adam.

'Well, I certainly wasn't going to think of under-paying for them. In fact they are fine, fit sheep, the best in the fair today. Let me make you an offer and see where we go from there?' Adam stood back and eyed the sheep over again. 'Five guineas for the lot? That includes the twenty that you still have back home, if they are as fit as these.' He waited and watched as the young lad thought about his offer.

'I'm loath to sell them, as these have been my pride and joy, but I've no option. My mother, sister and I need the money, but it means I'll have nothing to farm.'

'It's a good offer. Would it help if I were also to offer you first refusal on some of their lambs in October, when they are old enough to leave their mothers? You'd be receiving them back without the work, and would still have some money now. Times are hard, folk have no brass and us hill-farmers barely make anything at the best of times. That's the best I can do, but your sheep would have a good home and your flock would stay together.' Adam could see that the young lad loved his flock, but needs must, if he was to keep a roof over his family's heads.

'Where do you live? I want to know where they are going, before I agree,' the lad said.

'On the moor top above Denholme, at Black Moss Farm. I'd be asking for you to walk them up there, or do

you have a horse and cart? What's your name, lad?'
Adam asked.

'Reggie Ellwood's the name. I'll drive them up to you,
slow and steady, seeing they are all in lamb. It might take
us two days, but you'll get your sheep. I know where you
are. I know all the farms in that area. My grandmother
used to live at Low Withens, and we used to stay with
her when we were young. Your price is fair; you can have
them all, and I would appreciate the first pick of any
lambs this back-end. I'm from just above Ing Row, on the
way back towards your home, so I'll bring all forty
together. It breaks my heart to sell them.'

Adam counted out his money from his breast pocket
and handed it to the downhearted farm lad. 'There's an
extra two shillings in there: one for luck, and one in
payment for you driving them. Who's your landlord? He
must be a heartless devil to make you stoop this low,'
Adam enquired, as Reggie nodded his head in thanks and
quickly took Adam's money.

'It's Robert Baxter. He's wanting our land for one of
his sons, and putting up the rent is the only way he can
get us off it. That family will resort to anything, to get
what they want.' Reggie shook his head and looked
around him in despair.

'His land neighbours mine, and it isn't the first time
I've heard bad things about him. I haven't had many
dealings with Baxter up to now, but forewarned is fore-
armed and he'll not get far with me,' Adam growled.

'Well, I hope not. Keep an eye on my sheep, as he's
been known to claim stock that isn't his, but no one dare

stand up to Baxter.' Reggie looked at his sheep and hoped that none of them would come to harm.

'They will be in good hands. Now I see that my maid is looking for me, and it is time for us to be returning home. I'll see you in a day or so with the flock. I'll take you home, once you've delivered them. Take your time; they don't want to be rushed, as they are all carrying lambs, and some look nearly due.' Adam shook the young lad's hand and gave his new purchases another glance, then walked his way through the bleating sheep to where Lucy stood waiting for him.

'The more I hear about the Baxters, the more I think that I've got bad neighbours, although so far they've not done anything to me.' Adam stood next to Lucy and looked back at the sheep he'd bought.

'I know that the Baxters are a bad lot. Nobody has the time of day for them. And have you bought some sheep?' Lucy enquired.

'Aye, I've bought forty ewes, all in lamb. The lad I've bought them from is only selling them because the Baxters have put up his rent and he can't afford to keep them and pay the rent,' Adam growled. 'It was never like this when my father farmed. Everyone helped everybody else.'

'It hasn't altered – everyone does usually help out. It's just that family. I'd be thankful they have left you alone up to now. The youngest lad is a right bad lot. Archie doesn't have a good word for him.' Lucy looked at the worry on Adam's face.

'I think my problems will come when I put my stock

up on the moor. There's been none until now, but soon my flock of forty – and what lambs they produce – will tempt the Baxters, and then the fun will begin. But I'll be ready for them; they'll not get one over on me so quickly.' Adam sighed. 'Now, have you spent up? And what did you treat yourself to?'

'Coffee – I bought enough coffee for two drinks. I've never drunk it before, and I was curious about the taste of the roasted beans; they smelled so good while I waited to be served in the grocer's.' Lucy smiled.

'Of all the things you could have bought! You'll either like it or hate it. I want to see your face when you try it,' Adam laughed.

'I'll pretend to like it, even if I don't.' Lucy grinned. 'And I've got you some change.' She handed Adam the change from her pocket and looked at his face.

'You are a fair lass – you'll always keep me on my toes.' Adam looked at her. 'Now, let's be away home; in style this time. Madam, your donkey-cart awaits.' Adam pretended to bow, before making his way through the crowds of farmers and drovers, with Lucy following behind him. She would enjoy every minute of the journey back home, and couldn't wait to tell her mother that she had been shopping in Keighley with Adam Brooksbank.

16

Lucy could still hear her mother's words ringing in her ears, as she looked out the kitchen window at Black Moss. 'Don't you be getting too close to that Adam Brooksbank. Remember your position and don't let him ever touch you, because that's what he'll expect, if you encourage him.' She wished in the end that she had never mentioned how much she had enjoyed her time with him on her visit to Keighley, or had partly confessed that she admired him. 'These men take advantage of their maids. You'll mean nothing to him and then, before you know it, you'll be coming home with a baby in your arms and he'll deny everything,' Dorothy had gone on to lecture.

But she was wrong about Adam Brooksbank. He'd never shown her any sexual urges and it was the briefest of flirtations when he spoke to her. Lucy, on the other hand, would have welcomed more attention, and only wished that she could stop looking at Adam and feeling as if her heart was going to burst, if she didn't tell him the way she felt about him.

She watched Adam now as he waved to the lad who was herding his newly bought flock into the farmyard, and smiled, knowing how excited he was at putting his own flock of Rough Fell sheep onto the moorland. He'd been looking forward to receiving them, and she knew that with the arrival of the sheep his work as a farmer really started, because all the sheep were in lamb and would demand his attention over the coming weeks. Lucy wiped her hands quickly on her apron and walked out of the farmhouse, after seeing a lamb under the arm of the lad who was delivering the flock.

'Our first lamb at Black Moss. He's a bit of a surprise.' Adam picked up the small, tightly curled woolly creature from Reggie, while its mother bleated her worry that her baby was being harmed.

'He's lovely.' Lucy petted the bleating lamb's head and smiled at it as it struggled, trying to escape Adam's arms.

'He wriggles, does the little devil. The sooner he gets to where he's going, the better. And he's peed down my jacket.' Adam held the lamb tightly and groaned.

'He's christened you as his new owner.' Reggie laughed as he turned round and, with his walking stick, switched the flock up through the farmyard via the pasture gate, with his sheepdog nipping at the stray sheep when told to do so, by Reggie's instructions.

'Well, he can keep it to himself. I'm not impressed. Although we will keep this one and his mother in the back paddock, as he's a bit on the small side. Just until he builds up his strength, then he can join the rest of the flock on the high ground. So he's won my attention already.' Adam laughed and followed Reggie through the farmyard gate, holding the lamb up by its front legs for its mother to smell, and following it into the paddock, instead of going with the rest of the flock up the steep hillside and onto the moor.

Lucy followed Adam and leaned over the paddock gate, from where they watched mother and son nudge and comfort one another in their new home, oblivious to the rest of the flock being driven up the moorland.

'Now, that's a mother's love. Just look at her and listen to her – she loves that bonny little thing, no matter how much he's bleating.' Lucy smiled as the lamb searched for a drink from his mother, and she nudged him and directed him to her udder.

'Aye, she'll make a good mother. I don't think I need to worry about her. But I'll have my work cut out lambing, and watching the rest until they have all delivered and have survived the weather and whatever it throws at us. I'll be looking at them first thing in the morning and last thing of an evening, to make sure that all are well. I've never seen a fox on my land, but they are all too fond of a newly born lamb. And with that, I mean the four-legged kind, not the two-legged kind in the name of Baxter.' Adam walked away from Lucy and followed his flock and Reggie up onto the higher ground.

Lucy watched him as he walked up through his yard. She knew he was worried about the Baxter family; they were a bad lot, everyone knew it. But with Robert Baxter having a family of five sons and a foul temper, nobody dared challenge the family, for fear of reprisals. However, Lucy had a feeling that if they were to do anything against Adam, he would not turn a blind eye. And perhaps the Baxters had met their match in the quiet man.

Adam stood on the fresh green moorland and looked at his new flock. 'My father would have been proud, if these had been his. You have a good eye for a well-bred sheep. I bet it hurt, having to part with them.' He looked at the lad leaning on the wall, watching his years of work wandering to the corners of their new home, and felt for his loss.

'As long as they've got a good home and I can keep the roof over our heads for another year at least, it'll be worth it,' Reggie said with sadness.

'It shouldn't be like that, though. The Baxters might have the right to put up your rent, but not to that extent. Just because they want you off the farm, for their son's use.' Adam kicked a tuft of moorland grass.

'Aye, well, they couldn't find fault with the upkeep of the farm, so they had to get me some other way. It is how that family work – underhand and careful never actually to be caught doing their dirty business.' Reggie looked around him. 'You'll have to keep your eye on my lasses, as the Baxters will soon realize whose sheep they were, and that you've helped me out by buying them. They'll not like that. At least if they do make off with some of them, you'll soon recognize them, as they are the only

Rough Fell breed to be found for a good few miles around. I was also thinking about what to do if any of the Baxters fancied stealing them, so I've marked each ewe with a spot of red paint on its horn, just behind its ear, so that you know it's one of yours, if you come across it somewhere it shouldn't be.'

'That was good thinking on your part. They'll be fools if they do tempt fate and rustle any of them. I was a peeler in my younger years and still have contacts, but they won't know that. Perhaps it was fate that I've become their neighbour.' Adam laughed. 'Stop worrying. Now come and have something to eat and drink, and then I'll take you and your dog home. Lucy will have the kettle boiling and waiting for us, I'm sure. She bought some coffee when she was at Keighley and tried it for the first time yesterday. You should have seen her face when she sipped it – she did not like the taste one bit, so we are back to tea today, thank heavens.'

Reggie grinned and thought about Adam's maid, who had taken his eye on the quiet. 'She seems a good lass.'

'Aye, she's Bill Bancroft's daughter – Lucy from the flay-pits. I'd be lost without her. She's got the old farm looking exactly how it used to, and she's a really good hand around the yard. As well as keeping me fed.' Adam looked at the young lad and noted his interest.

'Is she wed? She's a bonny lass, I couldn't help but notice.' Reggie put his head down and then turned and smiled at Adam.

'No, she's not wed, nor does she have a beau. She's too feisty for a lot of people, I'd say. She knows her own mind, does Lucy.' Adam grinned, but at the same time felt a pang of what he knew to be jealousy, that Lucy had taken Reggie's eye.

'Then I'll join you for that drink and a bite to eat, and perhaps you could introduce us?' Reggie suggested. 'My mother keeps telling me to find myself a woman, and Lucy's rather taken my fancy.'

'She's a flirt, I'll warn you, and she says what she thinks.' Adam tried to dissuade Reggie, suddenly realizing that his maid was beginning to mean a lot more to him than he had recognized.

'I like a challenge, and she's about my age. Now these sheep seem to have settled, so my job is done here.' Reggie stood for a second and looked around him, before stepping out down the fresh-smelling moorland, with Adam not far behind him, pondering whether Lucy would be interested in Reggie's advances.

'So, Mr Brooksbank tells me that your father owns the flay-pits.' Reggie sat in a chair at the kitchen table and looked at Lucy, eyeing her up and down as she cleared it of the dirty plates from which they had just eaten their dinner.

'Yes, more's the pity. It's a smelly, dirty place, and I don't aim to spend much more of my life living there, if I can help it. Although I'll always be there for my mother and sister and brothers. Even Mam hopes that we can some day move from Providence Row and the smell of the pits.' Lucy stood for a second and looked at the sandy-haired lad of about her age, who seemed to want

197

to engage her in conversation, since Adam had gone out to harness the horse and cart in order to take Reggie home.

'Aye, I don't think I'd want to live there, either. Wasn't there a to-do over the fella that worked there, the other week? Somebody told me he'd died when drinking at The Fleece and arguing over some lass?' Reggie looked wistful and tried to remember the fella's name.

'Yes, he was called Thomas Farrington – the strangest man that you are ever likely to meet. I hated him. Trouble is, the lass he was arguing over was me. He'd got it in his head to marry me, which I knew nowt about, until he'd shouted his intentions to everyone in The Fleece.' Lucy decided to lie to Reggie; she didn't know him, and she wasn't about to open her heart to somebody she didn't know.

'Aye, well, I can see how he took a fancy to you. You're not a bad-looking lass, and you are free of a man, so Mr Brooksbank says. Would you like to walk out with me on Sunday afternoon? We could go and listen to the brass band at Ponden and perhaps have a picnic, if the weather is fine?' Reggie decided to chance his luck and not wait a second longer, now that they were both alone.

Lucy glanced at the good-looking lad in front of her. He was handsome; not that well dressed, in his corduroy trousers and checked shirt and waistcoat, but she could tell he took care of his appearance. As for money, she knew he wasn't wealthy, but that didn't enter into her decision as Adam stepped back into the kitchen. 'I thank you for asking, but I've already got a commitment for this Sunday.' She quickly turned her back on Reggie and went into the scullery.

'Perhaps another time then?' Reggie shouted, but got no reply.

'Are you ready for off? Rosa's waiting, and I could do with getting back before dark.' Adam looked at the crestfallen lad as he entered the doorway, overhearing the conversation. 'Never mind – I told you she'd a mind of her own.' He slapped Reggie on the back, guessing what the conversation between the two had been about, and felt slightly glad that Lucy had rejected him. 'You can come and see both of us any time you want, and try your luck again!'

'Nay, I've never any luck when it comes to lasses. I've nowt to offer, when it comes to brass, and that's what they are all after, when it comes down to it. Brass and stability, and I've neither.' Reggie pushed his chair back across the kitchen floor and made for the doorway, not even saying goodbye to Lucy, who had made herself scarce.

'Well, I have a bit of both, but no woman, so we make a good pair. But at least we have our health and nobody tells us what to do, so let's think ourselves lucky.' Adam laughed as Reggie hung his head and walked over to the donkey-cart, with Rosa standing patiently in harness. 'You are young yet, and the right lass will turn up when you least expect her to. Besides, let Lucy mull over your offer. You never know: if you visit her on another day, she might say yes.'

'No, she's not interested. I think she must already

have a fella, even if you say she doesn't. A lass like that doesn't stay single for long.' Reggie looked back towards the farmhouse as he climbed in the back of the donkey-cart, noticing Lucy standing at the bedroom window, watching as Adam flicked the reins over the horse's back. 'But maybe, like you say, I'll try my luck again another day. She's watching us go, so perhaps she's just shy.'

Adam said nothing to Reggie, but he knew Lucy as anything but shy. If she had fancied him, Reggie would already have known it and he'd be the one who was being pursued.

17

Even though it was nearly the end of May, the mist hung down around Black Moss. It was a fine drizzly mist, the kind that soaked you to the skin, even though you could hardly tell it was raining. The kind of rain that was not suitable for newly born lambs, which were being exposed to it on top of the moorland.

'I'm going to saddle up Rosa and ride up the moor and have a look at my flock. Although there's only one or two left to lamb, I'd better ensure that the weaker lambs are not taking any hurt in this miserable weather. Although their coats are fairly waterproof, this is the sort of weather that soon makes them shiver and go cold.' Adam looked at Lucy, who was busy darning his socks next to the fire as she moaned about the weather outside.

'Make sure you don't get too wet. It's a devil of a day, and the sheep and their lambs will have the sense to take cover under the walls.' She looked up at Adam, whose company she had enjoyed as she mended and darned his clothes. 'I'll stoke the fire, in case you bring one back to the warmth of the kitchen, and we can soon warm its belly with a bottle of cow's milk.' Lucy put her darning down on the table and added a log to the fire. She was used to the routine, as both of them had done just that on the few occasions when a sickly lamb had been born, and so far their tactics had paid off, with no fatalities to the small flock.

'I'll not be long – it will soon be dusk. It's best that I check them now and then. If any of them are struggling, they'll have the warmth of the kitchen overnight. You can get yourself home, if you wish. I'm sure your mother will be glad to see you, and I can get my own supper.' Adam pulled on his coat and put on his cap, then watched as Lucy sat back down in her chair and returned to her darning.

'No, sir, I'll wait until you return. I'm in no rush for home. Everybody will be crammed into the house on an evening like this, and I enjoy the peace of this kitchen and don't mind waiting to serve you supper.' Lucy looked up at him; she was content at Black Moss's fireside, looking across at the man that she had feelings for.

'Very well, I shouldn't be more than an hour. I just want to check all is well. I won't be long.'

Adam strode out of the kitchen and went round the back of the farmhouse to the stables. There he saddled up Rosa and led her to the mounting block, then rode her up the moorside, with his collar turned up to keep the rain from trickling down his neck. The moor was clouded in mist, and his sheep were hardly visible until he was nearly on top of them. Lucy was right; most of the sensible mothers were sheltering behind the drystone walls, protecting their offspring by sitting close to them and the wall. But some more foolhardy ones were still grazing on the wild moorland grasses, and their lambs looked a little dejected, although all of them seemed to be bearing up to the weather conditions.

Adam eased himself out of the saddle and walked across to where a set of twin lambs were curled up close together in the rushes for warmth, with their mother grazing a few yards away from them. The sheep bleated a warning to her offspring and, although cold and damp, they rose onto their legs and ran to their mother as Adam approached.

'So there's nothing wrong with you two then,' he whispered, as they both butted their mother for milk and she defiantly stamped her foot at the sight of Adam. He smiled and made his way back to his horse, but stopped quickly as, through the swirling mist and rain, he momentarily glanced the shape of a man. 'Hey, you! Stop right there. Do you know you are trespassing?'

The figure stopped for a brief second, and it was then that Adam noticed he had a lamb hanging down from one of his hands. It was Jacob Baxter. Adam recognized him despite the poor visibility, as he was the only red-haired man for miles around.

'Stop right there and put that lamb down, you bastard.' Adam ran quickly in the direction of the man, but his injured leg impeded him, as the figure disappeared once more into the mist. But Adam was not going to give up that easily. He knew the man had to climb over the wall somewhere along the border where both lands met. He ran blindly along the tufted heath of the moorland, guided slightly by the bleating sound of the distressed lamb being carried by Jacob Baxter, and not taking any notice of the moorland beneath his feet until it was too late. He'd forgotten to take care when approaching the wall and the boggy mire that he had talked about making safe, but had never got round to; and now he was regretting that, as his feet squelched in the peaty mire and he was being sucked down too quickly to escape the bog under his own steam. Before he knew it, the bog had sucked him down to above his knees and, try as he might, Adam could not pull his legs out of it, sinking deeper with every move made.

'Help – for God's sake, help me!' Adam shouted into the grey mist, hoping that Jacob Baxter would show sympathy with his situation and would help him out of the mire. But instead he heard the rumble of top-stones being dislodged from the dividing wall, as the thief made his way back onto his own land, leaving Adam sinking deeper and deeper into the dark, stinking bog. 'Help, Help!' Adam shouted, as his body became crushed by the clinging peat. He tried to pull on the moorland grasses and drag himself out, but with every move, he went further down into the bog. He was wet, cold and alone, and fighting for his life as he tried, again and again, to hoist himself out of the peaty grave. To make things worse, night was beginning to fall. His only hope was that Lucy would still be at his home and would perhaps realize that something was wrong.

As the darkness fell around him, and his senses started to become unclear, Adam prayed to hear Lucy's voice. He had no intention of ending his days crushed in a bog with his life only half-lived, but at the moment that looked likely to happen, as hypothermia started to affect him.

Lucy lit the oil lamps, placing one in the window and looking out into the gathering darkness. Adam should have been back by now, unless there was a sheep lambing and it had held him up, as he didn't like leaving them on their own, in case they had problems. She was going to be home late, and her mother would be worrying about where she had got to, she thought, as she pulled the boiling kettle and the pan of stew to one side of the fire to keep warm. She'd give Adam another half-hour and then, if he hadn't returned, she would have to leave the house unlocked and bank the fire up, and leave him to feed himself, as he had previously suggested.

She sat down at the table and looked around her. The house was warm and welcoming now and she enjoyed her time there, but she'd never stopped this late. She looked at the grandfather clock, which ticked steadily and made her aware of every minute that was passing. Nine-thirty – she couldn't wait any longer, but must make her way home and hope that Adam would understand. With the fire made safe and the kettle and stew to one side, she reached for her shawl from behind the kitchen door and stepped out into the farmyard. A full moon was starting to rise, shining briefly from behind the rain clouds, and it threw eerie shadows around the yard, as Lucy pulled the door behind her and made across the yard to the path down to the valley bottom. She drew her shawl around her and looked quickly about her, hoping to spot Adam coming out of the stable or perhaps from the pig hull, which now housed a recently bought piglet. But there was no sight of him. She was about to make her way home when she heard the sound of horses' hooves coming down the hard, stony path from the moor. She stopped and turned.

'I'm just about to go home, sir. Your supper is waiting for you, and I'll see you in the morning.' She looked up at the small horse as it came into the light of the yard, and found that she was talking to a riderless pony. There was no sight of Adam, but Rosa was still saddled and bridled and had made her way home without her master. 'What are you doing without your rider? Where's Adam?' She grabbed the horse's reins and patted its neck. 'Has he fallen or is he hurt? Oh Lord, what am I to do? You'd never have come back on your own if something wasn't wrong.' She stood for a second, wondering what to do. There was no option but to light a storm lamp and go and look for her master. Something was wrong, and she could not leave without knowing that Adam was safe and in his home.

With her head down against the rain, and with Rosa by her side, Lucy walked up the moorside, the lamp

206

lighting her way. Every so often she stopped and yelled out Adam's name, but it fell on deaf ears, with nobody replying – just the soft winds of the moor and the hoot of an owl, watching and waiting for its prey of moorland mice and voles. The light picked up the eyes of the sheep as they crouched behind the walls, and the illumination of the houses down in the valley, making Lucy realize how remote the moor was of a night. She didn't like the feeling of being alone and vulnerable on the wild moor, as she yelled out Adam's name again. Rosa paced patiently beside her and snorted, as Lucy stood in desperation and looked up at the stars that were starting to break through in the heavens above, as the clouds and rain began to clear above her, and the moon and stars won the battle for the night skies.

'Adam,' Lucy yelled out in desperation. 'Adam!' She turned as, faintly from a few yards away, she heard a feeble reply.

'Here – I'm here.'

She rushed to where she had heard the voice coming from, and by the light of her lamp and the moon she made out the form of Adam, buried up to his chest in the peaty bog, unable to move.

'Don't come any nearer – we don't want both of us buried in here,' Adam gasped, his voice already weak and exhausted. 'Go and get help. I only hope you'll not be too late.'

Lucy stared at Adam in disbelief and worry. 'I can't leave you. If you died, I'd never forgive myself,' she cried.

'You must go – there's no other alternative.' Adam sighed.

'No, I'll try and pass you Rosa's reins, if I can. Grab hold of them and I'll make her walk backwards, and hopefully we will be able to pull you out,' Lucy said as she pulled Rosa's reins over her head and led the pony as far as she dared to the bog's edge.

'Don't come any nearer, else you'll be joining me,' Adam whispered. He was soaked to the skin, frozen and exhausted, and he didn't know if he had the strength to hold onto the reins that Lucy was about to throw him.

Lucy unbuckled one side of the reins and threw the long strap of leather to Adam, lobbing it several times before he caught it successfully. She watched as he wrapped the leather rein around his hands and held on for dear life itself, as Lucy held onto Rosa's harness and pulled on the small, loyal horse to go backwards.

Rosa lifted her head and fought against the instructions given to her. And then, with coaxing and sweet words, she moved slowly backwards, a leg at a time, while Adam hung onto the rein. The peaty mire was reluctant to give forth its victim, but slowly and surely Adam was released from the life-sucking bog. He lay exhausted and shaking on the rough heathland, gasping for breath.

'Thank you. If you hadn't have come, I'd have been dead by the morning,' Adam whispered.

'You are not out of the woods yet. You are shivering, filthy and you sound terrible. Can you manage to climb onto Rosa, and I'll lead her back down to the farm?' Lucy looked down at a sodden Adam and tried to fight back the tears. She too was shaking, and her heart was beating fast as she bent down and offered him her arm to rest upon. He was weak, and she didn't know if she could manage to get Adam onto the back of the horse and take him home.

Adam took her arm, pulled himself shakily up and walked the few steps towards the horse. His legs were like jelly, and he couldn't stop shaking as he tried to put his foot in the stirrups and hoist himself up into the saddle. Lucy put her shoulder underneath him and helped hoist him into the saddle, then watched as he slumped down over the horse's neck, hanging onto its mane.

'We'll get you home and into the warmth. Then perhaps I should go for the doctor.' Lucy took the harness of the little horse again and, with one hand on one of Adam's legs and the other guiding the horse down the moorside, she slowly made her way from the wild moor down to the farmyard. She was thankful when she arrived in the yard and saw the lights and smoke rising from the farmhouse. She'd found Adam and he was alive – that was all that mattered for now, she thought, as she took the horse and its rider as near the kitchen door as she could, before holding out her arms for Adam to take, as he slid off the back of the horse.

'Steady now, take your time. Let's get you up these stairs and into bed. I'll bring the bed-bottle up, once you are in bed, and that will warm you up.' Lucy was Adam's crutch as he walked, step by step, up the stairs to his bedroom.

He sat, still sodden, on the edge of his bed and looked up at Lucy. 'Sorry, I haven't the energy to undress. Can you help me, please?' He shivered and shook, his voice feeble as he begged her with his eyes.

'Yes, sir. Let's get you into a clean nightshirt and washed, and then into bed.'

Lucy had never seen a naked man before, and she blushed as she started to peel the peat-covered clothes off her master's body. She was trying her best to ignore his manly parts as she pulled his breeches off and put a clean nightshirt over his head, before washing his face and hands and then lying him down in bed.

'I'll go and get the doctor, as you look to be running a fever.' Lucy looked at Adam and pulled the sheets over him.

'No – no doctor!' Adam protested. 'You'll find some laudanum drops in a bottle in the top drawer over there. Just give me one of those drops – it'll cure my fever and help me sleep.' He closed his eyes, too ill to worry that Lucy had seen him naked and that now she knew his secret addiction. She passed him the laudanum, which he took with shaking hands and then collapsed onto his pillow. He sighed and looked up at her. 'Thank you, you've saved my life. Now you must go home. Leave me – your parents will be worried about you.' He closed his eyes.

Lucy looked down at him as she stood up. How could she leave him in such a state? If she had been even an hour later in finding him, he would surely have perished in the cold of the peat bog. She tiptoed out of the bedroom and went to place the kettle back on the fire, and fill the stoneware bed-bottle to put under Adam's bedcovers. She hung her rain-sodden shawl back up behind the kitchen door and towelled dry her long hair, before taking her sodden boots off her feet and warming them at the fireside. The steam rose from her soaked skirt and she shivered herself, as she filled the bed-bottle with boiling water from the kettle, after taking her dress off and hanging it on the clothes drier above the kitchen fire. She was about to take the bottle upstairs, when there was a knock at the door and she hurried to answer it, opening it only slightly, until she knew who was behind it.

'You are here then, our lass. We thought something had happened to you. Mother's bothering to death, and she made me walk up to see what you are about.' Bill looked at his daughter, half-dressed and with her hair still damp, with a bed-bottle in her hand. 'It's like that, is it? Well, don't come running back to us when you are in trouble. I thought Adam Brooksbank was a decent man, but obviously not, as you have next to nothing on.' Bill scowled at his daughter.

'It's not what it looks like, Father. He's ill in bed – he nearly died tonight, sucked down into the mire at the top of the moor. I've just pulled him out, with the help of the horse. In fact the poor animal is still standing in the yard. I've only stripped my dress off because I was sodden to the bone. And this bottle is to warm Adam up, as he's feverish, shivering and exhausted. Come and see for yourself – he's in bed and all his peat-caked clothes are on the floor. I don't think I should really leave him on his own tonight.'

Lucy opened the door for her father and watched as he looked around the farmhouse, and at her clothes drying above the fire.

'He's up there – climb up the stairs and tell me what you think. He won't have the doctor. He's taken some drops of laudanum and says that will see him right.' Lucy ushered her father up the creaking stairs to the bedroom, where Adam lay, sweating but asleep, in his bed. 'He's caught a chill. Look at the beads of sweat running down his head. He doesn't want to be on his own tonight, and he should have the doctor.'

Bill looked concerned as he heard Adam mumble in a strange language under his breath. 'He's wandering in his mind – that'll be the laudanum and the fever.'

'I can't leave him, Father, he's too ill. I'll stop until the fever breaks or goes the other way, God forbid.' Lucy placed the bed-bottle under the bedcovers and picked the dirty, peat-covered clothes up from the bedroom floor and looked at her father. 'I'm going to stay, so don't ask me to come home. He needs me.'

'Well, he's not fit to be left, and I'm no good at looking after anybody. But at the same time, I don't like leaving you on your own with him. What made him unaware of the mire up there on the moss, as everyone local knows it's there? He might have killed himself, the silly bugger. You'd better stop – he's going to need you.'

Bill shook his head and looked at Adam who was still mumbling under his breath. 'Poor bugger, he nearly lost his life in the Crimea, and now he's like this.'

'That's why I can't leave him. He's a good man and he needs somebody by his side tonight. Besides, Archie will be here first thing in the morning, so I've only a few hours on my own.' Lucy looked at her father and knew that he respected Adam Brooksbank for serving his country, and for being understanding about the loss of the baby.

'Aye, well, stay with him then. It's only right and proper that you do. I'll stable the horse before I go, so don't fret over it not being looked after. You sit with him overnight. He'll get worse before better, by the looks of him. He's lucky to be alive – the devil must be on his side.' Bill started to go down the stairs, with Lucy following him, when he stopped at the kitchen door. 'You'll be alright, won't you? You'll not be frightened if anything happens to him? Locals always had it that this place is bad luck, and they might be right.'

'I'll be fine, Father. I only hope that he makes it through the night.' Lucy's eyes filled with tears.

'He's a good man, Lucy. But don't you get too close to him. You are just his maid. Your mother said your head was full of thoughts of him. Set your sights on somebody your own age, not somebody who's a cripple.' Bill sighed and opened the door. 'I'll see to the horse, and one of us will be up to see how you both are in the morning. Or send Archie down, if it's bad news.'

'I will, Father, thank you.' Lucy watched Bill grab

213

Rosa's reins as the pony stood patiently in the yard, then he led her to the stables behind the house. She closed the kitchen door, once he had disappeared out of sight. She was on her own and it was her task to make sure that Adam Brooksbank lived to see another day. Please God that he did, because she knew she loved him, no matter what her father said.

18

Lucy sat at Adam's bedside. It was the second day of him drifting in and out of consciousness, and she had heard him shout his dead wife's name in despair, as he relived his past. She had sat by his side, keeping him cool and giving him sips of water, for the last forty-eight hours, without securing any real sleep for herself – just the odd nap when she found herself slipping into an uneasy slumber as she sat faithfully by his side.

Archie had been her prop outside, keeping the farm working and lambing the last of the sheep, and making sure that all was in order there. He'd come to an understanding with Lucy's father that he would work for Adam Brooksbank until he regained his strength – if he ever did. Lucy prayed that Adam would survive. The more she soothed his head, the more she realized how she felt about the man whose life hung in the balance. She closed her eyes and felt her eyelids getting heavier as she dropped off to sleep in the uncomfortable

Windsor chair, as Adam for the first time in a while lay still and quiet. Perhaps the worst was over now and, with sleep, he'd recover.

Lucy awoke with a jerk, not knowing the time or day, but she quickly regained her senses and remembered where she was and what she was about.

'I didn't want to wake you. You looked so peaceful.' Adam looked up at a wide-eyed Lucy and smiled wanly. 'How long have I been in this bed? I've no idea of time,' he whispered, as she looked down on him with relief.

'I'm sorry. I didn't mean to fall asleep.' Lucy pushed back her long hair and looked down at her ward. 'You've been in your bed for two days now. I didn't think you were going to survive. Thank God your fever has broken. Do you remember why you are here? The bog you were stuck in?' She looked at Adam as he tried to ease himself up onto his pillows. 'Here, let me.' She helped him sit up and plumped up his pillows, so that he could sit more upright in his bed.

'And you've been by my side all that time? You've never left me? It seems that I owe you my life, because yes, I do remember you helping me out of the bog that was sucking my life away. If you'd not come searching for me, I'd surely have died of the cold and been sucked down into the peat's depths.' Adam closed his eyes, exhausted from the small amount of talking he had done.

'I couldn't have done any other. I couldn't have left you there. And you needed nursing. You were adamant not to have the doctor, and you administered yourself a dose of laudanum, which eased your pain and made you sleep. But it was when the fever came over you that I worried for your life,' Lucy said as Adam shook his head.

'Ah, you've found out about my weakness for laudanum. I only take it when I'm desperate – I'm not addicted,' Adam whispered with his eyes still closed, hoping that Lucy would not question him any more about his need for the painkiller.

'It makes no difference to me. Plenty of people take laudanum, and I've known my mother take it in the past, after giving birth. She says it helps dull her pain and her low mood, as sometimes life can be too painful to bear. Now, you just rest and keep quiet, and I'll go and get you some broth. You've not eaten for the last few days, so we need to build your strength up.' She stood up and looked down at Adam, feeling that a great weight had been lifted from her shoulders. He was alive, and now she would nurse him back to strength. She smiled and nearly burst into song at the thought of her Adam being back in the land of the living.

Adam sipped the broth being fed to him and looked at Lucy. 'What would I have done without you? I take it that it was you who undressed me and put me into bed? I'm sorry that I can only just remember. I must have been frozen to the bone when you got me home.' He sipped slowly at the spoonfuls of beef broth that Lucy gave him gently, then started putting together the past few days, from what he could remember.

'I did, sir. There was no one else to do it.' Lucy

blushed as she placed the spoon in the bowl and tried not to make eye contact with him.

'I hope I covered my modesty. I thank you, Lucy. You've done more than I could have asked of you, these last few days. Please stop calling me "sir". From now on, I'm "Adam". After all, you know more about me than any friend.'

'You don't have to worry, sir. You've been the perfect gentleman while you've been ill. You rambled a lot in your thoughts, and mentioned your late wife's name more than once, but whatever you said is already forgotten.' Lucy smiled and stood up as he looked at her.

'It's "Adam"! And thank you again, Lucy, I'll not forget your help. The sooner I'm back on my feet, the better. My flock will need attention, not to mention the rest of the farm. I've also the little matter of sorting out Jacob Baxter. It is his fault that I'm in this state. I caught him stealing a lamb, or at least I chased him to our dividing wall, but I'd forgotten about the mire and waded into it in the mist.' Adam scowled and swore under his breath.

'There's no need to rush getting better, for the sake of the farm. Archie has it all in hand, as my father's let him work here instead of at the flay-pits. He knew you needed Archie more. I'll ask him to check your flock. He lambed the last two sheep yesterday, and I think he said you had a pair of twins and triplets born. He was here early each morning and hasn't been going home until dusk. He's been worried about you, just like me.' Lucy shook her head. 'Those bloody Baxters are a bad lot, especially Jacob. I'll ask Archie to check the number of sheep, and then he can go down to the peelers in Denholme and tell them about your mishap, and that you saw Jacob with one of your lambs. It's time they were brought to justice, if you are up to it.' Lucy frowned.

'Aye, if he could do that, I'd appreciate it. Ask Archie to tell the sergeant there to come and see me. I might be in my bed for now, but I'll soon be up and about, and those bastards are not getting away with it.' Adam slumped back down into his pillows. He was tired, so very tired, but he'd see justice done to the Baxters, if it was the last thing he did.

Archie stood on the moor top. He'd counted and counted again, but he was still two sheep short. There should have been forty – forty sheep and their followers – so that meant two were missing; and if the lambs had been taken with them, it could be as many as six, if they both had twins.

He looked around him and spat out the grass that he had been chewing on. It was time to go down into Denholme and talk to the peelers. This time the Baxters would be caught, if they still were holding the sheep they had stolen. The speck of red paint, and the sheep's breed, would catch them good and proper. They'd swindled and stolen their way in the world for long enough, and hopefully now they'd get their comeuppance.

'Now then, Adam. You've been in the wars, I hear, and had a run-in with the tough boys of our patch. They've got a lot to answer for, have the Baxters. I wish they'd bugger off to where they came from. Since they appeared in the area there's been nowt but trouble: stock going missing, fences being broken down, not to mention folk being bullied into selling their homes to them. And I'm sure that they are up to no good, making counterfeit money, but I haven't been able to prove it as yet.'

The sergeant looked at Adam. It had been a long time since he'd talked to Adam Brooksbank, and memories of them both joining the constabulary in Keighley together came flooding back. They'd been close friends then; both of them young and full of hope for the future, ready to take on the world and change it.

'Aye, it's good to see you, Fred. We go back a long way, do you and me. So I'm glad that you are still a sergeant in these parts, because these buggers – as you say – need stopping. Archie will have told you what happened. They've taken two of my sheep, not to mention Jacob leaving me in the mire to die, without a second's glance. If it hadn't have been for Lucy, I'd have been a goner. Thank God she saved me.'

'You always do manage to get yourself into bother, one way or another, Adam. When I heard that you'd come back to live at home, I thought: Perhaps this time he'll settle, tend to his family home and, hopefully, find himself a woman. Then I hear that you were there when that strange bugger, Thomas Farrington, died at The Fleece. And now you've got yourself involved with the Baxters. I'm beginning to think you court danger and bad luck.'

Fred Dobson looked down at Adam. He'd been the

first one on the scene when Adam's wife had died, and he knew that Adam had never recovered from the loss of her and the baby she had been carrying. He'd lost his best friend that day, as grief had turned Adam into a different man: bitter and angry with the world. However, looking and listening to him now, Fred hoped that he had finally found peace.

'Now Archie Robinson tells me that these two sheep are marked on their horns, underneath their ears, with a dot of red paint. So if they are on the Baxters' property, they should be easy to find. This might be the excuse we've needed to raid their farm. It's the first time one of the Baxters has actually been seen thieving, so I'm grateful you are still alive to tell the tale.'

'It seems I'm just in the wrong place at the wrong time. But this time I might be doing my neighbours a favour, if you catch this family, who seem to be wreaking havoc on most of my neighbours. This used to be a quiet part of the world, unlike Keighley town.' Adam looked at his old friend.

'Things have changed. New folk have come to our patch, and industries have sprung up and, with them, a different sort of folk. There's no knowing who's who or what they are nowadays – not like the days when we were lads. Anyway, you are forgetting all the times you used to have to square up that lad from the parsonage at Haworth and deliver him back to his poor father and sisters. There's always one, and you should know it.' Fred smiled.

'He was just wild, rebelling against his father. I could understand that.' Adam looked down at his hands and knew that at one time Fred had been aware of his own rebellious nature, and that Adam too had fought against his father's wishes.

'Aye, well, we are all different, and we all learn the hard way. Now I'll send my lads to look around the Baxters' farm at High Ground. If we find anything, I'll let you know. If we do find your sheep, the Baxters are looking at a few years' hard labour or even being deported to Australia, depending on the judge.' Fred stood up. 'That seems to be the favourite thing at the moment: send the buggers out to the colonies and make them work for their freedom. A ten-year-old lad got sent to Australia on a convict ship the other month from Keighley, and he'd only pickpocketed a handkerchief. So with a bit of luck, you'll get rid of Jacob at least, as the judge will show no mercy if your sheep are found there.' He pulled on his helmet and watched as Lucy opened the kitchen door for him. 'You take care, old friend. Let this slip of a lass look after you until you are back on your feet.'

'I already owe her everything. Lucy here saved my life.' Adam smiled across at her. 'I'd be lost without her,' he whispered, as he closed his eyes and relaxed in his usual chair next to the fire.

'Well, you have a lot to be thankful for, and don't you forget it,' Fred said to him. 'Miss, you keep looking after him. You are just what the stubborn bugger needs.'

'If anybody can catch the Baxters, Fred can. He used to be a right stickler, when we worked together,' Adam said to Lucy, with his eyes still closed. It had been good to see Fred, even if the circumstances were not what he would have wanted.

'We'll see. It would be an answer to a lot of people's prayers if the Baxters were brought to justice – especially Jacob and his father. The other brothers aren't quite as bad. But don't you worry your head about them. Concentrate on getting better. We need you fit and strong, as it will soon be summer and there will be plenty of work to keep you out of mischief then.'

Lucy gazed at Adam as he slept. If only he knew how she felt about him, it would perhaps make all the difference to his life.

Sergeant Fred Dobson stood in the kitchen of High Ground. All five sons of Robert Baxter were sitting around the kitchen table, with their father at the head of it. The kitchen was low and dark, with no love and attention spent on it since the motherless family had moved into the farmhouse more than five years ago. Police constables stood around the room, and waited for instructions from their sergeant to handcuff the lot of them and place them in the police cart that was waiting for them outside.

'Those sheep are nowt to do with us – they must have strayed onto our land. There always have been gaps in the walls. That pillock of a neighbour should keep his house in order,' Robert Baxter scowled and spat out at Fred.

'And your Jacob here, I suppose, was nowhere near Black Moss when a lamb and he miraculously jumped over the wall and left Adam Brooksbank sinking to his

223

near-death in the mire,' Fred scoffed. 'Don't you lie to me, you old bugger. Besides, it's not just Adam Brooksbank's sheep. There's stuff in your barn and outbuildings that's gone missing from all over the district. Not to mention the coins found in your back place, which are counterfeit, made by clipping small amounts of metal from already issued coins. I suppose they appeared by magic. You and yours are looking at a good long stretch, if not deportation, once the Beaks at Keighley have seen you – and not before time. This time you can't deny it. You've been caught red-handed, or should I say "red-horned"?' Fred laughed.

'You bastard!' Jacob jumped up from his seat and turned on the nearest officer standing behind him, who pulled out his truncheon and showed no mercy, as he beat Jacob relentlessly with it. The rest of the brothers pushed back their chairs and threatened the remaining officers, but got nowhere, as they were handcuffed and marched out of the kitchen.

'Now, are you going to behave yourself and come without any bother, or are we to do the same to you?' Fred Dobson stood up and looked at the ageing Scotsman and watched as Robert glowered at the state of affairs he was in.

'You bastards always looked after your own. I knew, when our Jacob pinched those sheep, that you'd be knocking on our door. I should have told him to get rid of 'em. Bloody peelers.' Robert spat at Fred and walked past him with his head held high. 'They'll not hold me for long, I'll see to that.'

'It'll be at least a few months' voyage, you old bastard, if you are to take a visit to Van Diemen's Land or beyond, so hold your noise.'

Fred pushed Robert out of the farmhouse doorway, without even closing the door behind him. He'd been after the Baxter family for years, but had never had the evidence to nick them. Now, thanks to his old mate, he was going to have them off his patch for good. It was a blessing for one and all.

19

Adam stood in the public gallery of Keighley Assizes. He'd given his evidence against the Baxters and now the judge was passing sentence upon them. They all stood, looking rough and unkempt, in the witness box, shackled and unshaven, but still defiant. Their charges were as wide-ranging as theft, sheep-stealing, blackmail and counterfeiting. Since their arrest, many people had given accounts of harassment and theft by the Baxters, knowing that if they all banded together, the judge would have no option but to put the whole family behind bars for a good length of time.

The judge, in his white powdered wig and robes, leaned forward and looked at the motley group of offenders.

'I have taken into consideration all the charges and evidence given to me by the people you have wronged, and by the police findings. You, as a family, have been taking advantage of the good people around you. You have robbed and cheated, not to mention defacing the Queen's currency. I have no option but to give you the following sentences.'

The judge looked around him.

'Arthur Baxter, I sentence you to six years' hard labour. Charles Baxter, again six years' hard labour, along with your brother James. George Baxter and Jacob Baxter, yours are more serious crimes: one of sheep-stealing and one of counterfeiting. I have no option but to send you to the colonies, where you will work as convicts until the government thinks appropriate. As for you, Robert Baxter, you were aware of all that went on under your roof, and at no time did you take any meas-ures to keep your sons in line. In fact you encouraged them, from what I have seen. I therefore sentence you to ten years of hard labour.'

The judge rose and left, ignoring the cries and shouts of protest from the Baxters, as they were ushered out of the dock and downstairs into the holding cells, ready to be taken to serve their sentences.

'Bastards!' James Baxter shouted as he was dragged, kicking and shouting, out of the dock. 'I'll be back – you don't get rid of me that easy.'

Adam looked around him. All the locals, and the people over whom the Baxters had held sway, were jubilant at the news of their demise. At the far end of the gallery he spotted a face he recognized. It was Reggie Ellwood and he was making his way over to Adam.

'I hope you've got my lasses back? I knew the bastards

wouldn't be able to resist them. It was a good idea of mine to mark their horns.' Reggie held out his hand and shook Adam's as he patted him on the back.

'Aye, the sheep are all back safe on the moor. Archie went for them the other day.' Adam grinned. 'How do you stand with your home now? The Baxters can't demand rent from within jail.'

'I don't know. I've to see where I stand in a minute, with the judge in his chambers. No matter what is said, I can't be any worse off than having to pay an extortion-ate rent to that family of thieves. You can be proud of playing a part in their downfall. Just look at the folk whose lives the Baxters were making hell. It's a pity the lot of them aren't being sent to Australia. Some of them will rear their ugly heads again, if they survive the back-breaking work in Halifax jail.'

'I doubt old Robert will, but he should have thought about the consequences. Crime is a young man's game, and he should have kept his nose clean.' Adam shook his head.

'How are you now? I heard that you nearly lost your life, and if it hadn't been for that bonny maid of yours, you'd have been six foot under by now.' Reggie walked with Adam out of the gallery and to the top of the stairs leading down to the courthouse entrance and the judge's chambers.

'Aye, if she hadn't realized something was wrong, none of this would have happened and I'd be buried on top of the moor. I owe her everything. I'm good now; a little weak, but getting there.' Adam stood and looked at

Reggie, who had a twinkle in his eye as he thought about Lucy.

'Tell her I was asking after her. I'd still like to walk out with her, despite her refusal. She's a feisty one, but none the worse for that.' Reggie started to walk down the stairs and waited at the bottom of them, as Adam took his time with every step, still weak from his near-death experience.

'I'll tell her.' Adam looked down and then patted Reggie on the shoulder. 'Good luck with the judge. I hope he sees the sense in you keeping your home. And I'll see you shortly.' He watched as Reggie walked across the tiled floor and knocked on the judge's chamber door. He'd not encouraged Reggie about Lucy, as she had made light of his interest in her, and he knew that she wouldn't want Reggie to be encouraged. Also, Adam couldn't stop a pang of jealousy at the thought of Lucy walking out with Reggie, even though she was only his maid.

Adam returned to Black Moss Farm feeling that justice had been done. Now at least he knew his sheep were safe from the thieving hands of the Baxters. They'd be troubling no one for quite a while. He unsaddled Rosa and looked around him. The swallows had started to nest in the stable eaves, and they swooped and chittered above his head, mixed with a helping of swifts and house martins that screeched and dived in the sky as he crossed the farmyard and went into the house.

The front door was open, letting the warm summer's

light into the old building, and he heard Lucy singing to herself as he made his way into the kitchen. It reminded Adam of his mother singing when he was a child, and of the hugs and love she had given him, on his return from school in Denholme. The old homestead was beginning to feel like a home again and he was glad.

'Ah, you are back! How did it go? Did they all get charged and found guilty?' Lucy glanced across at Adam as she placed a bunch of dog daisies in a glass vase upon the kitchen table and stood back and admired them, before hearing what he had to say.

'Aye, they are all at this minute serving Her Majesty in the jail. They'll not be bothering us for a while. Jacob and his brother George are to be deported. The judge was not a forgiving soul, but Fred had warned me. They didn't go without a fight, though. The language they shouted at everyone as they were led down was terrible.' Adam sat down in his fireside chair and sighed. 'Lord, I'm tired. Today has really taken it out of me. Thank heavens for Archie – is he still here or has he gone home? He'll be glad to hear the news, for he hated the Baxters as much as anyone.'

'He's gone home. Everything's seen to, so you've nothing to do. Your supper's keeping warm in the oven, and I'm away home. It's nice to walk home on these early summer evenings. I went for a walk up the gillside earlier today and picked those daisies – they brighten up the place.' Lucy smiled.

'Just like you do. I heard you singing as I came in. It

230

was good to hear.' Adam looked up at Lucy and noticed her blush.

'I sound like a strangled cat! My mother says I've no voice fit for anything, and that I can't hold a tune. So I'll apologize now for the racket.' She hung on his words of praise as she looked up at the mantelpiece and the letter that had arrived for Adam with the post-boy earlier in the day. 'You have a letter awaiting you – it came when you were out.'

Adam stood up and reached for the letter, noticing the handwriting and recognizing it at once.

'Oh, she's written at long last! I thought she had abandoned me or, worse still, come to some harm.' He smiled as he held the envelope in his hand and looked at the delicate handwriting and smelled the perfume upon it.

'I thought it was from a lady. I could smell the perfume,' Lucy said quietly.

'It's from my dear friend, Ivy Thwaite. I do hope she says that she's going to pay me a visit. It would be so good to see her, after all these years. I'll have my supper and then I'll read it – it will end the perfect day.' Adam replaced the letter on the mantelpiece, not noticing the look of dejection on Lucy's face.

'I'll be away then. Don't let your supper go dry – it needs eating soon.' She looked at the excitement on Adam's face and knew that her words fell on deaf ears, as she stepped out of the farmhouse. Who was this Ivy Thwaite? Was she more than a friend? A lover, or a rival for Adam's affections? Lucy felt she had just started to enter Adam's life, as he'd noticed her of late, and now this woman was appearing on the horizon, with her posh perfume. Whoever she was, Lucy was going to make it her business not to like her, for this woman was a threat to her future happiness and, as such, she'd not give her the time of day.

'You look in a bad mood, our lass. What's wrong? Have you fallen out with Archie, or has a lad that you fancy not looked the side that you are on?' Dorothy Bancroft looked across at her daughter as she came home, throwing her shawl down into the chair before she sat in it, and not saying anything to her mother, as she stared into the fire. It was in need of attention, but Lucy couldn't be bothered to tend to it.

'Me – there's nowt wrong with me. I've just had a long day. Is our Susie not in her bed yet? Why do I always have to see to her?' Lucy growled and scowled at her younger sister, who sat drinking her cup of milk before bed.

'Now then, young lady, you usually like putting your sister to bed. Don't take it out on her because you are in a mood. And you are in a mood. I could tell as soon as you opened that door. Your face will stay that way, if the wind changes, and then no lad will look at you,' Dorothy said, smiling at her youngest daughter as she pulled her nightdress over her head. 'I hope you are not as grumpy as your big sister, when you are her age, Susie, else I'll be wishing myself into an early grave.' Dorothy smiled at Susie again, as she balanced her milk on her knee and said nothing to either of them.

'I'm not in a mood. In fact there's been some good news for us all around here. The Baxters got what they deserved in the courthouse today. They've all been jailed or sent to the colonies, and that'll stop them in their tracks.' Lucy still looked in a foul mood as she heard her mother gasp.

'They haven't sent old Robert Baxter to a penal colony, have they? He'll never survive the journey. Not that I'm that bothered, but he's old and some of them convicts don't even make it out there to Australia, the conditions are that bad on board ship,' Dorothy exclaimed.

'No, it's George and Jacob that have been deported. The rest have got hard labour in Halifax jail, I believe with sentences ranging from six to ten years. Adam was there, giving his evidence, and he waited for the sentences to be handed out,' Lucy said, without thinking. She had not yet told her mother that she and Adam Brooksbank were on first-name terms, and her mother would not like it.

'"Adam" is it, now? I've told you before, young lady: don't get too friendly. He's a nice enough fella, but he's still your boss, and you'd do well to remember that,' Dorothy chastised her.

'Oh, Mother, shut up. You don't know what it's like, working for him. He insisted that we are on first-name terms after I nursed him back to health. He's kind and understanding, that's all,' Lucy hit back.

'I know you nursed him back to health – and I hope that's all you did! It's not a healthy relationship that you have with that man. You think too much of him.

233

I'm going to have words with your father,' Dorothy warned.

'You do that and you'll look a fool. I'm off for a walk. You can put Susie to bed for once.' Lucy stood up and stared at her mother as she left by the back door. Mam would never understand how she felt – how could she? She'd never loved a man that she couldn't have, unlike her. A man who obviously already had a lover and had deceived Lucy into thinking there was no one in his life.

Lucy slammed the door behind her and heard her mother yelling for her to come back, but she wanted some time to herself; time to think things through, to ponder over what could be in the letter, and what this Ivy Thwaite might mean to the friendship that was starting to blossom between herself and Adam.

Adam pushed to one side the remains of his half-eaten supper and reached for the letter from Ivy. He'd nearly given up on her replying, but now he couldn't wait to read the contents of the letter. He'd not seen Ivy for such a long time and, hopefully, she would be sending news that she would be visiting him soon.

Lucy had been right: the letter did smell of perfume – expensive perfume, which was out of character for Ivy. She was a down-to-earth girl and had not in the past wasted money on fineries.

He opened the letter and unfolded the headed note-paper:

Laburnum House
22 New Street
Kendal

2nd June 1857

My Dearest Adam,

How surprised I was to hear that you are back in the country, and living at your old home too. I am so sorry to hear that the war in the Crimea has not been kind to you and do hope that your wound is healing. It must have been the most dreadful time for you and your fellow soldiers-in-arms.

I tried to keep abreast of affairs, but the news of our brave boys having to fight in such conditions made me feel so helpless, every time I read the newspapers. All those souls freezing and hungry on the Russian Steppes, and all for nothing really. No wonder you have chosen to return to the sanctity of your old home. Your mother and father would be so proud to know that at long last you are back where you belong.

Anyway, my darling, I too have got some news, but I will tell you it when I see you in person. It is partly the reason why I am late in replying to your letter, which filled my heart with joy at the news of your return. As you suggested, I aim to visit you, and perhaps stay a day or two, towards the end of next week, catching Wednesday's coach from Kendal and arriving in Keighley around 12 noon on the Thursday. Would you be able to meet me, my dear?

Please let me know post-haste if this is not agree-
able to you. Otherwise, I will look forward to sharing
a few glorious days with you, come Thursday.
  With love and affection,
  Yours in this world and the next
  Ivy

Adam smiled. Dear Ivy, he should have known that she would not have deserted him. They'd always been close, ever since they were small and she got teased for playing with the boys instead of the girls at school. She'd always been a tomboy, so what had she been up to now, which had kept her from writing to him sooner? No doubt all would be revealed on her arrival on Thursday, but before that, he must tell Lucy to prepare for a visitor – a visitor who was very dear to him and had to be made most welcome.

20

'I can't wait to see Ivy again. It's been so long, and we have been such close friends all our lives.' Adam smiled at Lucy as she cleared away his breakfast things and watched as she waved through the window at Archie, when he went about his work of cleaning out the cow shed. The warmer weather had finally arrived, and the cow had been turned out into the front pasture to feed on the lush growing grass.

'She must be important to you. You must have said her name ninety times since I arrived an hour ago,' Lucy commented, but didn't bother turning round to acknowledge Adam speaking to her. She was angry, as the first words Adam had said were that his beloved Ivy was coming to visit, and he was still wittering on about her.

'I'm sorry. I'm just glad that she's agreed to visit. We can at last catch up with one another, and Ivy might be willing to hold a seance, like she used to, so that I can speak to my Mary, whose words were of such comfort to me. I realized Mary had not left my life, simply gone into another room, which wasn't accessible to those of us who are still alive.' Adam hung his head and went quiet.

'She's a medium? This Ivy is a medium? One of those folks who prey on people's pain and grief, and tell folk exactly what they want to hear? Oh, I've no time of day for them. It's all a load of bunkum, and you want nowt with dabbling into that sort of thing.' Lucy shook her head and turned to look at Adam.

'It's not bunkum. Ivy told me things that only Mary and I knew. Ivy said she could see her, and that Mary was happy and I'm not to worry, because she was in a better world, with her parents and relations around her.' Adam scowled.

'She told you what you wanted to hear, that's all. That's what they all do. Con folk into paying them, for nowt,' Lucy scoffed.

'No, I'll not have you saying that. Ivy is as straight as a die. She's a good woman, and you'll treat her right while she is under my roof.' Adam looked across at Lucy. She was speaking out of turn about his friend, and he was not willing to put up with it.

'Hmm! Well, if you believe in that sort of thing, you do, but you won't convince me.' It seemed to Lucy that Adam was smitten with Ivy and that, no matter what she thought, he'd not hear any wrong of her. 'I'll go out and weed the garden today. I need the fresh air and it's a grand day – the sun's shining and everything's growing.' Lucy made an excuse to get out of her master's way. She was in no mood to be pleasant to him.

'You can put me some bread and cheese out for my lunch. I'm going up the moor on Rosa. I'm going to make that mire safe – fence it off – now that I've got my strength back. It should have been done before, then I'd not have fallen in. But I suppose some good came of it, with all the Baxters being sentenced. I'd rather you gave the house a really good clean, instead of doing the gardening. I need you to make the empty bedroom ready for Ivy, and we need to stock up on food and baking before next Thursday. I'll go into Keighley and get what we need, if you put together a menu for her stay. It needs to be a bit more refined than what you usually feed me,' Adam said as he got up from his chair and made for the door, not noticing the thunderous look on Lucy's face, as he left her standing in the kitchen after parcelling him his lunch of bread and cheese.

'Refined' – she'd give him bloody refined! What did he think she was? He'd never complained before about her cooking; in fact he'd relished it. This bloody woman, why on earth had she raised her head? Lucy looked around her and opened the front door, letting the sunshine flood into the house. She'd still go into the garden, where she could vent her wrath upon the weeds and check how the lettuce and radishes were growing. One of the meals for Miss High-and-Mighty could be a good ham salad, followed by rhubarb crumble; the rhubarb was growing pink and strong in the corner of the garden, and was at its best at this time of year, and it cost nothing. Which was exactly how Lucy rated Ivy – not worth a lot of time and money – although she would have to be decent with her, if she meant so much to Adam, to keep her job. She'd bottom the house and get it all spick and span, just as he wanted it, and would keep her thoughts to herself, rather than fall out with Adam; and she'd keep her mouth closed, when it came to the precious Ivy Thwaite.

Lucy looked around her. The sun was shining and she'd nobody to answer to all day. She untied her apron strings and placed her apron on the back of the chair. The housework could wait, as there was plenty of time before Thursday. The sunny day was calling her and she'd rather be outside, with the sun shining down on her. The mood she felt herself in might lighten with a bit of sunshine on her back. Because Lucy knew herself: she was not fit to be talked to, the way she was feeling. It was jealousy pure and simple – jealousy of a woman she had not even met yet, and of a friendship that she feared would come between her feelings for Adam and his for her, if he had any.

The rows of purple-and-green sprouting beetroot plants had never been so clear of the weeds that surrounded them. The chickweed, which had sprung up almost overnight, had been cleared and discarded, and the ground hoed and made tidy. Now it was the turn of the feathery green carrots, which they were starting to grow and which needed thinning, to enable the stronger ones to grow plump and large. Lucy concentrated on the job, bending down and pulling out the young seedlings, oblivious to the visitor who had just entered the farmyard.

'Now that's a grand sight to see – somebody working harder than myself.' Reggie Ellwood leaned on the garden wall and grinned at Lucy, with her hair in disarray and dirt on her face and hands.

'Oh, I didn't hear you there. I'm busy weeding; this chickweed gets everywhere, and I'm sure someone comes and plants it back in place overnight. I don't seem to get any nearer with it.' Lucy raised her head, stood up and pushed back her long blonde hair, which was hanging loosely over her shoulders. She looked at Reggie, whose dark hair shone in the summer sun, and who looked quite handsome in his checked waistcoat and white shirt with rolled-up sleeves, she thought, as she walked over to him. It was a pity he was a little too forward with his views, else she might have been attracted to him. But she'd lost her heart to Adam, whether he knew it or not, and whether he cared or not, and she'd no time for Reggie.

'Tha's a mucky devil. You've more muck on your face than in the garden.' Reggie laughed and looked at Lucy's face, with its streaks of dirt on it.

She lifted her hands and wiped her face as she blushed and looked at Reggie. 'I've been busy – a bit of muck doesn't hurt you.' She scowled. 'Are you wanting Mr Brooksbank, because he's not here; he's up the moor, fencing. There's Archie about somewhere. I think he's finished cleaning the cowshed and now he's in the stable.' Lucy looked around her, hoping that Archie would hear their voices and come and rescue her from the gaze of the lad that she knew was sweet on her.

'Aye, I came to see Mr Brooksbank, just to see how he's done and to reassure him that I can buy half his lambs off him this autumn, now that I'm not paying as much for keeping a roof over my head. At least I know that they are well bred, and it would be good to have them back on my land. But that's not the only reason I'm here. I'm not going to give up on asking you to walk out with me. I'll not let you ignore me. I've got to admit you've taken my eye, and I mean to have you on my arm before this summer's out, no matter what you think of me.' Reggie looked up at Lucy as she leaned against the wall next to him and watched as she listened to what he said.

'Aye, and I told you that I already have a fella and I'm not interested,' Lucy answered back, but smiled at Reggie. He was a cheeky devil and she admired him for his persistence.

'He'll not be a match for me. I'd buy you flowers every week and show you off on my arm for everyone to see. Everybody would say, "What a bonny couple them two make." And my home is secure now, so it'd be better than living down at the flay-pits.' Reggie reached out for Lucy's waist and squeezed it tightly over the wall top, before climbing over to join her.

'You are a cocky one, Reggie Ellwood. First, you ask me to walk out with me, and then you have me wed and living with you.' Lucy pushed him away gently.

'Who said owt about getting wed? I only said living with me, and we could live over the brush.' Reggie grinned and looked into her eyes. Both of them were oblivious to Adam walking up behind them, sweating with the heat of the sun, after pounding wooden posts and rails into the peat bog on the moor.

'Bloody hell, Lucy! I ask you to get the house ready for Ivy's arrival and here you are, flirting as usual, instead of working.' Adam came and stood next to them by the wall. He was not only annoyed that Lucy had not started on the house, but also that Reggie Ellwood was chancing his luck yet again with his maid. He felt a strange pang of jealousy as he caught her gazing at him.

'No, now don't get cross with Lucy. She was busy gardening up to ten minutes ago. It was my fault, I distracted her. I made fun of her mucky face while waiting for you.' Reggie saw the anger on Adam's face and rose to defend Lucy.

Adam looked at the newly weeded garden and at the muck on Lucy's face and wished he'd not been so quick to judge. 'Aye, well, that still leaves the house being neglected. I have got a visitor coming to stay next week and I want all just right for her,' Adam moaned.

'Her – a woman? So, you've got a woman in your life after all. I was beginning to think you were going to be living here on your own.' Reggie grinned. 'I've asked Lucy here to walk out with me, but she's still insisting on saying no. Perhaps you could convince her differently, seeing as you obviously have charms of your own?' he said and looked at both Adam and Lucy, as she bowed her head.

'Actually, Reggie, I've changed my mind. I will walk out with you this Sunday, if you are available. Perhaps we could have a walk around Haworth and have tea in that nice little tea-shop halfway up the cobbled high street. That is, if you can afford it?' Lucy lifted her head and looked at Reggie.

'Bloody hell! I didn't expect that. Aye, I'll pick you up, and tea in Haworth it will be.' Reggie smiled to himself.

'Now, if you'll excuse me, I'll go and wash my face and get on with my work,' Lucy said. 'I'm sorry I've disappointed you, sir, in putting the garden before your guest's needs. I'll go and see to her bedroom immediately, and plan what meals we can have for her stay.' She looked with steely eyes at Adam, as he'd shown her up in front of Reggie. She'd worked hard all day, and the housework would keep until nearer Ivy's stay. She would walk out with Reggie Ellwood, to spite Adam's assumption of her flirting with him, even though in her heart it was Adam she wished was on her arm. But that would never be, not now Ivy Thwaite was about to appear. Even Reggie had assumed that Ivy and Adam were lovers and not just friends, so how did she stand any chance to win her employer's heart?

Lucy could barely hold back her tears as she walked away from both men, entering the house and climbing the stairs to the spare bedroom, to make the spare bed up and dust the few pieces of furniture that were in the room. She wiped a tear away from her eye as she stood and looked out of the bedroom window, after opening it to let some fresh air into the unused room. The two men were leaning back on the garden wall, discussing sheep and no doubt other farming matters, unaware of how she really felt.

She sniffed and blew her nose. Damn the pair of them, but damn Ivy Thwaite more! She was responsible for the bad feeling between her and Adam, even though Ivy had not yet arrived. Lucy pulled out the spare pillows from the dark oak wardrobe and plumped them up with her fists, imagining the as-yet-unknown face of Ivy as she did so, and regretting accepting to walk out with Reggie that coming Sunday. He might be attractive in his looks, but she didn't find him attractive in any other way. She'd only agreed to make Adam realize that she was worthy of his love.

Adam stood at the farmhouse doorway. The light was dying and the moorland around him was quiet, apart from the odd bleating of a lost lamb from its mother, high above on the moor. He smoked his pipe and thought about the day he'd had, and the mood Lucy had been in all day. It wasn't like her. She'd been surly since break-fast time and she'd been far from decent in manner when he'd mentioned that Ivy was coming to stay. Then, when he'd come back down from the moor, to find her flirting and carrying on with Reggie Ellwood, he'd lost his patience. What did she want with Reggie? Surely she knew that he'd no money and that a life with him would be no better than the life she had at the flay-pits. Lucy could do so much better for herself. And it was only the other week that she said she wouldn't be giving him the time of day.

She'd hardly spoken all afternoon and had left that evening with barely a word, apart from giving Adam a list of meals that she thought appropriate for Ivy's stay, and a snide comment of it being fit for a queen, if not for Ivy. If he didn't know better, he'd say that Lucy had decided to slight his oldest friend, but she had no reason to do so; she didn't even know Ivy, and Lucy had no reason to be jealous of her. He only hoped that when Ivy arrived at Black Moss, Lucy would make her welcome and that she'd not show the petty side of herself, as she had done today.

There had been one good outcome of the day: the fact that Reggie had been able to rent his land at a cheaper rate, now the Baxters were in the jail. Reggie had also told him that the Baxters' home, and the adjoining land to Adam's, was to be sold. That was of great interest to Adam. He wouldn't mind buying and owning further land, especially the adjoining land of the Baxters, although he had no use for the farmhouse. However, he could always rent it to some deserving soul, he mused, as he wondered if he had enough savings for his plan. He'd have to watch what he spent in the future, and then he might be able to scrape a decent amount together, he thought, as he ventured into his home for the night.

'So who's this lad you are walking out with this afternoon?' Bill Bancroft looked at his daughter as she placed her best Sunday hat on her head, and dotted eau de parfum of violets on her wrists. 'Is he worth all this bother? In other words, has he got brass?' he growled.

'He farms just above Ing Row. But no, he doesn't have much brass. But he's asked me out for tea in Haworth, so I'm going to make the best of it. Nowt will come of it, Father, so you needn't worry. He's not my sort of man.'

'Then why are you walking out with him?' Her mother looked up from her darning and glanced at her wayward daughter, as she preened herself for a lad she didn't care for. 'You shouldn't lead him on, if you don't care for him – it's not right.'

'Nay. And if he's got nowt in the bank, then you can do better for yourself,' Bill added.

'Well, I've made up my mind now and he'll be here in a second. A stroll around Haworth, finishing with a cup of tea and a slice of cake, will be a pleasant change from stopping in this godforsaken place.' Lucy looked at herself again and felt her stomach churn. She didn't really want to go with Reggie, but she'd no option now.

'Lucy's got a fella . . . Lucy's got a fella . . .' Nathan chanted and egged Susie to join him in his teasing, as he danced around the kitchen.

'Shut up, our Nathan. He'll hear you. He said he was picking me up at twelve-thirty and it's nearly that now.' Lucy tried to swipe Nathan around the ear, but missed and swore as he put out his tongue at her, then ran upstairs to look out of his bedroom window at the man who was daft enough to court his big sister. 'Oh Lord, he's here. Now don't anybody come to the door and gawp at him.' Lucy picked up her small satin posy bag and glared at her parents, before going to open the door.

'Now then, Lucy, are you ready?' Reggie stood on the doorstep, cap in hand, and beamed at her as she opened the door to him. 'I've treated us to my next-door neighbour's horse and trap. I thought we'd go to Haworth in style. I'll stable the horse at the Black Bull at the top of the high street while we have a stroll.'

'So, who's this then, our Lucy? He's not leading you astray by visiting the Black Bull, is he?' Bill rose from his chair by the fire and went and stood behind Lucy, and looked Reggie up and down, noticing everything about him.

'Oh, Father, stop protecting me.' Lucy sighed.

'I'm not leading her astray, sir, just leaving the horse there. I'll not be sampling a gill while I have your bonny daughter on my arm. I'm Reggie Ellwood, it's a pleasure to meet you, sir. And thank you for letting Lucy walk out with me this fine day.' Reggie held out his hand to be shaken and looked up at Bill, as he surveyed the lad up and down.

'Aye, well, behave yourselves and have a good day. I'll expect her back by six – that'll be late enough. If you can't decide whether you like one another, after staring into one another's eyes for six hours, then the job's a bad 'un.' Bill shook Reggie's hand hesitantly and turned back into the house, leaving Lucy shaking her head at her father's forthrightness.

'He's alright, is your father. He says it how it is, and there's nothing wrong with that.' Reggie held Lucy's hand as she pulled up her skirts and climbed into the trap. 'Now isn't this fine? A bonny Sunday afternoon, all day together and enough brass in my pocket to treat you to tea. The other month I was near despair, but now that the Baxters have been dealt with – thanks to Adam

Brooksbank – my life's taken a change for the better. It's time I had a girl on my arm. And what a bonny one I have.' Reggie turned and looked at Lucy and wondered if he dared risk a quick peck on the cheek, as he sat up next to her and urged the horse forward down the shady green road to Haworth.

'It's just a day out and tea together. Don't get carried away, Reggie. It's nothing more than that.' Lucy looked at Reggie and saw the disappointment on his face. 'But we'll see how we get on.'

'Are you still courting this other fella you say you've got, because it's only right that I know?' Reggie looked ahead, not wanting to hear that he was only being used for a day out at his expense.

'Things are difficult at the moment. I think he's got another woman. So no, I can't say I am.' Lucy felt her eyes fill with tears, thinking about Adam smiling and talking about the dreaded Ivy's arrival, and how much he had missed her.

'Ah well, what's good for the goose is good for the gander. I'll have to make sure we have a good day and that I win you over. I'll give him a run for his money. And happen by the time I drop you off back at home, you'll have forgotten about him.' Reggie flicked the reins and started to whistle as they trotted along the blossom-filled hedgerows, thinking that he might stand a chance with the lovely Lucy, if he looked after her well.

The journey to the busy cobbled streets of Haworth was made up of polite conversation between Lucy and Reggie, both trying their best to be the person they wanted each other to be. Lucy was feeling a little bit guilty that, in her heart, she was leading Reggie on, when she knew he was not the right man for her. She was quite relieved when Reggie came out from the stables of the Black Bull, after stabling the horse, and linked his arm through hers without saying a word.

'The street is busy. There are lots of people walking out in their Sunday finest – don't they look smart.' Lucy smiled and watched all the ladies, dressed in their tight-waisted dresses with flowing skirts, in all the different colours that could be imagined, with their husbands or beaus, walking arm-in-arm with them and promenading up the ancient cobbled streets.

'Aye, and there's a lot of normal everyday folk, with not a lot of money, watching them. Not everybody's wealthy in Haworth. In fact it's quite the opposite, and everybody's scratching a living from carding wool, farm-ing or working in the iron foundry or mills. Don't let these few posh folk who walk out in their Sunday best fool you. They are only showing off, like us two,' Reggie said as he looked around him at the small cottage dwell-ings and the many businesseses that filled the narrow, dark streets of the old mill town.

'I know, but other folk seem to have so much more than I do. I'd like just a bit of what they've got. All I've ever done in my life is look after my sister and brothers, and be known as the lass from the flay-pits, which is not the best place to come from. It smells seven days a week and there are rats in the yard, and nobody worth any-thing looks the side I'm on,' Lucy moaned.

'Hey, your family love you, and you have a roof over your head and a full belly. Plus who says nobody looks the side you are on? Whose arm are you on today, and who doesn't give a damn where you are from? Stop feeling sorry for yourself, you moaning Minnie.' Reggie stopped in his tracks and looked long and hard at Lucy. 'I'm not the one you want, am I? There's somebody who's stolen your heart, and I can't compete.'

'I'm sorry, Reggie, you are right. I shouldn't have walked out with you. It's not fair on you. But I'm aiming too high and I can't have who I want, because he's already spoken for. Instead I'm feeling sorry for myself and spoiling your day.' Lucy bowed her head.

'Never mind. You never know, I might just win you over from this fella, who obviously doesn't know what he's got. Whoever he is, he's a fool. Now, a cream tea is calling to me, and I can't wait to get my gnashers into one of those cream scones in that window over there. I might not be the right fella for you, but we might as well enjoy one another's company. And seeing as I've got two bob in my pocket, we'll have a good day on it. Friends is what we will be, and if anything else comes of it, then it will be a bonus.' Reggie tugged on Lucy's hand and opened the door into a small, intimate tea-room. 'Sit back and think of yourself as Lady Muck, and I'll be Lord Muck, and we'll enjoy every mouthful and pretend that we eat cream cakes every day of the week.' Reggie grinned and pulled Lucy into the shop. 'Your chair, mi'lady.'

Lucy smiled at Reggie as he offered her a seat next to

the window. If only she could get Adam out of her thoughts, Reggie would be the perfect partner. She was glad he understood, as she hadn't wanted to hurt or deceive him. He might still be right: feelings might grow between them, she thought, as he winked at her and ordered a cream tea for two – something he could barely afford, and she knew it. But her head was still set on winning Adam's heart, regardless of Ivy Thwaite's intervention.

'Well, how did it go? Your father said he didn't look a bad sort, and at least he was polite.' Dorothy Bancroft looked at her daughter and noticed a flush on her face, as Lucy placed her bonnet on the kitchen table and sat down to unbutton her boots.

'We had a lovely day together, Mother. He treated me to a cream tea in Hattie Thorpe's Tea-Rooms and then we strolled around Haworth. It was a very pleasant day.' Lucy sat back and watched her mother smile.

'And will you be walking out with him again? He's brought some colour to your cheeks, if nothing else,' Dorothy said. She remembered when she had first walked out with Bill; she'd known from the very first moment together that he would be the man she would marry. She hoped it would be the same for her Lucy, after Bill had given Reggie his seal of approval.

'We might meet again, but just as friends, Mother – before you start insinuating anything more. He's a nice lad, a bit cocky, but he's good company. So don't say any more about it, Mother, because we will be keeping it at friends; nothing more.' Lucy shook her head as her mother sighed.

'Well, that's how all relations start out, and then they develop. It's a shame he's not got any money, though. I'd have been happier if he had. I wanted better for you.' Dorothy looked down at Bert, asleep in her arms.

'Mother, we are friends. I will not be marrying Reggie: not now, not ever,' Lucy said firmly as she walked away, leaving her mother with no doubt that a marriage was not in the offing, at least not between Lucy and Reggie.

21

It was Thursday morning and the farmhouse at Black Moss was as clean as a new penny. The stone kitchen floor was scrubbed to within an inch of its life, and polished so well that the pegged mat placed near the fire was prone to slipping when walked upon. On the kitchen table was a bunch of dog-daisies in a vase, while upstairs in the spare bedroom a vase of red roses took pride of place next to the iron bedstead, which was immaculately made up and waiting for their most important guest, who was about to be met at Keighley that lunchtime.

Lucy stood with crossed arms and watched as Adam looked at himself in the mirror. Not a hair was out of place, his sideburns were beautifully shaped, and he smelled of the new soap he'd bought the day before in Keighley.

'How do I look? Do you think Ivy will recognize me? I haven't seen her for so long.' Adam turned around and smiled at Lucy, who looked annoyed and had been moody all week.

'You look very handsome. I'm sure she will recognize you straight away when she alights from the coach.' Lucy wasn't lying; Adam did look handsome. He'd spent time dressing himself that morning, and his white shirt and dark suit with his favourite stud in the collar made him look younger than his years. He looked nothing like the farmer that he was, most days of the week nowadays. Instead he had reverted to the ways of a gentleman, as he had been when he first arrived at Black Moss. She couldn't help but stare at him as he made for the doorway. He was everything she wanted in a man, but he hadn't dressed to win her heart. Instead this was all for Ivy Thwaite, and Lucy felt angry and hurt at Adam not realizing how she, standing there, felt about him.

She watched as he walked across the farmyard and climbed into the donkey-cart to go and pick up his beloved Ivy from the centre of Keighley. She watched him go down the farm track for as long as she could, before turning back into the kitchen. There she sat down near the fire and burst into tears. She was going to lose him to Ivy and, to make matters worse, he'd no idea how she felt about him, and how hard it was going to be for her to serve and be polite to the woman who was her nemesis. Lucy hated every inch of Ivy's body, even though she had never met the woman, and the coming few days were going to be the worst week of her life.

Adam stood at the head of Church Green, awaiting the coach-and-horses arriving from Kendal, which was carrying his precious visitor. Ivy was his last link to his previous life, when he was married and happy. He was, therefore, looking forward to her arrival with a great deal of happiness, despite some discouraging remarks from Lucy. She knew nothing about Ivy and had no need to judge her, and he wouldn't put up with any of her skulking ways, if she was not civil to his guest.

He felt his stomach flutter and churn as he watched the coach and sweating horses arrive along the cobbled street. The coachman, looking red in the face, pulled his team of weary horses to a halt just outside the church gates, before climbing down from his perch and opening the door for his paying passengers to alight.

Adam held his breath and watched. A small, rounded gentleman with a traveller's case of goods was the first to appear, and then an elderly woman who was in need of assistance out of the carriage. And then finally, as Adam was starting to doubt that Ivy was on board the twice-daily coach into Keighley, he noticed her. There was no mistaking it was Ivy: she had on her head a hat set at a jaunty angle, decorated with the brightest of feathers, and her dress and bodice were of vivid purple – Ivy's favourite colour, he remembered. She looked around her, before taking the coachman's hand to steady her step down into the cobbled street. Adam pushed his way through the busy shoppers and called out Ivy's name, as she took a carpet bag from the hands of the coachman and tried to spot Adam.

'Ivy, I'm here!' He pushed past the other travellers and stopped in front of her and smiled at the face he knew so well.

'Oh, Adam, I didn't think I was ever going to see you again.' Ivy dropped her carpet bag onto the street and put her arms around the man she had known nearly all her life. 'You haven't changed a bit.' She stood back and looked at him. 'How come you never age, while Mother Nature has played her tricks on me and given me a few extra lines here and there?' She took his hands.

'Now then, Ivy, you are still the good-looking woman you've always been.' Adam bent and kissed her on the cheek, looking at the dark-haired woman with deep brown eyes and immaculate skin, who was as old as him, but still very attractive. 'Was your journey alright? The road from Kendal to here is not a good one. I take it that you stayed somewhere, to rest the horses last night?' Adam bent down and took Ivy's carpet bag, noticing that it was light, and not that full of clothes for her stay with him.

'Yes, we stayed over at Long Preston, at the Boar's Head. I was ever so grateful for a good night's sleep. The seats in the carriage were not that comfortable, and the road leaves a lot to be desired, it is that rutted. It was such an early start this morning – it was barely breaking light when we started out – but still, it's worth it, to be here and see you once again.' Ivy linked her arm through Adam's and started to walk down the road to where Rosa and the donkey-cart stood tethered to the church-yard railings, waiting patiently. She stopped for a second and looked at Adam. 'You've got a limp. How long have you had that?'

'It's nothing; it is nearly better now, although I think

I will always have a slight limp for the rest of my life. It's due to my falling out with a Russian's sword. Unfortunately, it left me like this, but he came out worse.' Adam smiled and held out his hand for Ivy to climb into the donkey-cart and sit next to him.

'Oh, Adam, life's not been kind to you. Perhaps now that you are home and settled, life will be better for you. I was so glad to hear from you, and to hear that you were back living at Black Moss. How are you managing on your own?' Ivy enquired, as Adam flicked the reins over Rosa's back and turned her and the donkey-cart in the direction of home. 'I never thought you were a domesticated man – most men aren't.'

'I could just manage. But no, I have a maid, Lucy. She's a good lass, and she looks after me really well. I couldn't wish for anyone better. I've also a farm man who comes and helps me two days a week with jobs that I find hard, so I have a perfect life – or so it would seem, to those looking in and not knowing me.' Adam sighed as they started the journey home.

'A perfect life, except that you are still missing Mary, I'm betting. Oh, Adam, you should learn to look to the future. She'd not wish your life to have stopped still since her death. You must learn to love again – it's what Mary would have wanted.' Ivy patted her close friend's hand as he held the reins and looked forward along the heavily travelled road to Halifax. 'Don't give up on finding a person to take her place. It's never too late,' Ivy whispered and decided to say nothing more about his loneliness, as they both made tracks to Black Moss and

Adam went quiet, remembering better days with Mary by his side. But he also wondered if Ivy's words had a double meaning, and if his absence had made her heart grow fonder of him.

Lucy stood on the doorstep of the farmhouse and watched as Ivy climbed down from the donkey-cart. She was everything Lucy had known she would be: tall, elegant, with striking features and a perfect figure. No wonder Adam had been so excited about his guest's arrival. Lucy curtsied as Ivy walked towards her and said, 'Welcome to Black Moss, Miss.'

Ivy smiled at her and waited for Lucy to open the kitchen door. 'Now, we'll have none of that. No "Miss" or "Ma'am". I'm Ivy, and I know you to be Lucy from the flay-pits. Adam has been telling me all about you on our way here. He tells me that he owes you his life, and that he will be forever grateful to you, as I am. I would hate to have thought that the wonderful Adam was left to his death, sucked down in the mire, when he had survived Sebastopol and many a blow from a thief, or even worse, when he patrolled Keighley and the district. He was always taking somebody on, fighting for justice and keeping the law. But it seems he's still at it, since he's also told me about these horrible neighbours of his, who have been dealt with as they deserve.'

Ivy leaned forward and kissed Lucy on the cheek, before walking into the kitchen, which she had known since she was knee-high.

'Oh, you have got this house looking lovely, Lucy. I've

never seen it looking so beautiful.' She turned and beamed at Lucy, then made herself at home by seating herself in a chair next to the table.

'Thank you. I try and keep it tidy and clean. It's a lovely house, and the view from the windows is spectacular. I love working here.' Lucy watched Ivy as she pulled a hat pin out of her hat and placed the elaborate headpiece on the table.

'And of course you have the perfect master in Adam. He always was a gentleman.' Ivy looked up at Lucy and smiled, before glancing over at Adam as he entered the kitchen, carrying her carpet bag full of her change of clothes. 'You never told me that Lucy was so attractive – you kept that quiet.'

Ivy grinned and made Lucy blush. She decided not to listen to Adam's reply, and picked up the carpet bag from Adam's hands and made for the stairs, to place the bag in Ivy's room. She stood halfway up the stairs, trying but not wanting to make out Adam's reply. But she only heard Ivy laughing, leaving her wondering what Adam had said about her. Ivy was a little forward with her eyes, and Lucy could easily see why Adam was fond of her. She had no edge to her, but at the same time she was confident and outgoing – everything that she thought herself not to be. Ivy was a better match for Adam than she ever would be, and more his age. Filled with despair, Lucy placed the carpet bag on Ivy's made-up bed and decided to accept that she would never be anything more than Adam's maid; not while Ivy was under his roof, and looking as she did. She knew her place in life and she'd been stupid to think that she could even dream of being anything other than Adam's maid.

Ivy yawned. It had been a long day and she was tired, but she still hadn't found the right time to tell Adam her news and was amazed that he had not yet noticed the band of gold on her wedding finger. To be honest, she thought the conversation had been a little one-sided, with Adam constantly singing the praises of his maid, Lucy, and what he had done since his arrival back at his family home. She smiled as he said farewell to Lucy and came to sit back down beside her.

'You think a lot of her, don't you?' Ivy looked across at Adam as he lit a spill from the fire and held it to his filled pipe.

'Aye, she's a good worker, and I wouldn't be here talking to you if she hadn't have saved me from the mire. This blasted leg of mine makes me so weak sometimes, but I try and overcome the pain it gives me.' Adam puffed on his pipe and looked across at his old friend. 'Now, how about you? You've not said a lot about yourself while Lucy's been about the house. What have you been up to with your time? Are you still giving sittings and doing the medium rounds, or has that come to an end?' Adam sat forward and looked at Ivy. She was a beautiful woman, but he had always seen her as a friend and nothing more; she was far too flighty for him, for a start, and liked to spend money on the finer things in life, as her clothes still showed.

'Well, the reason I didn't reply for a while was that I,

too, have been out of the country. I, we . . . have just come back from touring Italy, which was magnificent. But before I tell you about that, I'd better tell you the news that I said I had.' Ivy paused and held her left hand out for Adam to look at. 'I've gone and got myself married, Adam. I never thought it would happen to me, but I am a respectable married woman, with a husband I love dearly.' She looked at Adam as she held her hand out for him to take, and he looked at the gleaming gold band of the wedding ring and the delicately cut engagement ring above it.

'Now, that is a shock! There's me, wittering on about my life, and you have had all this to tell me.' Adam put down her hand and sat back in his chair, placing his smouldering pipe on the fire grate. 'Well, who's the lucky fella, and how long have you been wed?' he questioned Ivy, taken aback by her admission of no longer being a single woman.

'He's called Hugh Loveridge and he teaches at the workhouse. He's a good man and cares for the children there. He tries to make sure they have enough knowledge and education to stand on their own two feet, when the time comes for them to make their way in the world. He's introduced an apprentice scheme, for those who are old enough to work, but still gives them lessons if they need them. He's not a wealthy man, but that doesn't matter. He's kind and generous, and when my father he died left me with a nice legacy, so we want for nothing. For the first time in my life I am happy, Adam, and that counts for a lot.' Ivy bowed her head. 'It was

262

time I settled down. I was getting too old to look at spending my whole life alone, as we all need company in our old age.'

'I know. I still yearn for Mary and the love we had, although I know I should move on with my life. But sometimes it feels as if she is still with me, walking by my side and guiding me in what to do. When I was cold and freezing in the mire, I'm sure I heard her voice on the wind, faint and ghost-like. But then Lucy appeared, and I realized it had been her calling my name and that I had just dreamed it. Still, enough of me. I wish you and Hugh the best of marriages, and I'm glad that you have found a good man. Although schoolmaster to the work-house will not be that well paid, it will be a job of satisfaction, so that shows the character of your man to me.'

'As I say, money doesn't enter into it. I had money of my own, which is now his as well as mine. He's used to a frugal lifestyle and, now that I am his wife, I no longer move in the circles that I used to. Things have changed, Adam. I decided our honeymoon in Italy would be our last extravagance, before settling down and helping Hugh in his charity work with the poor and underprivileged of Kendal and the surrounding areas. So no, is the answer to your question "Do I still work as a medium?" Although I still hear the spirits talking to me and feel their presence. I will never be free of that.' Ivy looked across at Adam and thought that he looked slightly crest-fallen at her news.

'I was hoping that you might contact Mary for me.

Just one last time. I need the reassurance that she is still with me, even though I can't see her,' Adam whispered.

'Oh, Adam, Mary will always be with you. She's in here.' Ivy reached across and laid her hand on his heart. 'She will never leave you, and she will always know that you loved her. But now perhaps it is time for you to move on. She'd want you to be happy, and for you to have someone looking after you. I know she would – she's told me so.' Ivy took Adam's hands and watched as a single tear fell down his cheek.

'I loved her and I let her down. I should have been there for her,' Adam whispered.

'Stop it! What is done is done. Stop torturing yourself. If you truly want me to try and get in touch with the other side and talk to Mary, we will try tomorrow night. But I no longer feel her presence around me. I think she's moved into another of our God's rooms and is now at peace with herself.' Ivy smiled at Adam and let go of his hand.

'I think you are right. Her memory is not as strong as it used to be, even to me.' Adam blew his nose on the handkerchief from his pocket and looked at Ivy. 'Perhaps I should leave her soul in peace.'

'I think so. Look to the future, because your happiness is staring you in the face, from what I can see.' Ivy sat back and looked lovingly at a still-heartbroken Adam.

'What do you mean, Ivy?' Adam said, looking puzzled.

'There's love blossoming in this house, just like the

blossom on the trees. Now it is up to you to bring it to fruition and not let it slip away. Your maid Lucy looks at you with eyes full of love; and you, since I arrived, have never stopped talking about her. I may have got it wrong, but I don't think so. There are stronger powers than death itself working in this house, and it is for the good of both of you.' Ivy smiled.

'But she's my maid, and she's much younger than me! I do think a great deal of her, but I think you've got it wrong, Ivy. She doesn't care for me; in fact she walked out with Reggie Ellwood last Sunday. Plus she's not been her usual self this last week, moping around with a long face on her and not listening to what I needed her to do,' Adam retorted.

'I bet she's been like that since you announced my arrival? Does she think I have come to claim you as mine, and perhaps is a little jealous? That's what I think, so in the morning one of us must put her straight. Lucy will probably rejoice when she hears that I am now a married woman, and that you are still hers to admire from afar.' Ivy grinned. 'Men are so slow, when it comes to feelings. It is as obvious as the nose on my face that she worships the ground you walk on, and that you think something of her. Now, do something about it.'

'It's not easy for me, Ivy. Mary's shoes will always be hard to fill. And what if you are wrong? I'd make a fool of myself.' Adam sighed.

'Then do as you wish, but you are lucky to have Lucy looking at you with such love. And as for walking out with Reggie Ellwood, perhaps she was hoping you'd be jealous. Now, I'm going to my bed; it's been a long day and I hardly slept last night. Tomorrow is another day and we will see what it brings.' Ivy leaned forward and kissed Adam on the cheek. 'Goodnight, my dear friend. Don't worry, love has a way of showing itself even to the blindest. I'm just going to make sure that I help it along.' She smiled and then went up to bed, leaving Adam pondering her words.

Could Lucy be smitten with him? He did find her attractive and had enjoyed the intimacy of being near her, when riding Rosa to Keighley, and had nearly thought of kissing her while admiring the chicks at Easter, but had thought better of it, not wanting to be called a lecher by her or her family. He shook his head. Damn Ivy, she always did know him too well. And now he was feeling guilty for even thinking about his young maid and her winning smile, which had disappeared since his announcement of Ivy coming to stay. Ivy was right: Lucy had not had a good word for her, and she'd not said a word to him about her day out with Reggie Ellwood. But should he be true to Mary's memory, or should he perhaps follow Ivy's advice and open up his heart to a new, young love?

22

Ivy sat outside Black Moss Farm admiring the early-morning mist, which was following the river down in the valley below. She'd purposely awoken early in order to speak to Lucy on her own. The garden at the front of the farmhouse was abuzz with bees seeking pollen from the summer flowers, and the air was full of early-morning song from the newly fledged birds and their parents. The world was content, just as she was, now that she had found the right man to have by her side for the rest of her life.

She only hoped Adam could feel the same way she did, and could get over the loss of his late wife; and that perhaps a woman-to-woman talk with Lucy would help her dearest friend and make them both see how much they meant to one another. She'd caught signs of both of them having feelings for one another, and now she had decided to act as Cupid and make them realize how good life could be if they were together – regardless of

Adam's misgivings about the age gap and Lucy's place in society. Life was for living. Death came all too quickly, as well she knew from her previous dealings with the afterlife.

'Good morning. I'm just sitting here, admiring the scenery and this immaculately kept vegetable plot and garden. Somebody spends hours keeping this weed-free and in order.' Ivy smiled at Lucy as she came up through the farmyard, ready for her day's work.

'It's my guilty pleasure, along with Adam's help. It should supply him with all his needs over the coming months. The soil is good and rich, and things are doing well, with the attention that is lavished upon them.' Lucy caught her breath from the steep climb up to the farm and stopped to talk to the woman she had thought about, and had little sleep over, the previous night.

'Somebody has to look after him. I'm glad you get on with Adam so well, as he needs somebody to take him in hand and see that he looks after himself. He speaks very highly of you, and is grateful that you have been here for him.' Ivy smiled and saw the look of pleasure on Lucy's face for the praise she was giving her.

'It's nothing – I'd do the same for anyone. He's a good man, and I wouldn't wish to work for anybody else. Is he not awake yet? I'm sure he'd not want you to be up and about on your own. He likes playing the perfect host.' Lucy made for the front door and turned to look at Ivy.

'No. I could hear him snoring in the other room when

268

I tiptoed down the stairs. I left him to sleep. We talked until late last night, and I left him with a lot to think about. A lot was forthcoming in our evening together, and some things were quite revealing.' Ivy looked at Lucy with apprehension.

'I hope you didn't do as he wished and hold a stupid seance. He believes in you so much, and it's hurtful the way your sort fill people's minds with stories of loved ones still living on beyond the grave. You, and others like you, should not make a living from other people's grief,' Lucy spat out.

'No, I told Adam to leave the dead alone, and to look to making himself a new life. He could do worse than find himself someone to look after him, now that he has sowed his wild oats. He needs to be loved and taken care of. Mary would have wanted that for him. However, I think Adam knew that already, and that his heart already belongs partly to someone he owes a great deal to.'

Ivy looked at Lucy and saw the colour rise in her cheeks, knowing that her words would spark a reaction. She added, 'I fear my news of being a married woman came as quite a shock to him. I don't think he had ever envisaged me settling down and marrying. Poor Adam, he just needs a little encouragement to show him where his true feelings lie. Men are always slow at showing their emotions, don't you think?' Ivy reached for Lucy's hand and squeezed it. 'It's you he thinks a great deal of. But he doesn't know how to admit it. Perhaps, if you make the first move, then he will follow,' she whispered.

'You've got married! I thought you had come here to—' Lucy stopped short.

'What? Come here to fill your shoes and pinch him from under your nose? I do love Adam, but only as a true friend. Not like the love I've seen growing within you for him, and within him for you. Both of you needed to be told of one another's feelings, and you both need not to be scared of what folk might think. Happiness is hard to find. I should know. It has taken me plenty of years to find my Hugh, and although he did not have a penny to his name when I met him, I knew he was right for me – and to hell with the consequences.' Ivy smiled, but still held Lucy's hand, and closed her eyes as she searched for something to make Lucy believe in her power of knowing things that other people had lost the sense to feel.

'But he's my master! My parents would be furious if they knew how much I love Adam, and I would never have the courage to let him know. He'd think I was loose in my ways or, even worse, that I was only after his money. Besides, you often hear of masters taking advantage of their servants, only to cast them aside when they fall pregnant – or even worse.' Lucy looked at Ivy as she let go of her hand.

'You know Adam's not that sort. He's kindness itself. The way he spoke of you all yesterday, and I know that he loves you too. He just daren't admit it.' Ivy looked round towards the house, noticing Adam glancing out of the window. 'Now shush – he's coming. Think on. I never played Cupid's advocate between you two; let him think that he's done it all himself.'

'Morning, Ladies. What are you two about, this glorious morning?' Adam stood in the main doorway and looked at the two principal women in his life, and knew instantly that they had been talking about him.

'We were admiring the view. And I was complimenting Lucy on the size of her radishes, and how neat and tidy the garden looks.' Ivy smiled and winked at Lucy.

'Were you now! I think otherwise – you were both deep in conversation when I looked out of the window. It seemed something a bit more serious than radishes.' Adam grinned and watched as Lucy picked up her skirts and walked towards him to enter the house.

'Excuse me, I got waylaid. I'll light the fire and get the kettle boiling. I'll make you your breakfasts before I milk the cow – there's enough milk in the dairy for porridge. Would that be to both your likings?' Lucy put her head down and couldn't make eye contact with Adam. Her secret was out, she feared, and perhaps Ivy had led her on into thinking Adam felt the same.

'That will be fine, Lucy. But I'll bring the cow in from the bottom meadow, after we have had breakfast. I could do with a walk to clear my head, and then you two can carry on with your urgent conversation about radishes.' Adam looked at Lucy. It was true that he did feel deeply for the lass. He'd just needed someone to tell him it was alright to do so.

'She's as smitten with you as you are with her. What a pair of idiots you both are! Did not one of you have the gumption to tackle the matter? Would you still have been

271

skirting around the subject, if I hadn't talked to you both and found out that you both feel the same way?' Ivy whispered and sighed, looking out across the valley. Then she turned and looked at Adam.

'She still hasn't said anything to me. I'm still not sure,' Adam said as he noticed Archie making his way into the farmyard, ready for his day's work.

Ivy, spotting him, couldn't stop herself and shouted, 'Have you come a-courting Lucy? Because it seems everyone else knows how to go about it, apart from my friend here,' she yelled out to a startled Archie.

'No, ma'am. I'm just minding my own business, and hoping to start digging the ditches where Mr Brooksbank is going to be piping water from the springhead up on the fell to the house. I've no intention of courting Lucy or anybody else, come to that.' Archie seemed shocked at being confronted with such an accusation, and looked at Adam shaking his head.

'Be quiet, Ivy. Archie is my farm lad – let the lad on his way. As he says, he's starting to dig a ditch out for me so that we can have running water in the house. Something I need doing before winter sets in. So hold your noise. I don't want the world to know my affairs.' Adam nodded his head to Archie, as a sign for him to be on his way, as he took Ivy by the arm and entered into the kitchen of the farmhouse.

'Was that Archie I heard talking? He's late this morning. I hope everything's alright at home,' Lucy said as she set the table for breakfast and noticed the scowl on Adam's face, as Ivy sat down and winked at him.

'He didn't mention home, so I suppose everything is alright.' Adam pulled up a chair to the table and looked across at Ivy, as Lucy poured them both a cup of tea and went to stir the porridge that was now bubbling in a pan on the fire.

'He's a bonny lad. I asked him if he'd come a-courting you. I didn't realize who he was.' Ivy laughed.

'Oh, Archie wouldn't say a lot back about that. He's known me all my life. I tease him, but he's like a brother to me – we are close, but not that close. He works for my father as well, down at the flay-pits. He's a grand lad, but a bit shy.' Lucy spooned the porridge out into the blue-and-white willow-pattern china bowls and watched as Adam added salt to his, while Ivy added sugar before starting to eat. 'I'll go and get the cow in from the pasture. It will give you more time together. I could do with the walk myself.' Lucy felt awkward, knowing that she'd been discussed between the two of them, and she needed to gather her thoughts.

'Alright, if you wish, but I'd have done that for you.' Adam looked briefly at Lucy as she made her way out of the door.

'I've never got round to telling you, Adam, but I'll be returning tomorrow,' Ivy said. 'I'll not be staying as long as I would have liked. I didn't feel it right that I left my newly-wed husband on his own for too long, bless him. It was good of him to trust me to stay with a single man, and one with whom I have a lifetime's friendship. Besides, I don't want to outstay my welcome, now that we have caught up and I know that you are in safe hands.'

273

'That's disappointing. I was looking forward to you staying longer and to hearing more about the reformation that your husband has made in your life. You must love him dearly, from what I've heard about him and your new lifestyle. The next time you visit me, you must bring him with you. I'd like to meet the man who's tamed you.' Adam grinned.

'You'll meet him, as I expect us both to be asked on your wedding day.' Ivy smiled back at Adam and leaned back in her chair.

'Now you are expecting too much too soon. I've not even said that I'm going to make my feelings known to Lucy yet.' Adam looked out of the window and saw Lucy bringing the cow into the shed to be milked, as he replied to Ivy.

'Oh, you will, now that you've faced up to them.' Ivy watched as Adam stood up from the table. 'Go on, do it now – put the poor girl out of her misery and make your life complete.'

'You have a lot to answer for, Ivy Thwaite. If you've read this wrong, then I'm about to make an absolute fool of myself, and the whole of the Worth valley will know about it.' Adam looked back at Ivy as he opened the door and made his way to the cowshed, where Lucy was starting to milk the cow.

'I'd have brought her in for you. You've enough on, looking after my guest. Ivy can be quite demanding, and she's a devil for speaking her mind and poking her nose into other people's business.' Adam ran his hand along the

274

back of the docile milk-cow and looked down at Lucy, as she sat on the milk stool, busy at work. He felt awkward and didn't quite know how to approach her, concerning the way he felt. He looked at the cow munching happily away on the hay, which she had been given to keep her occupied while Lucy milked her dry.

'Yes, she certainly doesn't hold back in her thoughts.' Lucy stood up, her bucket full of creamy, frothy fresh milk as she placed it to one side and wiped her hand across her brow, moving a piece of stray hair out of her eyes.

'Is she right, when it comes to us two? Do you feel something more for me than just your master – do you have feelings for me? Because damn it, Lucy, I know I shouldn't, but I've been finding you more and more attractive by the day. But until Ivy decided to interfere with our lives, I had resolved to say nothing.' Adam looked down at the blonde-haired milkmaid, whom he now knew himself to be in love with.

Lucy stood silent for a moment and then decided to tell Adam the truth. 'Yes, she's right. I've tried not to show it, either. I know it to be wrong. My mother says I've to behave myself and look elsewhere, but I don't want to. Every time you brush past me or look at me with those hazel eyes, I feel my heart miss a beat. I can't help it. I'll leave, if you want me to, because I know I'm not right for you.' Lucy dropped her eyes from his gaze and felt tears beginning to well up in them.

'You will do no such thing!' Adam stepped forward and held her tightly in his arms. 'I've wanted to do this

275

for days now, but I didn't realize you felt the same way.' He looked down into Lucy's eyes and tilted her chin up towards him, then kissed her tenderly and passionately.

Lucy closed her eyes and felt her heart about to burst. She couldn't believe that Adam felt the same way as she did, as he kissed her again and again and whispered loving words to her. It didn't matter that they were in the cowshed, and that Ivy was waiting for her host to return. The words she had only dreamed of hearing were being said to her. She'd never wanted a young lad who only boasted and flirted with every glance. This was the man she had wanted. Lucy ran her hands through his dark, thick hair and whispered back words of love. She would never let him go now, no matter what folk thought or said.

'Milking a cow takes a bit longer than it used to.' Ivy grinned. 'And it takes two pairs of hands. I'd take that bit of hay out of your hair, Adam, else I might think you've been up to something you shouldn't.'

Adam reached up for the piece of hay that was telling tales on him and Lucy, and shook his head at Ivy's forth-right words, as Lucy made herself scarce by taking the milk into the dairy.

'I'm guessing you've both listened to old Ivy? About bloody time, if you ask me. Lord, how long would the pretence have gone on for, if I hadn't visited?' Ivy looked across at Lucy as she entered the kitchen. 'So, you've won the heart of my dearest friend – you make sure you look after it. Because Adam wouldn't be able to cope with it being broken again. And you, old devil, make sure you do right by Lucy. Not that you wouldn't, because you are not that sort. Once you love somebody, you give them your heart and soul. I know that all too well, after you lost Mary.'

'I never thought I'd love again. But you were right. Lucy has meant more to me with each day, and seemingly the feeling has been mutual.' Adam reached for Lucy's hand and they both stood and looked at one another.

'I promise I'll look after him. He is all I have ever wanted and, no matter what people say, I will always love him,' Lucy whispered as Adam squeezed her hand tightly.

'Well, this is lovely to see, I think. I take it that you've changed your mind about me, Lucy, now that I'm not a threat, but work for the good of people and don't prey on people's insecurities?' Ivy smiled. 'Well, I can see I'm no longer wanted here. I'd only get in the way, so it's a good job I'm going home tomorrow. I'd hate to play gooseberry between you two love-birds,' she said and looked at them both.

'Don't go because of us two. You are already leaving too soon, although I understand that you must feel lost without your husband by your side. I know I would. I hope we can prove to be good friends in the future.' Lucy left Adam's side and went and gave Ivy a tentative hug.

'I'm sure we will. I'm just glad I have made you two see what was plain to anyone who saw you both together. Now it is up to you two where you go next. But I must return. I promised Hugh I would return at least by Sunday to help him at the workhouse, so I must be true to my word.' Ivy laughed. 'You make a very handsome couple. I can see a grand wedding in a short while, and I'm never wrong.'

23

Lucy had felt as if she could explode with the joy she was feeling. She had hugged her pillow and whispered Adam's name to herself over and over again. He did love her, he'd told her so. And now she just had to hide her feelings from her parents, until she had summoned up the courage to tell them the truth. Her feet felt as light as air as she made her way down to the family kitchen, where Susie and her mother were still in their nightclothes and setting the breakfast table for the day.

'Does that man really want you to work for him on a Saturday? I don't know what he finds for you to do, up at that farm of his. But there's plenty you could turn your hand to here,' Dorothy moaned at her, as Lucy quickly buttoned on her boots and pinched a bit of bread from the bread-board to eat for her breakfast as she walked up to the farm.

'I always work Saturdays. And besides, today Ivy is returning to Kendal, so I need to say my goodbyes to her,' she said, with her mouth full of the first bite of bread.

'"Ivy" is it now! First, it was "Miss Thwaite", then it was "that bloody woman" and now it's "Ivy". You sound like best mates – I never saw that coming at the beginning of the week.' Dorothy wet the end of a tea towel from the warming kettle and wiped Susie's face free of the jam that she'd managed to smear on it, while eating her breakfast. 'You are a mucky pup, Susie Bancroft, and you should still be in your own bed. No more of this crawling in between me and your father once you are awake – you are too old for that now.' She glanced at Lucy, who was busy making sure her hair was in the right place before going out of the door.

'I'd still have been asleep, if it wasn't for our Lucy. She was pretending to kiss the pillow and whispering a name,' Susie mumbled as she ate her breakfast.

'Did she now? Well, you put the pillow over your ears next time and get back to sleep. And you, our Lucy, make less noise. Who was the fella she was trying to kiss?' Dorothy asked Susie, then turned to Lucy and decided to question her. 'I thought you reckoned nowt to Reggie Ellwood, and that he was just going to be friends?' Dorothy pried.

'It wasn't Reggie, it was—' Susie replied, but never got the chance to finish her sentence before Lucy stopped her in her tracks.

'You be quiet, our Susie. I was doing no such thing and if I was, I must have been dreaming. Reggie is only a friend, and that's the end of it. Now I'm going, else I'm going to be late, and Ivy is to catch the coach back to Kendal at ten.' Lucy glared at her younger sister as she made for the back door, hoping that Susie wouldn't say any more about her behaviour when she had gone.

'Aye, I suppose we will see you when you can fit your family in,' Dorothy sighed.

Lucy pulled the back door closed and set out to walk up the moorside lane to Black Moss. She scowled and groaned; she did have time for her family, it was just that life was better with Adam. He was, and had, everything she had ever dreamed of. And now that she knew how he felt about her, she was going to spend every minute that she could with him.

'I'm sorry I'm leaving so soon. You must come and visit us at Kendal and, of course, you must keep in touch.' Ivy looked over at Adam as he picked up her bag, after they had both sat and eaten breakfast. 'Bring Lucy with you – you will both be made more than welcome by Hugh and me.' Ivy looked across at Lucy, who stood next to the window and waited to clear the table after Adam's guest had left them.

'You will come with him, won't you, Lucy? I'm so glad you two have realized the love that has grown between you. And if you decide to tie the knot and get married, I expect to be the first to be invited.' Ivy smiled.

'It's a bit early for talk of that, I'm sure,' Lucy replied quietly.

'I'll go and put your bag in the cart and wait while you two say goodbye to one another.' Adam bowed his head and left the kitchen, with the two women standing together, embarrassed by Ivy's assumption of marriage.

'You get him wed. You are both made for one another, and don't listen to what folk say. He's a good man and he needs you.' Ivy hugged Lucy and kissed her, before standing back and looking directly at her. 'Before I go, I've something else to do for you, to ease your worries.' She breathed in and looked at Lucy. 'The babies your mother lost were never really formed, so they had no souls. I felt your worries when I held onto your hand the other day. Don't despair that your father buried them where he did; it was not his fault. They do not have a place in heaven or in the afterlife, as they never actually lived.' Ivy looked at the shock on Lucy's face.

'How do you know that? Who's told you?' Lucy gasped, feeling her eyes fill with tears.

'I felt your sorrow and worry, and I sense things that other people don't. It is as plain as the nose on your face, to those who have the gift. I'm only telling you this to put your mind at rest, and to prove that I'm not a fraud; that there are more things between heaven and earth that most people can't relate to. My lips are sealed, and your secrets are safe with me.' Ivy squeezed Lucy's hand and wiped a tear away from her cheek. 'Now you make your life with Adam, because that is where your path lies, of that I'm certain.'

'I'm sorry I implied that you were a fraud. I know better now. Nobody else knows my secrets, so you must have hidden powers and depths that are special.' Lucy wiped her eyes and looked at Ivy.

'Not special, just blessed. Now, you enjoy your life, because it is going to be a full and good one.' Ivy squeezed Lucy's hand again, before leaving for the door and her journey back to Kendal. 'Look after my Adam for me,' she yelled as she stepped up into the donkey-cart next to him and Lucy watched from the doorway.

'I will, of that you can be sure. Take care on your return journey,' Lucy yelled back. She'd a lot to thank Ivy Thwaite for, she thought, as she went back into the house and looked around her. A shiver went down her spine. What else had Ivy been able to tell about her, simply by a touch? She must know that her love for Adam was true, else she wouldn't entrust her with his love. She didn't know how, but Ivy definitely knew things that no one else did, and that worried Lucy slightly. Would she, as promised, keep her secrets or would she tell Adam? And, if so, would Adam still want anything to do with her?

Lucy still couldn't believe that her life was going to be as she had always wanted, from first realizing that Adam was the man for her. Surely something would go wrong. It always did, no matter how hard she tried to follow her own path in life.

'I tell you, Father, you are going to have to have words with our Lucy when she returns home this evening. She's up to no good with that Adam Brooksbank. He'll not give a damn about her. She's just his maid – something he can use for his own pleasure. Susie's been telling me that she heard Lucy saying his name over and over again

283

last night. The lass needs to come to her senses, and be told that men like that simply use young lasses.' Dorothy stood angrily next to her husband as he sat down, hoping for peace and quiet after a hard day's work at the tannery. But she was in no mood for her husband to be laid-back about the love affair that she had now realized was developing between Lucy and her employer.

'Aye, Mother, I think you are jumping to conclusions. Lucy's only fantasizing – it's what young lasses do. Besides, there's many a worse man for her to set her cap at. At least he owns his own farm, although he's perhaps a bit older than her. I think he's a decent sort.' Bill looked at the anger on his wife's face and saw that his words had antagonized her even more.

'He'll be using her. It'll be a different tale from you, when Lucy comes back home and tells you she's having his baby, and that he wants nowt to do with her. Because, mark my words, that's what will happen, Bill Bancroft. As soon as I saw him, I thought: Aye, you might think yourself a toff of a farmer, but keep yourself to yourself, when it comes to my lass.' Dorothy folded her arms and swore under her breath when Bill didn't reply. 'You say something to Lucy tonight, as soon as she steps through the door. She won't listen to me, but she will to you.'

'For God's sake, woman, can a man get no peace in this house? I've just finished work, I stink to high heaven and I'm bloody well hungry, and all you are bothered about is our bloody Lucy and a fella. I'll have a swill, feed my belly and then I'll talk to her. Now, hold your noise, and make sure the water for my wash is hot, and

284

I'll see what Lucy says after supper. I don't mind the man; he seems alright to me. Are sure you are not against him because you've got your head set on her marrying somebody with more brass?' Bill took his jerkin off and hung it at the back door, then watched as his wife filled the pot-sink with hot water from the kettle and placed a clean towel and a block of carbolic soap out for him to wash with.

'Money's nowt to do with it. Folk will talk. He's been wed before, and she's his maid. Lord only knows what they will be getting up to in that house, all on their own, every day.' Dorothy watched her husband as he stripped to the waist and lathered the soap and water.

'I'll speak to her after supper. But until then, give me a bit of peace. Not that it's likely in this house.' Bill glared at his wife, as Bert started wailing and the noise of his two sons fighting with one another in their bedrooms could be heard from above. 'Bloody young 'uns! I wish we'd never been blessed – they are nowt but bother,' he groaned.

'Now, just think on what you are saying. We are blessed, and Lord knows we've suffered enough losses. So step up and look after the ones we have, Bill Bancroft, else the devil must take you.' Dorothy went and picked up the bawling baby and scowled at Bill. He was a devil for getting out of his fatherly commitments, but this time she needed his support.

Lucy put her head on Adam's shoulder and enjoyed every second of having his arms wrapped around her, as she kissed him goodnight in the doorway of Black Moss. 'I wish I could be with you tomorrow, and that I never had to leave your side,' she whispered as he kissed her gently.

'It will soon be Monday. And besides, your family will need you. Your mother's got her hands full, with all your siblings in that small house. I'm not going anywhere, and now that we know how we both feel about each other, there will no longer be any need to be coy about our feelings. Bless Ivy, for making us face the truth. We would still have been fooling one another, if she had not stepped in.' Adam kissed Lucy's forehead.

'I know. And there was me, feeling jealous of her. I thought she was going to steal you from under my nose, and that I daren't say anything about how I felt.' Lucy held Adam close and buried her head in the warm, comforting smell of his jacket. 'I'd better go. It's getting late, and I don't want to make Mother and Father suspicious of my lateness in returning home.'

'We will have to tell your parents how we feel shortly. It wouldn't be fair not to do so. They might not approve, with me being married once before – and being your employer.' Adam tilted Lucy's head up and kissed her on the lips.

'They will have to, because I know that I will always love you. I've known it for weeks, but have never dared say so. My parents will not come between us – we can't let them. Not now, when we both know how we feel about one another.' Lucy looked up into Adam's eyes; she'd dreamed of this moment for so long, and she wasn't ever going to let it slip away.

'We will see. Let's give ourselves a bit more time to make certain of one another's feelings, then I will speak with them both. Make it clear that we are right for one another, and that my intentions are honourable. Now go, else they will be worrying about you.' Adam released Lucy from his arms and watched as she blew him a kiss on leaving the farmyard. He knew that in his heart there was still a place for his late wife Mary, but Lucy had already filled the empty space that had been left upon her death. It would, as Ivy had predicted, be only a matter of time before he asked Lucy to become his wife.

Lucy sat at the kitchen table and looked across at her mother. Something was wrong. Both her brothers had been banished from the room they sat in, and Bert and Susie were in their beds far sooner than usual, as the sun had not yet set. Her father looked at her from his chair near the fire and shook his head, as her mother spoke up.

'Your father's got something to say to you. And we want the truth, young lady, so don't give us any flannel,' Dorothy said sharply and looked at her daughter, as Lucy squirmed in her seat, waiting to find out what was to be asked of her.

'Aye, lass, I've had nothing but earache from your mother. She says she thinks that Adam Brooksbank is having his way with you, and that you are daft enough to let him. She thinks it's not proper, and that it'll only end up in shame.' Bill looked sternly at his daughter.

'It's not only me – you think the same, Bill. Now tell her that if it's true, she doesn't go back there. I'm not

287

having her carrying on with a man like him. He's her employer, and I've heard folk gossiping about him, saying that he thought more of his job as a peeler than he did of his first wife. It just shows what sort of man he is. I've kept that to myself until now, but it'll not hurt for the truth to come out.' Dorothy crossed her arms and looked at Bill and then at Lucy, her face stern and set.

Lucy said nothing, but she was filled with anger and annoyance at them, for not trusting her and Adam.

'Are you listening to your mother? If it's right, what she thinks, then we don't want you to work for him no more. And you'll have to make yourself useful around the house or find some work in Keighley. I know it was me who got you the job, but I didn't foresee this happening.' Bill looked at his daughter and saw that her eyes were filled with tears, but at the same time Lucy looked defiant.

'You don't trust me or him – you never will. Well, it is right: I do love Adam and he loves me. You can go and ask him yourself, because he is a gentleman and is thoughtful and loving, and he would never take advantage of me. And I'd rather be living with him – wed or unwedded – than living here in this stinking hovel, where I'm just used.' Lucy spat out the words, not worrying that they hurt the parents she loved and had always cared for. Adam was her world, her future, and she didn't care if they knew it now. No one was going to stop her from seeing him.

'You are talking rubbish, lass. What would he want with a slip of a lass like you? Your mother's right: you'll not be going back and working for him. I'm not having you trailing back here carrying his baby, because that'll be what happens.' Bill looked across at Dorothy, who was beside herself at Lucy's admission of love.

'He's not like that. Adam's never touched me in that way. He's not like you, always getting my mother with child and then burying them in the lime pit. That'll not happen to me or mine. You think I don't know about the babies that over the years have been buried there. And it wasn't only me; Thomas Farrington knew, but he can't say owt, now he's dead. You'll not stop me from seeing Adam and working for him, else I'll tell someone everything I know,' Lucy raged. How dare they think her so low as to lift her skirts up that easily. She loved her Adam, and that would only happen when she was wed to him.

'Get your bloody self to bed, madam, and don't show your face to us until you've thought about what you've said. By God, our Lucy, you've a fearful tongue on you. One that's hurt your mother. I never thought you could turn on your parents like that. Your mother and I were heartbroken over the babies we lost, but they didn't deserve a Christian burial because they were not born right. But for you to throw it in our faces, like you have done tonight, just for the sake of fighting for a fella that'll no more love you than look at you – I don't know if we will ever forgive you. If you were younger, I'd take my belt to you. As it is, get up the stairs out of my sight and your mother's.' Bill stood up, shaking with anger, and looked at Dorothy, who sat sobbing and shaking. 'Bugger off – get out of my sight, before I think better of giving your hide a good tanning.'

Lucy pushed back her chair, making it clatter and fall on the hard stone flags of the kitchen floor. Tears overcame her and she sobbed as she ran up to the safety of her bedroom, flinging herself onto her bed and crying into her pillow. She tried to muffle the noise of her grief, as Susie stirred in her bed. She must not wake her up, else she'd be in for another barrage of words from her parents. But she hurt, she hurt so badly. She had to be allowed to see her Adam; she loved him and she was not about to lose him. However, she knew that the words she had said in anger had hurt her mother the most, and she shouldn't have said them. It had been mean and cruel, and she shouldn't have lowered herself to coming out with such words.

Lucy closed her eyes and sobbed. The happiness that she had felt a few hours ago had disappeared, and now she was mortified and beside herself with shame, and with the knowledge that she would probably not be allowed back to Black Moss Farm again. Would Adam realize what had happened and come and look for her, or should she run away to him and defy her parents? She only knew that she couldn't live without him in her life, and that she had to be near him.

24

'Just listen to her, Bill, she's still crying,' Dorothy whispered and listened through the bedroom wall to the sobs that had been heard all night. Susie lay between the couple, after being woken by her big sister's grief, and stirred gently as Bill replied.

'So she bloody should be. Coming out with what she did, and threatening to tell everyone our business if we don't do as she wants. I've a good mind to go in and give her a good belting.' Bill looked up at the ceiling. 'That bloody Thomas Farrington was always creeping about the yard, knowing everybody's business, and Lucy's right when she says he's best dead.'

'It came out in anger, Bill, she didn't mean it. We've all said something we didn't mean, when roused. She was only fighting her corner. Perhaps Lucy does love Adam Brooksbank, but does he love her? I can't see it myself; she'll have read it wrong, and she's only young yet. It's best she has no more to do with him, although it sounds as if she is heartbroken. But he's not right for her, and she should have nothing to do with him.' Dorothy sighed; she was regretting saying anything about the matter now, as she lay listening to the sobs from the other side of the bedroom wall.

'Aye, well, I'll settle the matter this morning. It's Sunday, so I'll have a walk up that way and talk to him. Tell him that Lucy seems to have feelings for him and that she'll no longer be working for him. It'll be for the best.' Bill turned and looked at Susie, who was still fast asleep between them and appeared angelic. 'I wish children stopped at this size; they are nowt but worry as they grow older,' he muttered.

'They are always a worry, no matter what age they are, but usually I don't tell you the half of it.' Dorothy turned and looked at Bill. She remembered when she had told her mother and father that she had met the man she was going to marry, and their reaction to the news: that Bill Bancroft had not been good enough for her; that they'd hoped for better than the son of the local tanner. Listening now to the sobs of her daughter, she thought perhaps she shouldn't have said anything. That she should have let true love run its course, because she too remembered words said in anger, and the hurt that her parents had caused, when she was denied seeing the man that she eventually wed. Their words had only strengthened her resolve to be with Bill. And now here she was, still married to him twenty-one years on, and with children around her feet and not much money to their names. But she did love her Bill, despite his moods and his love of a gill. Perhaps she should have said nothing. But like any good mother, she just wanted the best for her daughter, and she thought that was not Adam Brooksbank.

Bill Bancroft strode out along the lane leading to Black Moss. He didn't know exactly how he was going to approach the subject of his daughter being besotted by Adam, but the more he thought about it, the more he became sure that it was all Lucy's doing. She was young and she knew she was attractive, and she got these fanciful ideas over fellas. Unfortunately, she had set her sights on Adam, whether he knew it or not. Despite telling Dorothy and himself that Adam said he loved her, it was all in Lucy's head, and the best thing for her to do was leave his employment and find somebody her own age and, hopefully, better prospects. After all, Adam Brooksbank was a small-time farmer, living off a few acres that his father had left him. Although he looked like a gentleman, he didn't own that much land, and Bill thought he'd never amount to much. A father wanted better for his daughter – particularly the daughter who had always been special to him.

Bill stood in the farmhouse doorway and looked quickly around him. The yard was tidy and well kept, with hens strutting and clucking around the few weeds that grew there, and the kitchen garden was weeded and full of vegetables. Adam Brooksbank was a tidy farmer, he'd give him that much; and the old farmhouse looked as if a lot of care had been put into it since his arrival. It was a pity that he had come with the news he had. But it was better for all if the man knew where he stood, when it came to Lucy's supposed love for him. Bill picked up his Sunday walking stick, tapped on the closed door with the handle and waited.

The door opened and Adam stood before him. He was in his shirt sleeves and looked surprised to see his visitor standing there on his doorstep.

'Good morning. I wasn't expecting visitors, with it being Sunday. Let me put my jacket on.' Adam looked at Bill and wondered why he was calling so early on a Sunday morning. He left the door open and reached for his jacket, feeling as if he was half-dressed in front of the man who had obviously made an effort that morning and was in his Sunday best.

'Nay, you needn't stand on ceremony for me.' Bill walked in behind Adam and looked around him. 'I'll not be stopping long. I'll say what I've got to, and then I'll be on my way.'

'You'll sit down surely and join me in a pot of tea. I've just brewed it and it's a good Darjeeling, which I treated myself to on my visit into Keighley when I dropped my visitor off.' Adam smiled and offered Bill a cup from the dresser, then waved for him to sit down. 'Everything's alright, I take it? Lucy is not ill or any-thing?'

Bill sat down, with his hands balanced on the top of his walking stick, and looked at Adam and his fancy tea and best china. He shook his head as he was offered a newly brewed cup of a tea that he had never heard of.

294

'Well, you could say that. You could class it as an illness – women get these funny dos, and they are hard to explain.' Bill gazed around the room. It was spotless and lovingly kept and, looking at the ornaments and furniture, it suddenly dawned on him that although he knew Adam Brooksbank to dress as a gent, he might also be worth a bob or two. 'My missus thinks it's best that Lucy doesn't work for you no more, because our Lucy has got it into her head that she thinks a lot of you – perhaps a little too much. It's not being right, seeing as she is your maid. She even thinks that you feel the same way about her, although we've tried to tell her she's probably dreaming.'

Bill looked across at Adam and gazed around the room again. It was full of good-quality furniture and was not what he'd been expecting. He was even more concerned that he was probably making a mistake in thinking Adam Brooksbank was just another farmer, rather than in saving the virginity of his daughter.

'But she's right, Mr Brooksbank. I do care deeply for Lucy. In fact I'd go as far as to say that I love her.' Adam sighed. 'It's taken a dear friend of mine to make me realize it. But Lucy and I have grown close, over the last months that she has worked for me. I owe her my life, and I will always be beholden to her for that. However, it's more than that; she brightens up my life and makes me feel young again, and I do feel for her with all my heart. But I know how it must look – after all, as you say, she's my maid. You must be thinking the worst of me. But believe me, my intentions are honourable. I'd never

295

do anything to hurt Lucy or take advantage of her, in the position she is in.' Adam looked at Bill Bancroft, who sat taking into consideration what he had said. He had not felt so awkward for a long time. His confession of his love for Lucy was not made lightly, and he tried to remain calm at the thought of Lucy's parent forbidding her to see him again.

'Aye, that will sit badly with her mother. She thinks the worst, you see, only seeing you taking advantage of our lass. You hear it so often, with these maids who go into service and are taken advantage of and then cast aside. She'll not believe that you think that much of Lucy. I must admit that I myself am not happy with the situation, and if you don't mind me saying, we had set the bar high for the man who was to marry our lass. She's a bonny one and turns many a man's eye. She could have the pick of the valley, if she played her cards right.' Bill shook his head. He was uneasy with the situation, and although it seemed that Lucy had told them the truth about the love that she and Adam had for one another, it still did not make it right.

'But would she be happy with anyone else? I might be slightly older than Lucy, but that makes me wiser. And perhaps I'm not a wealthy quarry owner or have huge estates, but I do love her and I will respect her, which is more than some of those young bucks that drink in The Fleece would do.' Adam said quietly as he watched Bill thinking it all through. 'I don't want to lose her as my maid, or as the love in my life. What if I was to say that I'd like to marry her and make her my wife? We have only just declared our love for one another, but if that would put both your minds at rest, then that is what I will do, for I know our love for one another is true.'

'Now happen you are being hasty man, and are as light in the head as our Lucy. You might wake up in the morning and regret every word you've said. I didn't come here today to wed her off to you. Just to tell you that she'd no longer be in your service.' Bill glanced across at the man, who obviously loved his daughter as much as she loved him.

'I'll not regret my words. I know Lucy will mean everything to me until my dying day. It's simply taken me this long to summon up the courage to say it. I've already lost a wife that I held dear, through my own pride in wearing my police uniform, but I'm not going to let myself lose Lucy. She's right: I do love her and always will do.' Adam bowed his head.

'Then I'd better walk back down and tell my other half what we have said this morning. It'll not please her, I expect. However, I can tell that you are a good man. You've looked after our lass well these last few months – perhaps a little too well, seeing as we are in this situation now. I've heard Archie Robinson talking highly of you, and he tells everyone what a good employer you are, and that you only show kindness towards him. You put me to shame, by the sound of it. I have to keep a firm grip on the motley lot that work for me in the flay-pits.' Bill rose from his seat and looked across at Adam. 'I never thought I'd come here and then go back and tell my old woman that you want to wed our lass. It's a shock to me, let alone to her. I'll not say anything in front of our Lucy, and then if you do happen to have a change of heart, she'll not be hurt even more. We both love her, and we only want the best for her.'

'So do I, Mr Bancroft, so do I. And I understand your concerns. However, love has no boundaries, and we can't stop the way we feel for one another.' Adam rose from his seat and accidentally knocked off the table the advertisement for the sale of High Ground, the Baxters' reclaimed farm, which he had been reading.

Bill bent down and picked it up, glancing at it as he handed it back to Adam. 'Are you interested in buying this place? Have you enough brass? It'll fetch a pretty penny, seeing as the courts are selling it.' He held out the leaflet in his shaking hand for Adam to take.

'Yes, I placed my bid yesterday – it's for sale by tender. The magistrate's dealing with it. I hope to secure it, for the land really. It would more than double my acreage, making this one of the best farms in the district. The house I'd be looking to let. I'd be staying here, this is my family home after all, and now that I've spent some time and money on it, I won't be leaving it.' Adam placed the leaflet on the table and opened the door for Bill to leave.

'My old lass always admired that house. It's set in the sunshine, not like where we are now. The houses on Providence Row are in a terrible state and aren't worth wasting any brass on, as they are all subsiding. It's only a matter of time and they'll start to crumble. It's a pity them bastards owned High Ground. Anyway, they got their just deserts and are all rotting in the cells now. I'll

298

go home and tell her what you've said, but I wouldn't hold your breath on seeing our Lucy in the morning. Once my Dorothy has got something into her head, it'll take the devil to make her change her mind, and our Lucy will have to do as her mother tells her. I've nowt against you. I think she'd be happy with you, and that's all I want for my lass in her life. It's her mother you'll have to convince.' Bill slapped Adam on his arm and then stepped out across the yard, ready to deliver the news that the situation was a little more serious than both he and Dorothy had realized.

Adam sat back down in his chair. He played with the poster for the farm sale in his hands and thought of Lucy. He should have gone down to the flay-pits and declared his intentions to her parents as soon as they realized how they felt about one another. She must have let her feelings be known to her mother, and now obviously Dorothy was worried about her daughter's reputation. Lord, he'd not awoken that morning with the intention of asking Bill Bancroft for his daughter's hand in marriage, not quite yet. He would have preferred to have taken his time and courted Lucy for longer, to stop any gossiping tongues from wagging and coming to the wrong conclusion about such a quick marriage. Ivy was right; she'd told him he'd be wed by winter, but he'd just laughed and told her not to talk so simple, although in his mind he had been thinking about it. Ivy might be proved wrong, anyway, if he couldn't convince Lucy's mother that he was serious, and that he did love Lucy and was not simply a letch who lusted over her. He only hoped that after talking straight to Bill Bancroft, Lucy would return to him in the morning as usual. If not, then he'd pay the flay-pits and the Bancroft family a visit, because he had to see his Lucy and reassure her parents once again that their daughter was to become his wife, whether they liked it or not.

Lucy had moped about the house all day. Her mother had been curt to her in conversation and had asked her to do several chores that were never expected to be done on a Sunday, as it was a day of rest. Her father had disappeared straight after his breakfast, saying that he was going for a stroll, which he did most Sunday mornings, so it was not out of character. But it had meant that she'd been left with her mother and younger siblings, with her older brothers leaving the house to wander the fields in the warm sunshine, sensing that there was tension in the usually happy home.

She sat on a stool with the front door wide open to her in the sharp summer light, as she darned the numerous pairs of socks and stockings that her mother had passed her way. Every so often Lucy wiped a tear away from her cheek and sniffed, thinking that she would never be able to see Adam again.

'Your face will stay like that, if the wind changes,' her mother said as she watched Lucy trying to concentrate on the job in hand.

'I don't care. I won't care what I look like, if you don't let me see Adam again,' Lucy wailed.

'Oh, Lucy, hold your noise. It's only for the best. We

are thinking of you – we don't want you to waste your life on somebody who's no good for you. I can tell you are upset, but you shouldn't let these fanciful notions get the better of you. He'll not think anything of you, lass, he'll just be stringing you along.' Dorothy rubbed her hand along her daughter's shoulders and felt her shaking, as she sobbed yet again. It wasn't like Lucy to be so upset; she was a fighter and always stood her ground. 'I'm only saying that you must finish working for him because I love you, and I don't want to see you hurt.' Dorothy sighed and looked towards Susie, who was playing with baby Bert with a pile of clothes pegs.

'How can somebody who loves me hurt me so? You are only saying that to keep me at home, to do some work for you. No matter who I meet, they'll never be right for you or my father,' Lucy moaned and then sobbed again.

'But Adam Brooksbank won't love you – he'll just be saying that. They'll tell you anything, Lucy, to have their wicked way with you, these men.' Dorothy wanted to hug Lucy and tell her how much she loved her, but knew that her hugs would not be appreciated by her heart-broken daughter.

'You are wrong, Mother. Adam does love me and he needs me. You've got to let me go and see him in the morning, and then he can explain.' Lucy sobbed and looked up at her mother.

'You are not going. Your father's gone to tell him that you'll not be working for him any longer, and then he's going for a gill at The Fleece. You can find work elsewhere.

Your father will take you into Keighley on Tuesday. The sooner you get out of that man's clutches, the better. He's not worth owt, Lucy, and I expect he's stringing you along. Now that's the last I want to hear about it.' Dorothy looked sternly at her daughter; the usual quiet Sunday was not to be ruined with her crying and carrying on, and Bill sinking his sorrows in The Fleece rather than face the world. How come it was always her that sorted the family problems, and was made out to be the bad one of the pair of them? Adam Brooksbank, in her eyes, was not a suitable match for her precious daughter, who needed to marry someone with money, and someone who would care for her.

Lucy knew better than to say anything to her father when he returned from The Fleece the worse for drink. Usually he was a quiet soul, but after one too many his mood changed and he was best left alone. She watched through the kitchen window as he staggered into the flay-pit yard, mumbling and cursing at the state of things around him, before entering the house.

'Get yourself up those stairs and make yourself scarce. Take Susie and the lads with you. It's best they don't see or hear their father in this state,' Dorothy whispered to Lucy and the rest of her family, as Bill opened the kitchen door wide and swore loudly.

'Well, I'm bloody well back to this stinking hole. Not that one of you will care.' He slurred his words and staggered across the polished flagstone kitchen floor, then slumped down in his usual chair.

'Hold your noise, Bill. You'll frighten the children,'

Dorothy lectured, staring at the man who had walked out of her house early that morning looking quite respectable, and comparing him now with the dribbling, swearing wreck he had come back as.

'Aye, we mustn't upset the children – not the children. They are precious, unlike me,' Bill growled.

'Oh, hold your noise, and stop showing this self-pity. Did you see him – did you tell that Brooksbank our Lucy will not be working for him any more?' Dorothy shook Bill by the shoulder as he sprawled in front of her, wanting to sleep now that he was home and in front of his own hearth.

Lucy listened from the safety of the bend in the stairs, while the rest of her family stayed in their rooms. It was only once in a blue moon that their father was in this state, but they knew better than to get in his way. She held her breath as he mumbled and swore under his breath, not coherent enough for either her or her mother to hear.

'Bill, tell me again! What did he say?' Dorothy shook his shoulder.

'Bloody well leave me be, woman,' Bill growled. 'I said: he said he loved Lucy, and the stupid bastard wants to marry her! Now bugger off, or get me to my bed.' Bill dropped his head, splayed out his legs and closed his eyes; all he wanted was some peace. He'd tell his nagging wife the rest of the tale in the morning, when his head was clearer and the drink had stopped him feeling so sleepy.

Dorothy stood back and looked at her sozzled husband.

She was not going to get any more sense out of him tonight. She looked down at him and whispered to herself, 'He wants to marry our Lucy' and put her hand to her mouth to stifle a gasp. Adam Brooksbank thought that much of her daughter that he wanted to marry her! Now what was she going to do? She hadn't expected that; she thought it had just been a fascination on Lucy's part. This so-called love affair was more serious than she had thought, and the man should have more sense than to lust after a young slip of a girl. There was one thing for sure: Lucy would not be working for him in the morning, not while she had a breath in her body.

Lucy sat back on the stairs and gasped, as she tried to hold back tears of joy this time. She couldn't believe that Adam had said that to her father. That he had declared his love for her, and had even said he had designs on marriage. She too knew that their love was true, but marriage! That was a huge show of Adam's devotion to her and she hadn't expected it so soon. Even though in her dreams she had whispered of being Mrs Adam Brooksbank, she had not thought it possible, for she was just his maid and, until the last day or two, they had not dared show their love for one another.

She listened as her father snored in front of the fire and her mother sat in her rocking chair, the sound of the runners gently hitting the stone floor, as she no doubt pondered the news that Bill had brought home with him. In the morning Lucy would be told by her mother what her thoughts on the subject were, and that would determine whether she could go to Black Moss to work, and to face Adam. Until then she would go to her bed, warm and content in the knowledge that he did love her, and that his intentions were honourable. And if she was allowed to marry Adam, she would be the happiest woman in the world.

25

Bill had eventually got himself to bed in the early hours of the morning, lying down next to Dorothy, who was still awake and fretting.

'Your feet are frozen and you smell like a brewery. I don't know why you get into such a state,' Dorothy lectured him as he climbed out of bed to relieve himself in the chamberpot.

'You know why – it's that bloody lass of ours. Not now, let me get some proper sleep. It'll soon be light and I'll have to see to the fellas out in the yard. My head hurts enough, without you yattering on about things now.' Bill grunted and pulled the sheets and patchwork quilt up to his chin, as Dorothy paid no heed to his request.

'So Adam Brooksbank said he loves Lucy and wants to marry her? That's all very well, but he's not the richest man in the valley. Our Lucy could do so much better; she could have any man she wanted, if she did but know it.

I'm against it, Bill. She'll not be going to work for him this morning. Both of them need to come to their senses.'

Dorothy looked up at the crack that was lengthening on the bedroom ceiling and thought about her own lot in life. She had wanted so much more when younger, but then children had come along and, with them, a lack of money; life was hard, and that was not what she wanted for any of her children. She wanted more for her two girls – especially Lucy who, with her startling good looks, caught many a wealthy man's eye, and them a lot younger than Adam Brooksbank.

'He might not be the youngest, but he's got brass,' Bill mumbled. 'I always thought he dressed posh, but I never thought he had that much money. He's thinking of trying to buy High Ground off the courts. She could do worse.' He closed his eyes.

'He's got money! I had him down as simply inheriting his father's farm and having nowt,' Dorothy said, with her eyes still focused on the state of the ceiling. Of late, she'd noticed a few cracks beginning to show on the walls of their home, and it was causing her another worry.

'Aye, now hold your noise and go to sleep. We'll talk about it in the morning.' Bill pulled on the bedcovers and turned his back on his wife. All he wanted was to sleep. He'd no concerns over Adam Brooksbank marrying his lass. In fact, from what he'd seen and from what the landlord in The Fleece had told him, Adam was a gentleman, and Lucy could do no better than to wed him.

*

'I've told our Lucy that she'll not be going to work at Black Moss this morning – or any morning, if I have my way. She's gone back up to her bedroom and is balling her eyes out and calling me all the names under the sun.' Dorothy thrust a cup of tea under Bill's nose and glowered at him. 'Don't look at me like that. I'm still not happy with the state of affairs. And as for you, I've no sympathy for you; you shouldn't have drunk so much. Look at the state of you.' She shook her head at her dishevelled husband. 'You'd better square yourself up, before you go and tell those men out there the business for the day.'

'It's not just me that needs to square up. You want to do the same yourself. I told you last night that Adam Brooksbank is a wealthy and good man. What I didn't tell you was what Ernest Shepherd said about him.' Bill took a long drink of his tea and looked at the annoyed face of his wife. 'After Thomas Farrington's untimely death, Adam Brooksbank gave the local peelers his account of how the death had been accidental, and Ernest Shepherd happened to comment that he'd been glad Adam had been there to give evidence, else it could have been a little awkward. Anyway, during the course of the conversation it turned out that the peelers all knew Adam, because he was once one of them, but, as you already know, left the force when his wife died tragically. But they were even more willing to accept his account of what happened because of his service in the Crimea. Adam Brooksbank was awarded the Victoria Cross, Dot – the highest medal anyone can receive!

He saved a lot of his regiment at Sebastopol from certain death, and put his own life at risk, after holding back an attack on his company on his own. That's how he's got his limp. Now, if someone who holds the Victoria Cross and has money and his own land is not enough for you, I don't know who is?' Bill looked at the dismay on Dorothy's face. 'You should be proud that our lass has fallen for such a good man.'

'Well, how was I supposed to know? Lucy's never said anything, and he's not made it known to us. The Victoria Cross – the Queen doesn't give them away for nothing! He must have been brave. That still doesn't make him any better, though.' Dorothy looked at Bill. She didn't want to admit that this time she was in the wrong.

'Dorothy, he's a decent man, and he doesn't brag about what he's done – and God knows, he should. You let our Lucy court him, and be right with them both.' Bill looked sternly at his wife. 'Give her a yell. Tell her to go and see to him, and give her your blessing. She's got herself a good one.' Bill got up from his chair and looked at his wife. 'You can't keep her at home forever. Let Lucy make her own way in life.' He went over and kissed Dorothy on the cheek. 'She's got a good man, so be thankful for that.'

'She's still my baby. I just want the best for her.' Dorothy hung her head.

'Well, you'll not go far wrong with Adam Brooksbank. Now shout her down here, and let her be away to him. I heard her sobbing this morning as I got up, and she'll make herself ill if she carries on like that.' Bill smiled at his wife. 'She'll be alright with him, so don't you worry.'

Dorothy went to the bottom of the stairs and yelled for Lucy to come down and join them. She listened as her daughter came out of her bedroom and, still sobbing, made her way down the stairs, to what she must have thought would be yet another lecture about herself and Adam. Her eyes were red and swollen as she stood demurely in front of her parents.

'Your father says I've to let you be; that you must go and see to him and that I should hold my noise and give you both my blessing.' Dorothy stood in front of Lucy. 'He says that Adam Brooksbank's an honourable man; in fact a hero, from what he's heard. That might not make him the right fella for you, but your father says he's to be made welcome into our family, so I'll not stand in his way.' Dorothy looked at her daughter, as the sobbing stopped and a broad smile came across her face.

'Oh, Father, thank you. Adam does love me, and I love him. He doesn't mean any harm to me. He's kind and gentle, and shows only the greatest respect towards me.' Lucy beamed. 'What do you mean by a hero? What have you been told?' She gathered her thoughts and looked at her father.

'He holds the Victoria Cross, lass – he's a brave man. The Queen will have given him that, and he's highly thought of by everyone that knows him.' Bill looked at the pride showing on Lucy's face.

'He's never said anything to me; he's not like that. He doesn't talk much about fighting in the Crimea, but he does talk about his wife, who he lost tragically.' Lucy spoke softly.

'Perhaps he doesn't like the memories of what happened out there. You often find that soldiers don't talk about the wars they fought in: too many bad memories, the poor buggers. Now, get yourself gone to him. He'll be wondering where you've got to, and will think we've stopped you from seeing him.' Bill looked at the joy on his daughter's face as Lucy glanced at herself in the mirror and then back at both her parents.

'Go on – get yourself gone. I'll be right with him. And, by the sounds of it, we've a wedding to be planning, although perhaps not just yet. Best if he takes his time courting you and makes it look more respectable.' Dorothy smiled wanly at her daughter.

'I love you, Mother, and you'll not regret giving us your blessing.' Lucy rushed forward and hugged her mother, then kissed her father on the cheek, before grabbing her bonnet from behind the kitchen door and flying out to go and tell Adam her news. She couldn't wait to see him, and with every step on the path to Black Moss her heart grew lighter, knowing that she had the man of her dreams waiting at the other end of the path for her.

'I didn't think I was ever going to see you again.' Adam beamed as he watched Lucy enter the farmhouse. He met her with open arms and embraced her tightly, looking down into her eyes as he stepped back from kissing her.

'You've my father to thank, as he made my mother see sense. That and the fact that he found out about your

311

secret.' Lucy smiled. She loved Adam for what he was, and the medal awarded to him did not mean much to her, other than that she was proud of him.

'My secret?' Adam looked puzzled.

'Yes, Father found out last night that you had been awarded the Victoria Cross for bravery, and that finally swayed my mother's views on you.' Lucy buried her head in Adam's shoulder and held him tightly.

'Oh, so folk around here know. I was trying hard to forget, and every time I look at the blasted medal it reminds me of the lives that were lost, and the pain and misery my fellow colleagues went through. It's still in its presentation box in the chest of drawers in my bedroom. I have no intention of ever wearing it, or celebrating the fact that I was awarded it. There were much braver people than me on the battleground. I was lucky and survived; or perhaps not so lucky, with the dreams and memories I find myself having sometimes.' Adam stood back from Lucy. 'It makes me no different from any other man, and your mother should realize that.'

'I'm not bothered what medals you have, how much money you have – all the things I heard my mother and father discussing as I lay on my bed, crying and thinking I might never be allowed to see you again. I love you for who you are, and I will always love you. I think I've known that from the first day we met,' Lucy said with feeling.

'Then we will be wed, because I feel the same way about you, and I have not felt this way about a woman for a long time. Just as long as you know that I'm not perfect; I have my flaws. I take laudanum for my pain, both physical and mental, and sometimes I cannot lift the mood that I find myself in. It's a weakness I wish I didn't have, but it helps me forget sometimes. But I will always love you and provide for you well – there is no doubting that.' Adam looked down at Lucy and saw that she loved him, despite his addiction.

'I don't care that you take laudanum. And besides, with time, I might ease your memories and fears and you may not be so dependent on it. I love you, Adam Brooksbank – flaws and all – and I am only too happy to become your wife.'

'Then I will go and speak to your mother and father, and we will both visit the parson at Haworth and arrange a date for our marriage, if you are in agreement for us to be married there. I have a great fondness for the parson, and he has always been there for me when I've needed him, and I'd like us to wed at Haworth.'

'Yes, of course, that would be more than suitable.' Lucy shook her head. 'I just can't believe this is happening to me. I'd kept my love to myself for so long.'

'Well, it is, my love. Now today I have to go into Keighley to see if my bid for the Baxters' farm has been accepted. I won't be away long, and I hope to come back with the good news that my farm has doubled in size. I would rather have bought the land and house under better circumstances, but I wasn't going to miss the opportunity to clear my neighbouring land of the Baxters forever.' Adam smiled and kissed Lucy on her brow.

'I didn't know you were thinking of buying their land

until I overheard my father telling my mother. It will make a difference to your workload – are you sure you will be able to cope?' Lucy looked across at Adam as he went into the far room, which was hardly ever used, but where the desk containing his cheque book and savings were kept.

Adam returned and smiled. 'Yes, I will manage, although I might pinch Archie completely from your father's employment. I'm sure he would rather be farming than working at the flay-pits. But, I haven't secured the property yet. I'm sure there will be more than just my interest in the land and house. It will depend on how much everyone else bid for the property. It would benefit me – or should I say "us" – the most, so I'm hoping that my offer has been successful. '

'I hope you come back with a smile on your face, after securing what you want.' Lucy watched as Adam stopped in the doorway, before setting off to ride Rosa into Keighley to see the magistrate.

'I've secured the one thing I wanted most, when you walked in through the door this morning. The land and house at High Ground I can live without – unlike having you in my life. If I'm successful, I will be happy, but I think I am already more than blessed this morning.'

Lucy watched as Adam rode down the hillside towards Keighley, before she returned into the kitchen. There she sat down in the chair and looked around her. She breathed in deeply and smiled. In a few months, or perhaps even weeks, this would be her home, and she would no longer be the maid. She would be Adam's wife, and the house would be her domain. Her days at the flay-pits would be at an end, and she would always be smelling the clear moorland air of Black Moss. Her wedding day could not come soon enough for her liking.

Adam stood outside the magistrate's chamber and looked at the deeds in his hand. He'd been one of only a few to bid for the Baxters' confiscated assets, with the money generated by the sale going back into the coffers of the Crown, to replace the counterfeit coinage that old man Baxter had been issuing. It was the Baxters' loss, but Adam's gain, and although it had made his bank balance a whole load lighter, he was happy with his new assets.

His life was changing for the better. He now had a good large farm, and he also had the heart of a young woman whom he would always love and cherish. He looked up towards the spired tower of St Andrew's. He had one more thing to do before he returned home, and that was to visit the grave of his beloved Mary, at rest in Haworth churchyard. To go and seek her blessing to get on with his life, and hope that she would understand his needs, in whichever world she was now. It was time to put the past behind him and look to the future.

26

'Bill, I swear these cracks are getting bigger.' Dorothy stood with her hands on her hips and looked up at their bedroom ceiling. 'And have you noticed the one running up the front of the house? You can nearly put your hand in it, in parts.'

Bill moaned and looked up. 'Aye, I think you are right. Kenny Lawson and Jim Willan was at me the other day about the state of their houses, and I noticed the same in Thomas Farrington's old house when I went to look round it yesterday. The whole row seems to be crumbling.'

'It had better not crumble on our heads. Don't you think you should get somebody to look at what's going on, before we're left with just a heap of bricks and nowt else?' Dorothy lectured.

'I know what's wrong. I don't need anybody to tell me. Trouble is, I don't know what I'm going to do about it. We haven't the brass to do what's needed.' Bill sighed.

'What is it, then? Is there nothing we can do?' Dorothy asked with concern, thinking that she and her family were living in a hovel already, without it collapsing around their heads.

'My grandfather used to say there was underground workings around here – coal or copper, or something of the sort. He always told my father that he'd made a bad buy when he bought this row of houses and the flay-pits. I think his words are coming true and it's subsidence that's causing these cracks. The row is sinking, Dorothy, and there's nowt me and you can do about it. The houses are buggered, but the flay-pits will be alright.' Bill shook his head and looked at the worry on his wife's face. 'We'll have to move, and the fellas that rent from us will either have to move out or stay until their house falls around them. It might be years or it might be months, but we'd better look for somewhere else as fast as we can. But with not a lot of brass in the bank, we'll have to rent, and it will have to be nearby.'

'Oh Lord, Bill – that'll mean no rent money coming in, and us paying rent to someone else for the first time ever. There's little enough money to go round, without losing our home. Thank heavens Lucy will soon be gone; at least she's one less mouth to feed, although we will be her wage down and all.' Dorothy looked anxiously around her; nothing ever went simply in their lives, it seemed. 'Talking of our Lucy, Adam Brooksbank and she will soon be here. She said to expect him coming down to see us about eleven this morning. He wants to do things properly and ask for her hand correctly, she said, and she assured me that he is honourable. He's worried about me perhaps thinking he's too old for Lucy, and he's here to put me right, so she said. But he'll not change my mind over that – he is too old and he can't change that fact, no matter how much brass he's got.' Dorothy folded her arms and looked out of the bedroom window. 'I know I've moaned about the smell of the yard, but we've had some good times here, and I don't want to leave.'

'Well, you are going to have to. And you are going to have to accept Adam Brooksbank as one of us, and wish them both the best. I'll keep my ears and eyes open for somewhere to move to, but it might mean the five of us living in a one- or two-bedroomed house; it can't be nowt grand.' Bill put his arm round his wife. She moaned enough, but only when things were not right, and he wished he could do right by her more often.

'Oh Lord, Lucy's here – I can hear their voices in the kitchen. Does my hair look alright? Is my apron clean? I've got to look tidy for him, now that I know he's seen the Queen and been honoured by her,' Dorothy flapped.

'It doesn't make him any different from the man you spoke to before. He knows what we are. He isn't marrying our Lucy for her money or, if he is, he'll be sadly disappointed.' Bill laughed at the panic on Dorothy's face.

'She's got a full wedding chest; she's been making quilts and cushions and rugs since she learned to sew. I hope he isn't thinking of a dowry, because we can't offer him a penny, especially now.' Dorothy sighed.

'He'll not be here for that. He just wants our blessing,

318

and then they are going to see the parson at Haworth. Now, come on. Don't worry, something will sort itself out regarding the house. Let's go and give those two love-birds our blessing, and welcome Adam to the family – money or no money.' Bill squeezed Dorothy's hand tightly. 'Things will take a turn. Our luck will change – it has to.'

Lucy looked nervously around her. At least the house looked tidy, her mother had made an effort, and baby Bert was asleep in the old drawer that served as a cot when he slept downstairs. Where Susie was, she didn't know and, quite honestly, Lucy didn't care, seeing as Susie had been the cause of a weekend of heartache, after giving her secrets away. And she knew the boys were at school.

'I can hear my mother and father upstairs. They'll be with us in a minute.' Lucy smiled as Adam sat down at the table and looked around him.

'I know it sounds daft at my age, but I feel nervous about asking for your hand, even though I blurted it out like a fool when I was talking to your father about my love for you.' Adam glanced round the room. Providence Row was not the best of houses to live in. It looked neglected and crumbling, and he noticed a stain of damp down the back of the kitchen wall.

'You'll be fine. My father is in awe of you holding the Victoria Cross, and my mother has come round to me wanting to leave the family nest. I'll be so glad to leave here – not only because I'm marrying you, but because this house and yard are just terrible to live in. The smell and the damp get to you after a while.' Lucy noticed Adam looking around him and comparing his now-spotless house to this one, and she hoped he wasn't thinking twice about marrying a lass from such a humble background.

'I can understand that. I've been wondering if—' Adam cut his sentence short as Bill and Dorothy came down the stairs, with Bill smiling at him and Dorothy, as ever, reserved in her outward show of feelings.

'Now then, Adam, it's good to see you.' Bill held out his hand and Adam shook it. 'Put the kettle on, Mother, and butter us all one of those scones that I smelled you baking in the oven this morning.' Bill sat down at the table, along with Lucy and Adam, and watched as Dorothy quickly made cups of tea and placed a plate of newly baked scones on the table, the butter dripping down the sides of them from their warmth.

'You know there was no need for you to be this formal. After all, you made you intentions well known the other evening, and I think we all know how you both feel about one another, after this weekend's upset. Your mother didn't realize it was that serious between you, so she's regretting being a bit hard on you both.' Bill looked at Dorothy.

'Yes, I didn't realize that you, Adam, felt that strongly for our Lucy. I thought it was simply her dreaming and fantasizing. After all, you are her employer, and there is an age difference.' Dorothy was determined to say what was on her mind as she looked across at the two lovers.

'Mother!' Lucy blushed and looked at Adam with concern.

'I can understand your worries, Mrs Bancroft, but believe me, I do love Lucy. And hopefully my age will be an advantage to us in having a good, stable marriage. After all, I've my own farm and I am not short of money. She will not want for anything.' Adam smiled and helped himself to a scone, as he watched Dorothy's face for a sign of acceptance.

'We can't send her to you with a dowry. We don't have that kind of money,' Dorothy said sharply.

'I don't expect one. Your daughter's hand and her heart are enough for me.' Adam smiled and reached for Lucy's hand. 'In fact I was just about to tell Lucy a plan that I have been hatching and, if you accept, then that is my dowry to you, for letting me marry your beautiful daughter.'

Adam glanced at both Lucy and her parents as all of them waited to hear what he had been planning, and what had made him want to visit them that morning.

'I was successful with my offer for High Ground, so now I own an extra fifty acres, along with the large farmhouse there. The house is no good to me. I aim to stay in Black Moss because, after all, it is my family home. However, I wondered – as Lucy has often complained of the living conditions down here, being so near the flay-pits and her room being so damp – I wondered if I could possibly offer the farmhouse to you and your family to live in? It would be more roomy, and your family would be away from the flay-pits and the smell of them.' Adam sat back and hoped he'd not insulted his new family, but it had been Bill himself who had said that Dorothy would love to live at High Ground, if they had the money. Well, now she could, and perhaps she could forgive him for being not quite suitable for their daughter.

Lucy gasped and looked at both her parents, unable to judge by the look on their faces what they thought of the suggestion. Her father was a proud man, and Providence Row had always been his family home.

Bill nodded his head slowly. 'Aye, lad, I don't know what to make of this. Me and Dorothy here have just come from upstairs, looking at a crack in the ceiling that's getting bigger by the day. Likewise, there's gaps appearing in all the houses along this row – the whole lot is subsiding. Do you know how grand your suggestion is to us? We were beginning to despair, and to wonder what we were going to do. But we will not take charity; we will pay you rent.' Bill looked at Dorothy, who had tears running down her cheeks, and reached for her hand and shook it, while smiling at her.

'No, I've pinched your daughter from you – the house is yours for as long as you and your family need it. It's for purely selfish reasons, because at least I'll know that nobody will steal my sheep. And perhaps, when they are older, Lucy's brothers might help out around the farm.' Adam relaxed and smiled at Lucy as she went and put her arm round her mother.

'Don't cry, Mother. You've always admired High Ground. I remember you used always to stop and look at it lovingly when we walked past it. Well, now you can live there.' Lucy kissed her mother on the brow.

'God bless you, Adam Brooksbank! You have caused me sleepless nights, when I worried about Lucy here, but you are our saviour this morning. And I must confess that our daughter could not be marrying a finer man – a hero not just to his country, but to our small family. I will not say another bad word against you for as long as I live,' Dorothy sobbed.

'As long as I have not offended you. But I was aware that all of you must suffer one way or another, living so near the tannery, and I'm glad my offer has come at such a good time.'

'It takes a lot to offend this family. We've heard it all. After all, we are not in the most popular trade. You've done us a big a favour and, when it comes to marrying Lucy, you have our blessing. And we hope you'll both be as happy as me and my old lass have been.' Bill stood up and shook Adam's hand. 'We are proud to welcome you into our family, and I and Dorothy can't thank you enough for your offer of a new home.'

'You are welcome, sir. I love your Lucy and I will always do right by her. We are to travel on to Haworth next and arrange a date with the parson there. I hope you don't mind us getting married there, instead of Denholme. It's just that the parson's a dear friend of mine and I'd like him to take the service.' Adam looked at the couple and smiled as Dorothy wiped away her tears.

'No, we have no objections. Haworth will be a grand

place for a wedding. We haven't many relations, so there will not be many attending from our family.' Dorothy glanced at Lucy. She was beginning to realize Adam's attractions for her daughter. He was a gentleman and was more than worthy of her hand in marriage.

'No, nor I. You can probably count the number of my guests on one hand. It's better to ask the ones you love than those you think you are obliged to invite.' Adam grinned.

'You can both meet Ivy. She's the one to thank, for us realizing how much we thought of one another. She predicted that she'd be coming to our wedding soon.' Lucy looked at her mother and father, then went to stand next to her Adam and linked her arm through his.

'Aye, she's a lot to answer for, but we will forgive her – it's all for the good. Now, get yourselves gone to Haworth. No doubt you'll tell us the date and arrangements when you come home tonight, Lucy?' Dorothy smiled at her daughter. She was still feeling guilty for thinking the worst of her daughter and Adam.

'I will. I'm hoping – if Adam is in agreement – for a late-September or early-October wedding. The chrysanthemums in the garden will be flowering, and I can make my own bouquet.' Lucy looked at Adam and beamed.

'Whatever you want is right with me. We will have to see if Patrick can fit us in then, and we won't know until we get to Haworth. So, my love, we must be away, and you can tell all this evening.'

Dorothy opened the door for the handsome couple and gently took Adam's hand as he passed her, and kissed him on the cheek. 'Welcome to our family. And thank you for all your help with the house. We will never be able to repay you.'

'There's nothing to repay. You are my family now.' Adam smiled down at the woman he knew had been against the marriage. His timing of a new home had swayed Dorothy, and now he was free to place a ring on her daughter's finger.

'So, Adam, you are looking for me to wed you.' The parson looked at the couple sitting across from him and saw the happiness and love that flowed between them. 'You've decided to look to the future instead of dwelling in the past.'

Lucy looked down at her feet and felt uncomfortable in the parson's gaze. His reputation, and that of his family, was well established in the district. He was a good man, and tragedy had made him stronger rather than weakening him, but she couldn't understand how he kept his faith in God, after losing five daughters, a son and his wife at such early ages.

'I have, sir. And I have been lucky enough to find Lucy, whom I love dearly. It would mean a great deal to me if you yourself would marry us. I befriended all your family, and I will always remember you marrying Mary and me here at Haworth. It was a joyous day, and I wish the same for Lucy and me.' Adam glanced at Lucy and saw her drop her head.

'Are you sure you want to wed here, for those very reasons? Aren't the memories still too tender for you?

And perhaps Lucy here does not want to follow in dear Mary's footsteps?' Patrick looked across at Lucy.

'Oh no, sir. Please, I would like to marry Adam here at Haworth. It would be a great honour to be married by you, and it is what Adam wishes.' Lucy looked at the elderly grey-haired parson and noticed him smile.

'Marriage is a joint decision, my dear, and I'm willing to wed you both, as long as you are in agreement and the decision is not just Adam's. Being married is all about a compromise between man and wife, and one should never be stronger than the other. I am glad someone has won Adam's heart. He's too good a man to live life on his own, and he needs a woman to be there for him and comfort him. You, my dear, will be exactly that in his life. God bless you both. Now, what date am I to look at? Of course the banns will have to be read in each parish, so I hope you are in no rush.' The parson looked across at the couple in front of him and noticed Lucy blushing. He had to ask that, because so many couples came to him with the wife-to-be already with child and needed to be wed quickly.

'No, there's no rush, sir. But Lucy has shown a liking for a date in late September or early October, and I'm in agreement with that. Only because she is growing chrysanthemums in the garden and would like them in her bouquet. However, we'd like it to be held on a Saturday, if possible,' Adam said.

'I'd be happy if you could wait just a little while longer, Adam.' The parson flicked through his diary, struggling to read the appointments, as he looked at the weeks that had events next to them. 'I have the twenty-fifth of October free, and that would give you ample time for the banns to be read, and for you to prepare yourselves for this change in your lives.'

Adam looked at Lucy, who seemed a little disappointed at the date being later than expected, but she nodded her head in agreement.

'Yes, that will be acceptable. The twenty-fifth of October. At what time?' Adam asked.

'We usually hold weddings at two o'clock – is that acceptable?' The parson looked at them both as they nodded their heads. 'Then I will see that Arthur reads out your banns in both churches, and I will fill in the relevant forms. It is a joyous day, Adam. I'm glad you have found happiness once again. And you, young lady, have got yourself a good, kind man. He's strong-willed but dependable, and I know you will have a good life together.'

'I know. He means everything to me.' Lucy linked her arm into Adam's and smiled up at him.

'Those chrysanthemums will have to be protected from the frost, if you are to use them in your bouquet. We have several cloches in the garden and you are welcome to place a plant or two within them, if the weather does get frosty, to protect them for your day.' The parson examined the young girl, who was obviously deeply in love with Adam.

'Thank you, sir. I might just do that. I had set my heart on using them, as my mother had the same flowers on her wedding day.' Lucy smiled.

'Well, the offer is there. And for now, that is my part done. Unless you wish to speak to me each week to make sure that neither of you has any reservations about the marriage, and to explain to you what marriage entails? However, I think Adam already knows about commitment, and I can see that you love him without reserve.' The parson patted Lucy's hand and looked up at Adam.

'Thank you, sir, but we will have no regrets about our decision. We are both looking forward to a happy life together and – who knows – perhaps children?' Adam looked lovingly at Lucy.

'Not yet, Adam, else the Reverend will think we are in a rush to wed,' Lucy chastised.

'Oh no, not just yet. I wasn't thinking.' Adam backtracked on his words.

The parson smiled. 'Children will be an extra blessing, whenever they arrive. Now go and prepare, and look after each other. And I will pray that the weather keeps warm and kind to us until then.' He watched the happy couple leave his study and shook his head as he looked at the date in his diary. Adam Brooksbank had found love once more; he was a lucky man. And she was a lucky young woman.

27

The weeks till the wedding had flown by so quickly. The whole of the Bancroft family had flitted from Providence Row and were now living happily at High Ground. Dorothy loved her new home; the boys had a bedroom each, and Susie – once Lucy was married – would soon also have a bedroom of her own. But the most noticeable thing was that the air was fresh and clear every morning, and the drinking water from the well outside was clean and pure every day, not discoloured on some days, as at Providence Row.

'I can't believe you get married this Saturday. It doesn't seem five minutes since Adam and you sat across the kitchen table from us at Providence Row.' Dorothy looked at Lucy, who was busy stitching buttons onto her wedding dress in front of the fire.

'Time does seem to have flown, but it's because we have all been so busy. Adam has been putting his stamp on his new land here, and you have been making this place your home. Perhaps we should have waited until spring to get married, with one thing and another. And just look at the weather this morning – when will it ever stop?' Lucy looked up from her delicate lace dress and watched the rain pouring down outside. It had rained hard for the last four days, and the land was saturated and the rivers were swollen. Adam had told her to stay at High Ground until the weather improved, and she was missing him deeply, as well as worrying about the bad weather continuing until her wedding day.

'Aye, your father's not suited; he's getting sodden each day at the flay-pits and he says the river is rising and flooding into the terrace. It's a good job we all found new homes. He said the kitchen was a-swimming, and the water was running around the end terrace that Thomas Farrington lived in. He's never known it to flood like that before; he said even the rats were having to swim for it.' Dorothy sighed and looked at her daughter. 'We've a lot to thank your fella for.'

'Well, I only hope Adam's remembered to dig up my chrysanthemums and put them in plant pots inside the barn. Else they will be battered to death and not fit to use on Saturday, and then I'll have no bouquet. It isn't frost that I've had to worry about, it's this bloody rain.' Lucy twisted the cotton that she was using around her finger and broke it off beneath the beautiful small silk-covered button that would fasten the high collar on her wedding dress. 'There – all done; that's my dress sorted anyway, if nothing else.' She held it up in front of her and inspected her needlework. Every stitch on the

330

tight bodice and long, flowing white skirt she had sewn and decorated with lace and embroidery, and now it was finished and she looked at it with a critical eye. 'What do you think: should I have had a lower neckline? I like these high-standing collars, but do you think it makes me look as if I've got a double-chin?'

'You've not got a double-chin at your age! It's perfect, and so is Susie's bridesmaid dress. I'm going to have all on not to cry. My precious girls looking so beautiful, and I'm to lose you – I don't know how I'm going to cope.' Dorothy's eyes filled with tears. Her eldest was getting married and she would miss Lucy so much.

'Mother, I'm only just over the moor. You live in Adam's house, and I'll never be away really.' Lucy scowled. She herself couldn't wait to leave home and start her new life with Adam, and Saturday could not come fast enough. She even disliked staying away from Black Moss while the rain poured down. It was only the knowledge that after Saturday it would be her permanent home, and that she would no longer be simply the maid, that made her stay at home and feel partly satisfied with her lot.

Bill looked around him. He was drenched to the skin and the flay-pits were overflowing with water, which swirled around his feet and those of his workers, who looked miserable and disheartened.

'Bugger this for a lark! You wouldn't send a dog out to work in this,' he shouted, as even the men scraping the hides in the shelter of the shed looked dejected with the wet weather. 'Get yourselves home. I'll pay you for the rest of the day and we will see what tomorrow brings.' He shook his head as his workers put down their tools and thanked him, then made their way back to the warmth and dryness of their own homes. They were sodden and frozen and knew that, come winter, their working conditions would be even worse when it froze outside, but the rain today made work impossible.

Bill looked across at his old home. He missed living there, as he'd been able to go and get a warm-up and a quick brew, if he'd been cold. But now he used it just to hide from the rain, and to scan the empty house and recall his childhood and that of his own family when they were young. High Ground was alright, Dorothy liked it, but it would never be home, he thought, as he glanced at the row of desolate, near-derelict houses in the grey of the autumn afternoon. The waters from the river had swollen and burst its bank, along with the excess water from the flay-pits, and they were now lapping at his old home's door as well as at three other houses along the terrace. If he had still been living here, the cosy kitchen they had lived in would have been flooded, and he could imagine the chaos that a flood in his old home would have entailed. It was a good job the row was empty now, although what to do with the houses, he didn't know. They were only really fit for workshops, although even then he wondered if they would be safe.

'I'm off now, Mr Bancroft. I'll come tomorrow if the weather is decent. Otherwise it'll be Monday before you see me. Although I'll be at Lucy's wedding on Saturday,'

Archie Robinson said, disturbing Bill from his thoughts as he gazed across the yard at his old home.

'Listen – can you hear that noise?' Bill held Archie back and pulled off his cap to listen to the noise that was building in volume, from the row of houses. It was a low, rumbling noise, and Bill and Archie stood still as it grew louder and louder.

'Bloody hell, the houses are collapsing! That chimney's on the wobble, and look at the end house, which used to be Farrington's: the wall's collapsing. Let's get back, else we will be buried in all the debris.' Archie pulled on Bill's jacket, dragging him to the back of the yard and putting the flay-pits before them, as the whole terrace started to lose slates and chimneys, and the walls buckled like wet paper. It deafened the two of them, as they watched the devastation unfold before their eyes. Both were covered with dust and rubble from the collapse of the row into a gaping sinkhole that opened up in the ground before them, taking the once-loved homes into its depths.

'My houses – they've gone, there's nowt left! My home has been washed away. Another minute, if you hadn't talked to me, and I'd have been inside it. I was just thinking to stay there for another hour, to see if the weather faired.' Bill looked dumbstruck and ashen-faced as he turned to Archie. 'God help us, if my family had still been living there, or the lads working here – I'd have had their deaths on my hands. Thank God everybody had moved out.' He walked gingerly towards the gaping sinkhole and the remnants of Providence Row, with

Archie following him. They both looked at the one piece of red-brick gable end that stood teetering on the edge of the hole. The inside walls were still covered with a bright-yellow wallpaper, reminding them both that up till several months ago it had been home to the flay-pit worker Thomas Farrington. The rest of the house was now deep down in the cavern that had once been the underground workings.

'Well, I don't think you'll be moving back in there in a hurry,' Archie said. 'But at least there's no damage done to the pits. You've still got them and the yard. Things could have been worse.'

'I don't know whether to laugh or cry. But aye, lad, you are right: things could be a lot worse. I could be buried down there with the house, and nobody would know. At least that saves me from pulling the bloody things down.' Bill looked out from under his dripping wet, dust-filled hair. 'Now I've just got to tell the wife and put a brave face on it all, because there's nowt we could have done to stop it. Now get yourself home, and I'll see you when I see you. If it's stopped raining in the morning, we will have to have a tidy-up and make the most of what Mother Nature has left us with. That wall will have to be knocked down, else it'll fall on some-body's head. I don't know about you, but my legs feel shaky. I've never seen anything like that before.'

Bill drew his fingers through his hair and stood and looked around him. His past life had disappeared before his eyes, and he knew it could so easily have been him along with it. He watched as Archie, with his bait box under his arm, picked his way around the rubble on his way home, leaving Bill to think how lucky he was not to have been in the house when it collapsed. He was hesitant to leave the pits as they were, but it would soon be dark, and he needed to get home to change out of his sodden clothes and tell Dorothy of the disaster that had taken place. It was the end of their home at Providence Row. It was just as well they had all settled into their new home, and that Adam had been kind enough to let them stay there.

'Oh, Bill, you could have been killed! And is there nothing left of all of the houses?' Dorothy and Lucy looked at Bill, as he shed his sodden clothes in front of the fire and stood in his undergarments, shivering and shaken by the day's events, while Lucy put some dry clothes in front of him and Dorothy made him a hot, sweet drink of tea.

'No, only a wall end, and I bet that collapses into the same hole by the morning. I only hope it doesn't take any of the flay-pits with it. I've never seen the rivers rise as quick, and for there to be so much water on the land. The bridge over the river at Four Lane Ends is near to flooding. It's got to stop raining soon.' Bill's hands shook as he took hold of his warm mug of tea and looked at his wife and daughter. He'd lost his home and nearly his livelihood, but at least he was still alive.

'I hope it stops raining for Saturday, although that's of little concern, compared to what you've been through today, Father.' Lucy looked at her shaken father and knew that losing Providence Row would be hurting him. 'You'll have to rebuild,' she said quickly.

'No brass, lass. And anyway the land's not fit to build on, and who'd want to live next to the flay-pits again? We were glad to leave it all behind. No, we've got to let it go and make the best of what we've got. At least we will have got you off our hands, come Saturday, and we know that you'll be looked after and cared for. It's up to me to make sure the rest of the family are looked after and get decent jobs. I don't want my three lads working in the pits; they deserve something better. It's a mucky, hard job and it doesn't pay that well. Let me be the last generation to work there.' Bill looked at his family and silently thanked the Lord that he was still with them and had survived the afternoon's events.

By the following morning the rain had eased and the sun was trying hard to break through.

'There's enough blue sky to make a sailor a pair of trousers,' Lucy said as she opened the front door of High Ground and looked out on the sodden moorland, with abundant white-watered springs gushing down the hillside. 'I'll go and rescue my chrysanthemums from Adam. They'll keep now, if I pick them for Saturday. But I'll walk to the flay-pits with you first, Father – not that I'll relish seeing the devastation the storm has brought.'

'Well, you both take care. I'll not be coming with you, as it'll break my heart. It was our first home, and I know it wasn't the most glamorous of places, but it hurts to think there's nothing left of it now.' Dorothy sighed. 'I bet folk will come to look at it from far and wide – there's nothing they like more than revelling in somebody else's misfortune.'

'Aye, I know. That's why we've got to be away. It'll be a shock for the workers that left early yesterday – they'll not know what's happened.' Bill pulled on his jerkin and donned his cap as he made for the door. 'Your skirts will be sodden by the time you get to Black Moss, there's that much water on the ground.' He looked at Lucy, thinking she must be more desperate to see Adam than the flowers, if she was to accompany him to work and then go on to Black Moss.

'It doesn't matter, it's only water. If I don't go today, I'll never get there, as it's the eve of my wedding tomorrow and we will all be too busy. Adam's got Ivy and her husband visiting, although they are staying at the Brown Cow in Keighley. And I want my last day of being single to be with my mother at home.' Lucy pulled her shawl around her shoulders and waited for her father.

'Very well then, but you'll be upset by what you see.' Bill looked at Dorothy and shook his head. There was no convincing Lucy to stay at home, despite the mud and rain that would ruin her skirts.

Bill was right. There was a crowd gathered around the sinkhole and what remained of Providence Row when they arrived at the flay-pits. The gable end, which had been upright when Bill left, had now also fallen into the abyss and, along with it, a small part of the yard. Bill felt his stomach churn and his head go light as he realized it was the lime pit that held their secret that had slipped into the chasm. He looked down into the depths of the hole and hoped that nothing of their deeds was visible. People around him shook their heads and patted him on the back, muttering words of consolation, before talking amongst themselves and looking at Bill and his daughter.

'Well, there's not much left, is there?' Lucy looked around her at the destruction. 'Looks like it's taken the lime pit as well,' she said, not adding any other comment, but knowing that her father knew full well what she was thinking.

'Aye, happen for the best, lass. Things always happen for a reason. Perhaps it was time to move on. The old place knew it had been abandoned, and so nature reclaimed it.' Bill paused. 'At least I still have my living, and that's the main thing. Time to get these gawping workers of mine back to work, else they'll look down that hole all day. They can do that when they help me fill it in, with the rubble and soil from up above the flay-pits. Time to bury the past and move on. What's done is done, and there's no going back. You go and see that fella of yours and enjoy your life, because it will be over all too soon, and there will be things that come and challenge you both in your life that you can do nothing about.' Completely out of character, Bill gave Lucy a swift hug and then pushed her on her way to the man who had replaced him in her heart. She had all her life in front of her, and he was sure it would be a better one than he could ever offer her, if Lucy stayed at home.

*

'I've missed you.' Lucy held Adam close. 'I know it's only been a few days, but I've counted the minutes, even the seconds,' she whispered as he kissed her and looked into her eyes.

'And I have missed you. The place doesn't feel the same nowadays if you are not here,' Adam whispered. 'Not long now, and you'll be here permanently as my wife.'

'I'm not staying, as we both have so much to organize and do. We have had a disaster down at Providence Row – or should I say what used to be Providence Row. It got washed away when the ground collapsed from underneath it yesterday evening, and my father's there now, trying to make sense of it. You do realize that we owe you our lives. If it hadn't been for your offer of a new home for my family, we would still have been living there. Just another thing that I have to love you for.' Lucy kissed Adam again and watched as he in took the news.

'That's terrible. And the flay-pits, are they untouched?' He stood back and looked worried.

'Yes, thank the Lord. My father's still got his business, so we are thankful for that. Go down and see the damage, if you have time. There's already a crowd of people there and no doubt it will grow, once word gets out of the damage that's been done.' Lucy looked out of the kitchen window down to the valley bottom, but could not quite see her old home.

'No, I've got Ivy and her husband to meet at Keighley this afternoon. They have asked me for dinner with them this evening. I might go tomorrow, if I get the time. But my head is full of thoughts about our wedding. Saturday will soon be here, and when I walk you down the aisle I will be the happiest man in the world. All is in place, and I've guarded your chrysanthemums with my life. They are safe and dry in the barn and ready for you to take.' Adam held Lucy by the waist and kissed the nape of her neck.

'I can't believe this is happening to me. I've dreamed of it so much that I never thought it would truly happen,' she whispered.

'Well, it is to happen, my darling. Saturday is our day, and whether it rains or shines, I care not, because I will have you by my side forever.' Adam kissed her once more.

'Oh, let the sun shine for us, Adam. Even though it is autumn, there are still a few flowers surviving and the leaves are such a beautiful colour when the sun shines.' Lucy returned his kiss and smiled.

'It will shine for us, my love – it has to; it's our special day and I won't let it do anything other than shine.' Adam held her tightly. Saturday could not come soon enough, whether it rained or shone.

28

Lucy looked at herself in the long mirror of her bedroom. She was still not used to her new room at High Ground and had not made herself at home in it, knowing that she would be leaving it shortly for her new life with Adam. She gazed at herself critically, noticing every stitch and tuck that she had added to her own hand-made wedding dress. Was the waist too tight? Did she look too fat? Was it even the right colour? Although she knew the last point to be fine, she had chosen a white lace to show that she was still virginal and to stop any gossips accusing her of having a rushed wedding. Her heart was fluttering like a trapped butterfly as she noticed her mother standing behind her in the reflection of the mirror.

'You look beautiful, our Lucy.' Dorothy swept a tear away from her eye. 'I know I shouldn't, but I can't help but cry. You are still my baby, and yet here you are getting married.'

'Oh, Mother, don't cry. I'm not going far – only two

or three fields away – and you are welcome any time, you know you are.' Lucy turned and hugged her mother tightly.

'I've brought you this; it was your grandmother's before you. She gave it to me on my wedding day, so now it is yours.' Dorothy held out her hand and opened it up to reveal a silver necklace set with a blue sapphire – a necklace that Lucy had always admired, when allowed to look at it. 'The blue will bring you luck.' She leaned upwards and fastened the necklace around her daughter's neck. 'There, your gran would be proud of you; such a bonny lass and marrying such a good man. Now he might be different in bed – you'll just have to take the rough with the smooth and let him have his way, as that's the way of the world when it comes to men.' Dorothy looked at her daughter. They'd never talked of such things before.

'I know, Mother. You don't have to say any more.' Lucy blushed.

'Well, I'll be away then. Archie's come for me and for your brothers and sister, with his cart all done up like a dog's dinner. He's got ribbons and the odd flower or two on it. Lord knows whose garden he will have raided for them! Your father's having a drink with the landlord of The Fleece downstairs in the kitchen; he's waiting for you to join him in The Fleece's coach. Don't be long, as they are already on their second whisky. Besides, you don't want to keep your man waiting at the altar.'

Dorothy stood in the doorway and gave her daughter a second glance, before going downstairs and joining

342

Archie and her younger family. She felt a lump in her throat as Archie climbed up into the cart with the excited youngsters. She must not cry; today was a good day: the sun was shining and it was Lucy's wedding day. She must not let her feelings spoil her daughter's big day.

Lucy picked up her spray of chrysanthemums and ivy from the marble washstand and gave herself one more glance. Her blonde hair lay long over her shoulders, and she'd made herself a small halo out of the chrysanthemum buds and placed it on her head to match her bouquet. After today she'd wear her hair in a plait; it was not right to flaunt her long golden locks, once married. This was the beginning of a new life for her, she thought, as she left her unloved bedroom behind her and walked down the stairs – a life that she had only dreamed of a few months ago.

'By heck, lass, tha's bonny.' Bill looked at his daughter and caught his breath. 'I hope Adam realizes what he's got.'

Lucy smiled as the landlord from The Fleece opened the kitchen door and then rushed to help her into his coach. She made room next to her for her father, then put her dress in order and battled her nerves as Bill slapped her knee and grinned. There was no going back now – not that she wanted to. She was about to become Mrs Adam Brooksbank, for better, for worse, for richer, for poorer, until death did them part. And she could not be happier.

*

343

Adam turned to look at his beautiful bride on the arm of his father-in-law-to-be. Lucy looked radiant, and the parson beamed as Adam held out his hand for her to join him at the altar. Little had he known that, before the year was out, he would marry the flippant, flirty young girl he had employed as his maid. But now he had room in his heart only for her; his first wife Mary would always be with him in his memories, but Lucy was the one he loved.

As he slipped the wedding ring onto Lucy's finger he looked across at Ivy, who winked at him. She too knew that Mary had left his life, and that Adam's happiness now lay with Lucy. He leaned forward and tenderly kissed his maid from Black Moss Farm – now his wife. Together they would live and love and make a new life for themselves, until the day they were parted by death; and even then their love for one another might survive the grave.

Lucy walked proudly down the aisle of the church, her arm linked through Adam's. She had got the man of her dreams, despite everyone telling her that Adam was wrong for her. She smiled as she noticed Reggie Ellwood standing in a pew near the back of the church. Next to him stood a pretty brunette lass, who obviously had eyes only for her man, as she grasped his arm tightly and whispered in his ear. Lucy was glad that he had found someone; she would never have been right for Reggie, for her heart had belonged to Adam from the first day they had met.

As they both walked out of the church and stood under the archway of the porch, the sun suddenly broke through the clouds and shone down on Lucy and Adam, warming their already-flushed faces. Under a shower of flower petals and rice, Lucy looked up at her man – the man she had always dreamed of since she was young. She was now Mrs Adam Brooksbank, mistress of Black Moss Farm, and she had a husband to be proud of.

For the Sake of Her Family

DIANE ALLEN

It's 1912 in the Yorkshire Dales, and Alice Bentham and her brother Will have lost their mother to cancer. Money is scarce and pride doesn't pay the doctor or put food on the table.

Alice gets work at Whernside Manor, looking after Lord Frankland's fragile sister Miss Nancy. Meanwhile Will and his best friend Jack begin working for the Lord of the Manor at the marble mill. But their purpose there is not an entirely honest one.

For a while everything runs smoothly, but corruption, attempted murder and misplaced love are just waiting in the wings. Nothing is as it seems and before they know it, Alice and Will's lives are entwined with those of the Franklands' – and nothing will ever be the same again.

OUT NOW

For a Mother's Sins

DIANE ALLEN

It is 1870 and railway workers and their families have flocked to the wild and inhospitable moorland known as Batty Green. Here they are building a viaduct on the Midland Railway Company's ambitious new Leeds to Carlisle line.

Among them are three very different women – tough widow Molly Mason, honest and God-fearing Rose Pratt and Helen Parker, downtrodden by her husband and seeking a better life.

When tragedy strikes, the lives of the three women are bound together, and each is forced to confront the secrets and calamities that threaten to tear their families apart.

OUT NOW

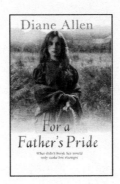

For a Father's Pride

DIANE ALLEN

In 1871, young Daisy Fraser is living in the Yorkshire Dales with her beloved family. Her sister Kitty is set to marry the handsome and wealthy Clifford Middleton. But on the eve of the wedding, Clifford commits a terrible act that shatters Daisy's happy life. She carries her secret for the next nine months, but is left devastated when she gives birth and the baby is pronounced dead. Soon she is cast out by her family and has no choice but to make her own way in the world.

When further tragedy strikes, Daisy sets out for the bustling streets of Leeds. There she encounters poverty and hardship, but also friendship. What she really longs for is a love of her own. Yet Daisy doesn't realize that the key to her happiness may not be as far away as she thinks . . .

OUT NOW

Like Father, Like Son

DIANE ALLEN

From birth, Polly Harper seems destined for tragedy. Raised by her loving grandparents on Paradise Farm, she is unknowingly tangled in a web of secrecy regarding her parentage.

When she falls in love with Tobias, the wealthy son of a local landowner of disrepute, her anxious grandparents send her to work in a dairy. There she becomes instantly drawn to the handsome Matt Dinsdale, propelling her further into the depths of forbidden romance and dark family secrets.

But when tragedy strikes, Polly is forced to confront her past and decide the fate of her future. Will she lose everything, or will she finally realize that her roots and love lie in Paradise?

OUT NOW

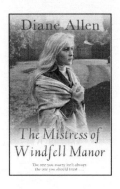

The Mistress of
Windfell Manor

DIANE ALLEN

Charlotte Booth loves her father and the home they share, which is set high up in the limestone escarpments of Crummockdale. But when a new businessman in the form of Joseph Dawson enters their lives, both Charlotte and her father decide he's the man for her and, within six months, Charlotte marries the dashing mill owner from Accrington.

Then a young mill worker is found dead in the swollen River Ribble. With Joseph's business nearly bankrupt, it becomes apparent that all is not as it seems and Joseph is not the man he pretends to be. Heavily pregnant, penniless and heartbroken, Charlotte is forced to face the reality that life may never be the same again . . .

OUT NOW

The Windfell Family Secrets

DIANE ALLEN

Twenty-one years have passed since Charlotte Booth fought to keep her home at Windfell Manor, following her traumatic first marriage. Now, happily married to her childhood sweetheart, she seeks only the best for their children, Isabelle and Danny. But history has a habit of repeating itself when Danny's head is turned by a local girl of ill repute.

Meanwhile, the beautiful and secretive Isabelle shares all the undesirable traits of her biological father. And when she announces that she is to marry John Sidgwick, the owner of High Mill in Skipton, her mother quickly warns her against him. An ex-drinking mate of her late father who faces bankruptcy, Charlotte fears his interest in Isabelle is far from honourable. What she doesn't realize is how far he's willing to go to protect his future . . .

OUT NOW

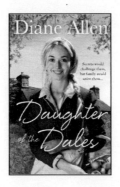

Daughter of the Dales

DIANE ALLEN

The death of Charlotte Atkinson, the family matriarch, at Windfell Manor casts a long shadow over her husband Archie and their two children, Isabelle and Danny. With big shoes to fill, Isabelle takes over the running of Atkinson's department store but her pride – and heart – is tested when her husband James brings scandal upon the family and the Atkinsons' reputation.

Danny's wife Harriet is still struggling to deal with the deaths of their first two children – deaths she blames Isabelle for. But Danny himself is grappling with his own demons when a stranger brings to light a long-forgotten secret from his past.

Meanwhile, Danny and Harriet's daughter Rosie has fallen under the spell of a local stable boy, Ethan. But will he stand by her or will he cause her heartache? And can Isabelle restore the Atkinsons' reputation and her friendship with Harriet, to unite the family once more?

OUT NOW

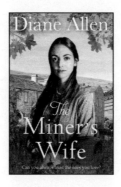

The Miner's Wife

DIANE ALLEN

Nineteen-year-old Meg Oversby often dreams of a more exciting life than the dull existence she faces at her family's farm deep in the Yorkshire Dales. Growing up, she's always sensed her father's disappointment at not having a son to help with the farm work.

So when Meg dances all night at the local market hall with Sam Alderson, a lead miner from Swaledale, a new light enters her life. Sam and his brother Jack show Meg a side to life she didn't know existed. But when her parents find out, she's forbidden from ever seeing them again.

Although where there is love, there is often a way. When Meg's uncle offers her the chance to help run the small village shop, she leaps at the opportunity, seeing it as a way to escape the oppressive family farm and see more of her beloved Sam. But as love blossoms, a darker truth emerges and Meg realizes that Sam may not be the man she thought he was . . .

OUT NOW